continued . . .

Chance of a Ghost

"Alison has a wry sense of humor and is written so well it is easy to imagine her as your sardonic sister or friend . . . With an outstanding cast of characters, a well-plotted mystery and some sentimental reunions, this is a standout series."
—*The Mystery Reader*

"An enjoyable escape for any reader wanting to laugh and sympathize with a woman who succeeds by working with unreliable ghosts." —*Lesa's Book Critiques*

"I love the concept of this series. Ghosts helping the living solve crime . . . The characters, both of this world and the world beyond, are realistic, smart, and quirky. You won't want to miss this ghostly cozy mystery, full of enough wit, charm, and supernatural hijinks to keep you turning the pages well past midnight." —*MyShelf.com*

Old Haunts

"Wisecracking though level-headed, Alison is the kind of person we'd all like to know, if not be . . . Great fun with a tinge of salt air." —*The Mystery Reader*

"An entertaining and spellbinding tale in which the ghosts come across as real, as each brings melancholy and humor."
—*The Mystery Gazette*

"Copperman's Alison Kerby is my kind of protagonist. She's realistic and knows her weaknesses . . . Best of all, she has a dry sense of humor . . . Leave your disbelief behind. Pretend you believe in ghosts. You'll certainly believe in Alison Kerby as a perfect amateur sleuth."
—*Lesa's Book Critiques*

"I knew *Old Haunts* was gold before I finished reading the first page." —*Fresh Fiction*

"*Old Haunts* is like an old friend (or your snuggy blanket)—dependable, solid and just what you need it to be."
—*Night Owl Reviews*

An Uninvited Ghost

"A triumph . . . The humor is delightful . . . If you like ghost stories mixed with your mystery, try this Jersey Shore mystery." —*Lesa's Book Critiques*

"Funny and charming, with a mystery which has a satisfying resolution, and an engaging protagonist who is not easily daunted . . . Highly recommended."
—*Spinetingler Magazine*

"There are several series out now featuring protagonists who can interact with ghosts. Some are good, but this one is the best I've read. Alison's spectral companions are reminiscent of Topper's buddies: funny and stubborn and helpful when they want to be . . . I look forward to Alison's next spooky adventure." —*Over My Dead Body!*

"E. J. Copperman is certainly wonderful at weaving a great mystery. From the very get-go, readers are in for a treat that will leave them guessing until the final chapter . . . Alison Kerby is a wonderful character . . . If you love a great mystery like I do, I highly recommend getting this book." —*Once Upon a Romance*

Night of the Living Deed

"Witty, charming, and magical." —*The Mystery Gazette*

"A fast-paced, enjoyable mystery with a wise-cracking, but no-nonsense, sensible heroine . . . Readers can expect good fun from start to finish." —*The Mystery Reader*

Inspector
Specter

E. J. COPPERMAN

BERKLEY PRIME CRIME, NEW YORK

THE BERKLEY PUBLISHING GROUP
Published by the Penguin Group
Penguin Group (USA) LLC
375 Hudson Street, New York, New York 10014

USA • Canada • UK • Ireland • Australia • New Zealand • India • South Africa • China

penguin.com

A Penguin Random House Company

INSPECTOR SPECTER

A Berkley Prime Crime Book / published by arrangement with the author

Berkley Prime Crime Books are published by The Berkley Publishing Group.
BERKLEY® PRIME CRIME and the PRIME CRIME logo are
trademarks of Penguin Group (USA) LLC.

For information, address: The Berkley Publishing Group,
a division of Penguin Group (USA) LLC,
375 Hudson Street, New York, New York 10014.

ISBN: 978-0-425-26926-8

PUBLISHING HISTORY
Berkley Prime Crime mass-market edition / December 2014

PRINTED IN THE UNITED STATES OF AMERICA

10 9 8 7 6 5 4 3 2 1

Cover illustration by Dominick Finelle/The July Group.
Cover photos: *Flock of Birds* © AlexusssK/Shutterstock;
Painted Backyard © iStockphoto/Thinkstock.
Cover design by Judith Lagerman.
Interior text design by Kristin del Rosario.

For Sid Caesar, Harpo Marx, Harold Ramis,
Zero Mostel, Larry Gelbart, Chuck Jones, and Robin
Williams. There aren't enough funny people in the world.

ACKNOWLEDGMENTS

I fear I'll sound like a broken record pouring out thanks to some familiar names, except nobody listens to records anymore and sounding like a broken MP3 file just doesn't have the same pizzazz.

Still, it would be wrong for me to let you think that the book you're holding in your hand—on either paper or pixel—is my work alone. It's not. I get the original idea and try to make it come out perfectly, and thankfully there is a team of people to let me know just how far off the mark I have wandered. And to them many, many thanks are due. If they are thanks you've read before, well, thank *you* for reading acknowledgments.

For inspiration, I refer back to the Topper films and TV series, which apparently had more of an impact on me when I was six than I would have guessed. But if you're going to write about ghosts and you're not that interested in scaring the pants off people, there is no better place to look.

The Haunted Guesthouse Mysteries would not exist but for two people who liked and believed in it: Thanks to Christina Hogrebe of the Jane Rotrosen Agency for bringing me first to the incomparable Shannon Jamieson Vazquez. Shannon, this is our ninth (!) book together—who could have seen *that* coming when we met for coffee in 2005? Thanks for your good taste, your unerring sense of logic and your undying confidence in me. It means more than you can know.

A special belated thanks to Stacy Edwards, the production editor on almost all the Haunted Guesthouse books, whom I should have acknowledged five books ago. Sorry and thanks, Stacy!

Of course thank you to Josh Getzler, Danielle Burby and all at HSG Agency. It gives an author confidence—something we don't generally produce independently—to have such an accomplished and dedicated team backing up the work. Thanks for all your hours trying in vain to convince me I'm a good writer.

Don't ever think the author is responsible for the cover of the book in your hands. Authors by nature are word people—images, thankfully, are in the hands of those like Dominick Finelle, who did the illustration, and Judith Lagerman, who created the cover design. They are as responsible for the look of this series as I am for the words.

A huge debt of gratitude to every reader of the Haunted Guesthouse Mysteries. You have taken these characters to your hearts and welcomed them into your minds. There is nothing that makes an author more proud than the reader who wants more as soon as the current book is finished. Believe me, I'm working on it.

And as ever, thanks to Jessica, Josh and Eve, who give me three reasons to get out of bed in the morning.

One

I was stripping white paint off the paneling in the new home theater (formerly game room) of my guesthouse when the cell phone in my pocket vibrated, indicating a text.

Normally, I wouldn't have bothered to check the phone immediately, at least not before I'd finished the task at hand and showered—and very likely changed my clothes, ordered dinner and straightened up a couple of rooms—but my daughter, Melissa, was at her friend Wendy's house this afternoon and might have been texting to let me know she needed a ride home or (more likely) to ask if she could spend the night there.

Such are the thrills of summer vacation. You're only eleven once.

I wiped my hands off the best I could, then let the rag fall onto the drop cloth I'd carefully placed under the work area. I am nothing if not prepared.

But the text I'd received was not from Melissa; it was

from Detective Lieutenant Anita McElone of the Harbor
Haven Police Department. My breath stopped for a second. When your eleven-year-old isn't at home, you really
don't want to get a call from the police. I knew McElone a
little, but we weren't what I'd call "friends," and she'd
never contacted me out of the blue before.

The text read: "COME OUTSIDE TO YOUR PORCH."

That took some of my panic away but piqued my curios-
ity. I looked out the window of the home theater—therein
lies a tale; it was slated to become a fitness center for the
guests until I found out how much exercise equipment
costs—and sure enough, McElone was standing on the front
porch next to the glider, hands clasped behind her, pacing.

I sighed. The big scaredy-cat. Lieutenant McElone, one
of the most unflappable people I have ever met, is afraid to
come into my house because she thinks she'll see a ghost.
Which is silly. McElone can't see the ghosts who stay in
my house.

Perhaps I should explain.

Melissa and I moved to Harbor Haven, the town where
I grew up, about three years ago after a divorce from a man
I call "The Swine," although that sometimes makes me
feel like I'm insulting actual pigs. I bought the property at
123 Seafront because I wanted to start a new life for us
here on the Jersey Shore, and I'd been in the process of
renovating the place when things changed after a freak . . .
we'll call it an "accident" . . . left me with a severely
bruised head, a concussion, and the ability to see ghosts.
Specifically, Paul Harrison and Maxie Malone, who had
been inhabiting the old Victorian since they'd been murdered on the premises. Once they realized that I could see
them, they'd wanted me to find out who had killed them.
But that's a story told elsewhere.

As it turned out, I was not the only member of my family who could see Paul and Maxie, though I was the only
one who'd had to sustain a head injury first. My mother

and Melissa were both professional-level ghost communicators and had been keeping that little fact from me for, let's say all *my* life in Mom's case and all *her* life in Melissa's. But I have forgiven them. I am magnanimous. And it comes in handy now that my father has passed away. I'm sad he's dead, but he's still around a lot. My family is an emotional roller coaster. Probably in a different way than yours.

I took a breath before heading outside to McElone. I'd specifically chosen this moment to work on the theater because I was, for once, alone in my thoughts, something that almost *never* happens around the guesthouse. With Liss at her friend Wendy's and all six of my current guests out at the beach on this scorching-hot day, the only "company" I'd normally have had would be the ghosts. But Maxie, who'd recently developed the ability to leave the property, had decided to go visit her mother, and Paul, who still can't wander farther than my property line, had been . . . not upset, and not exactly broody lately, but showing signs of some ennui, which he had not explained. I decided he was a grown man—if a dead one, which would understandably bum *anyone* out—and I'd let him work out his issues until he brought them up himself.

Wiping off my hands again, I walked out of the theater, down the corridor to the entrance, and opened the door. A blast of heat and humidity, which you tend to forget about when you're living in air-conditioning, smacked me hard in the face.

McElone wasn't even sweating. I'd been exposed to the tropical wave for three seconds and was already feeling moist, but she had no human responses. She was, I had decided long before, not so much a regular person as a cop who occasionally took in air to survive.

"This is what it's come to?" I asked. "You text me from my own front porch because you're afraid of my house?"

"I'm not *afraid*," she protested. "I'm just not interested

in seeing any more than I already have." The lieutenant had been witness to a few of the less conventional events that take place in my house. Events that several of my guests pay good money to witness, but the novelty of it is lost on McElone.

"You sure you don't want to come inside?" I tried. "I promise there are no ghosts around at the moment, and it's got to be a hundred degrees out here."

McElone held up a hand at the very suggestion, which made her look a little like a very imposing cigar store Indian. Cigar store Native American? "I'm fine here."

There was a tentative quality to her that I'd never seen before. McElone doesn't actually have a sense of humor, but she's usually sharper in conversation than this.

Something was bothering her.

It probably would have been bothering her more if she'd known that despite my assurances about the lack of ghosts, Paul had just risen up from the crawl space under the front porch and was watching her closely. "You didn't call the lieutenant, did you?" he asked, knowing full well that I wouldn't answer him directly with her there.

"What brings you here, Lieutenant?" I asked for both our sakes. "Have there been complaints about the guest-house again?" Locals in Harbor Haven know the stories about the place, and I had recently installed a prominent sign, just to the left of the front door, that read proudly, "Haunted Guesthouse," replacing a temporary one Melissa had made on poster board.

But occasionally the odd—and some of them are *very* odd—tourist or a townsperson with an especially prickly nature makes a complaint at the police station about "weird goings-on" or "strange noises" emanating from the house. None of which is actually true, since the ghosts can't be heard at all if you don't have the ear for it.

"Do you remember Martin Ferry?" McElone asked, out of nowhere.

"Detective Ferry?" I asked. I remembered him as a sour-natured detective in Seaside Heights, who had once reluctantly shared some information with me. We hadn't hit it off so much as we'd tolerated each other. "Wasn't he your partner before you came here to Harbor Haven?"

McElone nodded. Then she shuddered a little, bit her lip and looked like she was fighting tears. "He's dead," she said finally, forcing the words out.

"Oh, Lieutenant," I said. I've never called McElone by her name, only her rank. We don't have that kind of relationship. "I'm so sorry to hear it. Was it sudden?" I recalled Ferry as a middle-aged man with a prodigious belly; I wondered if his heart had given out.

"Very sudden," McElone answered. "Somebody shot him."

TWO

"Come inside," I said again to McElone. I was getting really hot out on the porch. "I promise nothing strange will happen." I might have said that last part a little louder than was necessary; I wanted to emphasize it to Paul. I had to admit, the heat and the news of Ferry had me just a little off balance.

"No," the lieutenant answered. "Really."

"At least sit down," I suggested. I have a glider on the front porch, and gestured toward it. McElone surveyed it up and down, as if trying to determine what these puny humans do on such things, but eventually sat down and let out a breath.

"I'm going to get myself a glass of lemonade," I told her. "Would you like one, Lieutenant?"

McElone turned her head suddenly, as if she'd just realized I was there. "Yeah. Sure. Thank you." This *was* serious; she wasn't even being snide. Snide is McElone's baseline attitude when I'm around.

I opened the door again and let the cool, dry air envelop me as I walked into my supposedly terrifying house. Paul slipped through the door (and when I say *through the door . . .*) and followed me, as I'd hoped he would.

"Why do you think she came here?" I asked him quietly. "She seems really shaken by what happened to him."

"I think it's obvious," the spook to my right answered. "She wants our help in finding Detective Ferry's killer."

Paul, who'd been a fledgling private investigator when his life was cut short on his first solo case—guarding Maxie—and I had an arrangement: He and Maxie would help me guarantee an interactive experience for some of my guests (those who booked through Senior Plus Tours, looking for the "value-added" aspect of staying in a haunted house) if I helped him. As it turns out, eternity is a long time, and being a ghost stuck within my property lines was a little dull. Paul wanted to keep his hand in the investigation biz. He'd need "legs" outside the house on occasion. And since Melissa was (at the time) nine years old and Mom was not exactly as spry as she used to be, Paul chose me.

Suffice it to say that while I was not completely thrilled at the prospect of working PI cases, I *was* thrilled with the idea of guaranteed guests for my business, which is what Senior Plus assured me they'd send if I could deliver the spooks. So after a while I'd caved and sat for the private investigator's exam, Maxie reluctantly signed up for the "spook shows," the guests started coming and I forgot all about my PI license until Paul started insisting that I keep my end of the bargain and actually take cases.

He can communicate with other spirits—I call it the Ghosternet—and he let it be known that "we" were open for business. So once in a while a ghost will ask him for help, and I have to go along for the ride if I want to keep my real business running. Which is also how I know Lieutenant McElone (who doesn't respect my detecting skills much, and she's right).

Now I looked at Paul carefully. "You know, there are times when you overestimate the draw of your imaginary detective agency," I told him. He frowned at the word *imaginary*, but I didn't give him time to answer. "McElone is a detective herself, and a good one. She doesn't need me—and as far as she knows, the whole 'agency' is me—to help her on an investigation. She has the Harbor Haven Police Department."

I opened a cupboard and took out two glasses. Melissa would have been impressed that I used the actual glass ones. When it's just the two of us, we drink out of plastic cups I buy at the Acme. We're a classy family.

"No, she doesn't," Paul countered. "Keep in mind, Detective Ferry was a member of the Seaside Heights department. Unless he was killed here in Harbor Haven, his case is not within the lieutenant's jurisdiction."

I went to the fridge and got out the pitcher of lemonade (which, in the interest of full disclosure, Melissa had made, following a recipe her grandmother had given her; I'm either the world's worst or the least-inspired cook, depending on whether you ask me or the my mother, who's diplomatic to a fault) and walked to the counter.

"I guarantee the cops in Seaside would be all over the murder of one of their own," I told Paul. "Even if McElone wants to look into it herself, she has to trust them to handle it. There's no reason to ask me." I got a tray from the cabinet under the microwave oven.

Paul raised an eyebrow and put his hands into the pockets of his jeans, a sign that he was getting stubborn about something. This was different from when he's thinking, when he'll feverishly stroke his goatee. You get to know someone when they inhabit your house, even if they died before you got there.

"I'll bet you that the lieutenant asks you for help when you go back out to the porch," he said. "I'll bet you I'm right."

I put the glasses and the pitcher on the tray and lifted it, heading for the kitchen door. (Perhaps it should be noted that this was a special favor for the lieutenant—the guesthouse is not a bed-and-breakfast, so even my guests don't get more than a morning cup of coffee or tea out of me.) "Fine for you," I said. "But it's not like you can pay off when I win. What are you betting?"

"If I win the bet, we take the case for Lieutenant Mc-Elone," he said.

"And when *I* win?" We were almost to the front door.

"*If* you were to win, we turn down the next investigation we're offered, and I won't complain about it. How's that?"

"Double or nothing," I said.

He looked puzzled. "Double or nothing?"

"When I win the bet, I get to turn down the next *two* cases you cook up on the Ghosternet. Deal?"

Paul didn't even stop to think. "Deal."

I tilted my head toward the knob on the front door. "Do you mind?"

Paul reached over and opened the door for me, which was a vast improvement over what he could do when I first met him (at the time, picking up a quarter was a chore requiring intense concentration). I thanked him quietly as I carried the tray back into the blast furnace.

I put the tray down on a wicker table next to the glider where McElone was still sitting, looking uncomfortable but amazingly not sweaty. I poured the two glasses and handed her one as I leaned on the railing facing her.

"I'm really sorry for your loss, Lieutenant," I said, and meant it. "I know Detective Ferry was a friend, and this must hurt. I wish there were something I could do."

"There is," Lieutenant McElone said. "You can help me find out who killed Martin."

Paul's grin was so wide I swear I could see his rear molars.

I concentrated my attention not on my usual terrible luck in gambling—I lose money driving *past* Atlantic City—but on the woman inhabiting my glider. "I don't understand," I told McElone.

Her face showed no emotion; her voice was not the least bit wavery. She looked at me with her un-sweat-stained face and said, without hesitation, "I'm asking you to help solve my ex-partner's murder. Will you do that for me?"

Now, the fact of the matter is that bet or no bet, Paul or no Paul, I owed Anita McElone my life at least once and probably more times than that. She had been there for me at times when I most needed someone. She deserved to get what she wanted from me in her time of great need.

But what she really needed was a good detective, which I wasn't. "Are you sure you want me?" I asked her. "Don't you want a more . . . experienced investigator?"

McElone looked at me for a long time, so long that I started to think maybe she was staring into space, thinking of her lost friend. Maybe she was trying to bore a hole in my face with her eyes.

Then she did the oddest thing I could have imagined: She laughed. Not long, not uproariously—she laughed like she'd been taken by surprise by something so unbearably absurd that there was no other logical response.

"I'm not asking you to *investigate*," McElone said. "Believe me. I've *seen* you investigate. No offense."

"None taken," I said. I am very objective about my (lack of) detecting skills. But Paul looked a little put off. "But then, how can I help solve Detective Ferry's murder?"

McElone's face lost any hint of amusement, not that there had been much to begin with. She broke eye contact and looked off toward the street. She bit her lip, but not like she was trying to fend off tears; it was more like she really didn't want to have to say what was about to come out of her mouth.

She was embarrassed, and I'd never seen her embarrassed before.

"I want you . . . that is, I'm wondering if you would . . . please . . ."

Paul broke the silence, but only I could tell. "She thinks

there might be something you can do with people like me," he said. "She wants you to get in touch with ghosts."

I almost shook my head to deny it, and then remembered my track record today betting against Paul. I turned toward McElone and tried out his theory instead. "You think a . . . ghost can help?" I asked gently.

McElone closed her eyes quickly, as if I'd said something dreadfully painful. And she nodded, an almost imperceptible gesture, and let out her breath. Make that Paul two, me zero, for the day.

"But you don't believe in ghosts," I reminded her, though she probably didn't need the help. "You've always made fun of me when I say something about them."

"She's afraid of us, and you know that," Paul admonished me. "She's lost a friend. Let her up off the mat."

McElone turned back to face me, something like the usual fire back in her eyes. "I have seen stuff go down in this house that I can't explain away," she said. "I have watched things fly around with nobody holding them up. I have heard you talk to people who weren't there and get answers to questions that I couldn't hear. I have seen you get out of situations you had no business surviving. A friend of mine is dead, and I want to find out who did it. I'll use anything—*anything*—to accomplish that. If you can get me some good information, I don't care where you get it from, understand? I'll find the way to make it admissible in a court of law later. Now," she said firmly, "Can. You. Help. Me?"

I didn't give Paul time to interrupt, because I wanted him to hear me say it without prompting. "Yes," I said. "I can, and I will."

Three

Contrary to my expectations, Wendy's mom, Barbara, dropped Melissa off at home just a few minutes later. Turned out Barbara and Cliff, Wendy's dad, had plans for the evening, so instead of Melissa spending the night at their place, I offered to provide a roof over Wendy's head so they could cancel their babysitter for the night.

It was a shame from my point of view, though. As soon as they showed up, the girls headed up to Liss's room to "hang out" (kids don't "play" anymore), depriving me of my daughter's input when Lieutenant McElone told Paul and me (one intentionally) the details of Martin Ferry's death. She may be only eleven, but I value Melissa's perspective on the investigations Paul makes me take on; she has a really good sense of people and a way of cutting to the logic of a point that helps.

Instead, she said hello to McElone, gave Paul and me a look that said she wanted an explanation when it was possible and led Wendy up the stairs to the dumbwaiter/elevator that leads to her room. She loves that thing.

Turning back to McElone once the girls were gone, I asked (at Paul's prompting), "Why do you need to investigate the case? Isn't Detective Ferry's own department doing everything they can to solve it?"

McElone, standing now and ignoring the excellent lemonade (I was on my second glass), held up her hands, palms out, to indicate that she didn't want to misspeak.

"They did everything they thought they should do," she answered. "Between the boardwalk fire and how Hurricane Sandy messed up the town, the Seaside Heights department has had more to deal with than they should've. But that's not the issue—it's that Martin's death was ruled an accident. From the trajectory of the bullet and the way the room looked, they determined that his weapon accidentally discharged as he was removing it. They said there was no sign there was anyone else in the room with him. There were no signs of forced entry. There were no prints on the weapon except Martin's. They truly believe it was an accident."

"Then why don't you believe it?" I asked, without Paul's help that time.

McElone did not pause to organize her thoughts. "Because I knew Martin, and that is not a possible scenario. He was so careful with his weapon—and I never once saw him draw it—that the idea he'd just idly toss it on the table and let it shoot him is outside the area of plausibility."

"Ask if his current partner would agree with her assessment," Paul suggested. "Perhaps his behavior has changed in the years since he and the lieutenant worked together."

I passed the suggestion along, but McElone shook her head. "Martin hasn't had a partner since I left," she said. "He wasn't always the . . . easiest guy to get along with."

"No kidding," I said. My memories of Detective Ferry were that he'd had a somewhat condescending and irritable manner, which I'd attributed to the usual disdain cops feel for private investigators. I gave him the benefit of the doubt that it wasn't run-of-the-mill misogyny.

She gave me a warning look. "He was my partner, and he was my friend."

"Okay," I answered. "So what do you want me to do?"

The ice in my lemonade had melted, so now I had lemon-flavored cool water. But I took a sip anyway while McElone gathered her thoughts. Paul was watching attentively.

And then Maxie appeared from overhead, like a vulture. Maxie is sometimes a little thoughtless, I think, in the way she flaunts her ability to travel outside my property, particularly in front of Paul, who is frustrated that he can't. She floated down from above my roof wearing a pair of jeans and a black T-shirt whose legend read, "Seriously?"

"What's the lady cop doing here?" she asked with her usual high level of tact. "Somebody get iced?"

"As a matter of fact, someone did," Paul told her. "Be quiet for a minute." He was all attention on McElone.

"You don't get to tell me—"

"I need you to try to get in touch with Martin's . . . spirit," McElone said, practically trembling with the weight of her embarrassment. "I want you to ask him what happened, and how I can find the person who did that to him."

Involuntarily, I looked at Paul, my conduit to other ghosts. "Ask her," he said.

"What are you looking at?" McElone asked me.

I dodged the question. "How long ago did this happen to Detective Ferry?" I said.

"It happened Sunday."

Paul raised his eyebrows and shrugged.

"Two days ago," I said. "That might not be enough time."

The lieutenant squinted at me as if I were far away and speaking Finnish. "Enough time for what?"

"People don't become conscious ghosts right away," I explained. "The ghosts that I know—"

"Please," she said. "I'm not ready for that yet."

Despite her protest, I continued. "In my experience, it can take a few days before a ghost even knows where he or she is, and a while after that to figure out they aren't alive anymore." McElone was a cop and a good one, and she needed the facts in order to function at her best. "So it might be another day or two—or more—before Detective Ferry can be contacted."

McElone's eyes were serious and focused now. She was on a case and getting the information she required. "That's doable," she said.

"Yeah, if it works," Maxie snorted.

Paul nodded at me. "She has a point. Tell the lieutenant."

"There's something else you need to be prepared for," I told her.

She looked concerned. "He won't know me if he sees me?" she asked.

"It's not that. What you have to prepare for is that not every person who . . . passes away"—I try to be sensitive and avoid using the words *die* or *dead* in front of Paul and Maxie—"becomes a ghost."

"You mean it might *never* be possible to contact Martin about this?" McElone said. The disappointment in her voice was thick; she'd clearly enlisted me as a last resort, and now I was telling her even that could fail her.

"I'm not saying that for certain," I said. "There's no rhyme or reason to it. The rules seem to be different for everybody. Paul says the afterlife comes without a handbook."

"Who's Paul?"

That was a conversation for another day. "Don't worry about it," I told the lieutenant. "What I'm saying is that it might be a few days until I can give you a definitive answer, okay? I promise we'll—*I'll*—do everything I can."

McElone stood up straight. "Thank you for doing this," she said.

"Not at all. I know it wasn't easy for you to ask."

Her eyes narrowed. "You have no idea," she said, then simply nodded, as if dismissing an inferior officer, squared her shoulders and walked to her personal car (she'd never drive the department-issue vehicle on what she considered to be personal business), got in and drove off.

So she probably didn't see me turn toward Paul and ask, "What did we just sign up for?"

"From your standpoint, I would think it's a dream case," he answered. "All you have to do is tell the lieutenant what I tell you. You should be thrilled."

My lip curled a little bit; I didn't agree with his assessment. "I knew Detective Ferry a little, Paul. He wasn't my favorite person on the planet, but I'm not happy he's dead." I walked back inside to the air-conditioning.

Paul scowled, following. He doesn't like it when I call him out on things, especially when I'm right. "That wasn't what I was saying," he said.

Now *I* scowled, and for the same reasons. "Well, let's move on," I said magnanimously. "Can you get on the Ghosternet and look for the detective?"

"He's not gonna be there," Maxie kicked in. I hadn't even realized she'd come inside with us—*she* doesn't care if it's a hundred degrees out. "Like you told the police lady, he hasn't been dead long enough." Maxie doesn't mind the word *dead* as long as it's not being applied to her.

"Nothing is uniform," Paul told her. "We don't know that I can't find him. It's all I can do, anyway. I'll get on it immediately. I will let you know if I get a message back." (That's what he calls the communication he gets from other users of the Ghosternet.) Without another word, Paul sank through the floor of my front room to the basement, which is where he prefers to commune telepathically with those of his own kind.

Knowing my guests would likely be coming back from the beach shortly, I decided to go clean up the game room, where I'd been working, since there wouldn't be enough time now to finish stripping the white paint off the paneling. Maxie followed me, which wasn't astonishing but is unusual. She doesn't often seek out my company and relishes time she can spend on the roof, by herself.

I walked into the movie room (as I'd decided to call it) and assessed its condition. The room was a long rectangle with windows on two sides and hadn't seen much use as a game room. Maxie had suggested turning it into a home theater, while Paul actually thought we should turn it into a "consulting room" for the detective business (I shot that down in a hurry), so obstinately I'd decided to make it a fitness center for the guests—until I asked a few and discovered they had no interest, combined with the high cost of the equipment I'd need to buy. And my father, a former handyman, agreed with Maxie.

As usual, I realized that Maxie, who'd been an interior designer when she was alive, had actually had the best idea first, and subjected myself to her endless crowing when I announced my change in plans. I sold the pool table on Craigslist, and now the space was becoming a movie room.

First step: Strip off the white paint I'd used to cover the paneling because it made the room too bright for viewing movies, especially during the day. And because it was just ironic enough to fit my life. Paint on, paint off. Maybe the first movie we'd show would be *The Karate Kid*.

Maxie stopped at the door and considered. "How dark are you going to go on the stain?" she asked.

"Light," I said. "Just not a real high-gloss finish, because I don't want glare and I don't want it to be reflective." I started to clean up the site, first removing the can of paint thinner. It was extra hot in this room because I had some windows open to reduce the fumes.

"Probably a good idea," she agreed. Ah, so I was going to get the reasonable Maxie this afternoon. Reasonable Maxie was a rare sight, and disturbing in her own way.

I put the lid back on the can of thinner, placed the morning's front section of the *Asbury Park Press* on the lid and stood on it. That way you know the can is closed properly. But there's not much to do when you're standing on a paint can, so I looked at Maxie. "How's your mom?" I asked.

"Fine! She's fine! Can't I do *anything* without being questioned like a criminal?" She flew up into the ceiling and kept going.

I got down off the can of thinner. The reasonable Maxie had left the building.

Four

With Paul downstairs, Melissa upstairs with Wendy and Maxie's whereabouts anyone's guess, I didn't have much time to consider why a young female ghost would fly (literally) off the handle (figuratively) at the mention of her mother.

What I *did* have to do was clean up the movie room, or more specifically, the construction area. I put the paint thinner, stepladder and other tools in a utility closet handily located in the room and did a little quick sweep-up, and the room was presentable again.

I, however, was not, so I went upstairs to shower and change before any of my guests returned from the beach or the town.

I'd barely gotten myself into a presentable pair of cargo shorts and a blue top before my cell phone rang. The Caller ID indicated the call was coming from Jeannie Rogers, my closest friend.

"Hey, Jeannie."

"Heeeeellllloooooo." The mournful elongation of Jeannie's

greeting indicated either that the world had just come to an end and it was left to Jeannie to break the news to me, or that her one-year-old (pardon me, *eleven-month-old*) son, Oliver, was already tracking below the necessary requirements for a terrific preschool he wouldn't be able to attend for at least two years. Equally unmitigated disasters in Jeannie's world.

"What's wrong, Jean?"

A sigh that could have driven a hyena to Xanax emanated from my phone, but I've known Jeannie for a while, so I was expecting it. "Nora broke her leg," she moaned. "She fell down the basement stairs going for a suitcase."

Nora? Who was Nora? Oh, yeah: "Tony's mother broke her leg? Oh, that's too bad." Tony Mandorisi, my friend and home improvement guru, is also Jeannie's husband.

"It's beyond bad," she went on, intimating that I had clearly missed the tragic implications of her—Jeannie's—misfortune. "She and Jimmy were due in tomorrow morning."

This rang a vaguely familiar bell, but I couldn't quite remember what it was that bore significance here. "Well, I'm sure Tony's parents can visit after her leg is better."

Now Jeannie's voice took on a decided edge, since I had not picked up on her deep and lasting misery. "You don't understand. Tony and I are leaving on the cruise tomorrow afternoon. Nora and Jimmy were going to watch Oliver for five days."

Oh, yeah. It had been surprising enough that Jeannie—who defines the term *helicopter mom* to the point that she should be decorated by the Air Force—would agree to leave her young son for five full days, but Tony had insisted that they celebrate their wedding anniversary with their first solo trip since Oliver's birth. So Jeannie had reluctantly agreed to go on a romantic cruise to Bermuda with her husband.

Now that idyll was being threatened by a freak accident suffered by a woman trying to accommodate them, which Jeannie, of course, saw as the queen mother of inconveniences. I probably would have seen it as a dark omen indicating I should stay off the cruise ship at all costs, and that is the difference in our personalities.

Another is the fact that Jeannie absolutely won't believe there are ghosts in my house. She's known me for a very long time but still will not admit to the possibility that Paul and Maxie are real. She thinks I'm a master con woman, taking in gullible tourists who want to see spooky things go on, and that all the evidence of Paul and Maxie (which include flying objects, conversations that seem to have only one side and the occasional hole in one of my walls—it's a long story) is just prestidigitation on my part. Her husband, Tony, however, has taken to the idea of the ghosts, and occasionally even tries to communicate with Paul. He's a little afraid of Maxie.

"Well, there must be someone else who can take care of Ollie," I said, slipping as I used the nickname that Tony used for their son but Jeannie disdained ("It makes him sound like he should be hanging around with a guy named Stan and getting into fine messes"). "It's just a few days, right?"

"It's five days, tomorrow through Sunday," Jeannie answered. "And it's impossible. My brother can't get here from Omaha in time. And none of our friends have children."

That irked me a little. "Hey, *I* have a daughter, you know."

And even before Jeannie responded, I knew I had done something very, very stupid. I had walked into the middle of the highway as the tractor-trailer came barreling down from the mountain with its brake line cut. I had stood in front of the wall during the firing squad's daily target practice. I had seen the funnel cloud and gone driving toward the tornado.

"Really? You wouldn't mind?" Jeannie squealed. "Oh, Alison, I can't thank you enough—you're saving my marriage!" Jeannie is, among other things, given to hyperbole; as far as I knew, there was no trouble between her and Tony.

But that wasn't the point. I had inadvertently just volunteered to bring Oliver to my house and care for him while his parents were on a ship at sea. Now don't get me wrong: I adore Ollie and think he's the sweetest baby on the planet since Melissa, but Jeannie is, let's say, a little exacting about his care. She had interviewed seven different day care centers before deciding on a private babysitter, who had undergone every possible vetting mechanism short of a polygraph test. That was canceled only because Jeannie couldn't find a qualified technician. And even after all that, Jeannie wouldn't trust poor Katie the babysitter with her son for five whole days.

"Whoa, hold on there, Jeannie." This required a moment. I'd volunteered, sort of, and I did want my friends to have a good time. Tony, especially, needed the break (mostly from watching Jeannie hover over their son). I wasn't going to renege on what she saw as a promise, despite its stemming simply from my mention of having a daughter. "I'm happy to help you out, but I want to get a few ground rules straight before we start."

I could hear her eyes narrow. "Ground rules?" she asked.

"Yeah. You need to understand that Liss and I are crazy about Oliver"—I avoided using his nickname so that this time Jeannie could concentrate on what I was saying—"and we're happy to have him visit for a few days."

Jeannie's audible eyes were down to slits now. "But . . . ?"

"*But*, we're not going to be able to do *everything* exactly the way that you do. He's going to be on vacation, too. You have to be prepared for the idea that some things in Oliver's day might be just a little bit different than normal."

"How different?" Jeannie asked.

"Well, for example, I'll try to stick to the foods he eats already, but if I have to make substitutions based on what we have in the house or what my mom might bring one night, I'll do so. Carefully."

Jeannie made something approaching a chewing sound, which indicated that she was rotating her jaw, something she does when confronted with an idea she had not considered before. "*How* carefully?" she asked.

"I'm a gift horse, Jeannie. You want to look me in the mouth?"

There was a long pause while Jeannie undoubtedly considered her options. She had none. "Okay, you're hired," she said.

"Try not to sound too grateful," I told her. "You don't want me to get a swelled head."

"Oh, come on, you know I love you, and I'm thrilled you're taking Oliver! But . . ."

I smiled, but she couldn't see it. "But you've never left him alone this long before, and you're nervous. I get that."

Jeannie had the nerve to sound amazed. "How did you know?"

"I told you. I have a child."

We arranged for Tony and Jeannie to drop Oliver off at noon the next day. I started mentally calculating how much I'd have to pay Melissa to help me out with the baby whenever I couldn't care for him myself but was interrupted by two of my Senior Plus guests, Don Coburn and his "better half," Tammy, returning from their day at the incredibly hot beach.

In addition to the Coburns, I had another couple and two single guests at the moment, and while six people are plenty to deal with, at the height of the season, having any guest rooms vacant was not a great sign. We were still struggling to get back to normal after the Sandy damage, no matter what the TV commercials told us about being "Stronger Than the Storm." I wasn't worried about making the mortgage payments, but the knowledge that college tuition was just seven years away could send me into a cold sweat at night.

Red as beets, walking slowly with fatigued legs, the Coburns nevertheless appeared to be the two happiest people on the planet. Tammy was from Grinnell, Iowa, she had told me, and she was getting a look at the ocean for the first time in her life. Don, who'd moved to Iowa and met Tammy forty years earlier but had grown up in Avon-by-the-Sea, not far from Harbor Haven, just seemed tickled that she was so pleased.

They agreed that the Shore was the best ever (although Tammy really didn't have a basis for comparison) and went up to their room to shower and change before heading out to dinner. A lot down the Shore is different since the storm, but sand still gets into your clothes and hair.

Paul rose up from the basement at that moment—it was clear I just wasn't going to get much cleaning done this afternoon—with a puzzled look on his face. "I tried to contact Detective Ferry, and as we suspected, he is not yet in contact, if he ever will be," he reported. "It would be much easier if everyone evolved the same way."

"The lack of rules really bothers you, doesn't it?" I asked him.

"A lot of things bother me," he said. That was unexpected. Paul usually didn't do the passive-aggressive thing; that was Maxie's territory. And sometimes my mother's.

"What do you mean?"

He waved a hand. "Nothing," he said. "I am a little concerned, however."

"Why?" I decided to go into the kitchen in case any more guests arrived. The Senior Plus tourists are used to my conversing with people who aren't there, and since I'd publicly declared the guesthouse to be haunted, I'd been getting fewer "civilian" guests. Still, it can be unnerving to see your hostess talking to the ceiling or the wall, so I try to keep the kitchen a guest-free zone and conduct conversations with Paul and Maxie there.

Besides, since I don't cook, the guesthouse is not a bed-and-breakfast—no breakfast—so the kitchen is usually unoccupied.

Paul followed me. "After trying to contact Detective Ferry and failing to find him, I sent out a general message asking about him. I got a number of responses from people who had some interaction with the detective while he was alive."

I looked into the freezer, pretending I might actually cook something if I could find the right kind of food there.

This was really just a ruse; I knew perfectly well that with Wendy in the house, we'd be ordering pizza. Luckily, Mom would be over tomorrow to help Melissa cook dinner, when I'd have Oliver around. "So people knew Ferry," I said to Paul. "Is there something suspicious about that?"

"Not on the face of it." Paul, when he's thinking hard, doesn't pay much attention to his positioning, so he drifts. He was about halfway in the air to the ceiling fan now, stroking his goatee. "You would expect that a detective would have interacted with a number of people who are somewhat unsavory, criminals and such. There was one who said the detective had solved his murder."

"I imagine that guy's pretty grateful. Does he have any information that might help McElone?" I asked.

"No," Paul answered, looking uncomfortable. "His information was not specific to the detective's death."

Something about Paul's tone was disturbing. I turned to face him. Paul's head was an inch from the ceiling fan, and I suppressed the urge to tell him to look out, because there was nothing the fan could possibly do to him. "I don't like the way you sound," I said.

"You shouldn't. The man who contacted me said that Detective Ferry was a corrupt officer, and that even his investigation into the man's death was motivated by a chance to help the people who were, as he put it, 'running' the detective."

"You're saying—"

"*I'm* not saying anything," Paul said. "The man who says Detective Ferry solved his murder is claiming the detective was involved with a local mob."

Five

Detective Martin Ferry had mob ties? That wasn't good news, and it certainly wasn't anything I was going to tell Lieutenant McElone unless I absolutely had to. Paul couldn't get any more information out of the "connected" ghost—apparently these guys won't break the code even after they're dead, and *that's* loyalty—to the point that he didn't even know the name of his contact, though Paul noted that the ghost "could be holding a grudge."

I spent much of the night, when not listening in on the latest fifth-to-sixth-grade (summer is an odd time for kids) gossip from Wendy and Melissa or dealing with the needs of my guests, wondering what else I could do to help the lieutenant.

Let me save you the time: I didn't come up with anything.

The next morning, my Senior Plus Tour guests Don and Tammy were the first up and out. They headed off to Point Pleasant to spend the day on the boardwalk, giggling like a couple of teenagers. It was inspiring.

Another couple from Senior Plus, Stephanie and Rita Muldoon, wandered down around eight thirty and took some of the orange juice I'd made available. Even though I don't cook, I do put out coffee, tea and juice in the mornings. This time of year, I also make sure we have plenty of ice in case any of the guests want their morning beverage cold.

Stephanie asked about breakfast places in town, and I directed her to the Stud Muffin, our local bakery, or the Harbor Haven Diner (where I have an arrangement to get a small percentage for every customer I send their way).

"The next ghost experience is at ten," I let them know. Rita laughed lightly. You can tell the ones who are a little bit scared by the way they act like they're not scared.

"I think we'll be seeing some ghost juggling," I told her. It's not that hard to juggle when nobody can see your arms. Paul and Maxie can just hold the stuff in their hands and move it around, and people think it's juggling, I'm told.

"Sounds like fun," Stephanie said. "But there's another one in the afternoon, right?"

Maxie dropped down through the ceiling—early for her—just in time to hear that. "If they're not going to stay, we don't have to do the morning show, right?" she asked.

With my back to the guests for the moment, I threw Maxie an irritated look. "Yes," I answered Stephanie. "Around four."

"Good. I think we might just hang out on the beach this morning before it gets too hot." Rita looked at her wife. "Right, honey?"

Stephanie put her arm around Rita. "Don't worry. I'm here to protect you." She smiled indulgently.

"There's nothing to worry about," I said sincerely. "I assure you, the ghosts in this house are absolutely not dangerous."

"Depends on your definition," Maxie said, but instead of proving her bad-ass-ness by throwing something, like she often does, she just smiled at me. "So, am I off this morning?"

She knew I couldn't answer in front of a skittish guest, but it's hard for her to contain herself. Maxie has, let's say, impulse-control issues.

I ignored her as I got Rita and Stephanie some towels from the downstairs linen closet, reminded them to make sure they used sunscreen and hydrated regularly (I'm such a mom) and saw them out the back door toward what would be my private beach if my beach were, indeed, private. It's not. The borough of Harbor Haven's zoning laws have seen to that. I don't really mind, but I do have to buy beach badges for my maximum number of guests (and myself and Liss) every year. It adds up.

As soon as they were outside, I turned sharply toward Maxie. "All of a sudden you need your mornings off?"

Maxie made a point of studying the ceiling, like Michelangelo sizing up the Sistine Chapel and deciding one of Adam's fingers needed nail polish. "I'm going to see my mom," she said.

"Again?" I asked. "What's going on with your mom? Is she all right? Should I give her a call?" It occurred to me that Kitty hadn't come by the house to visit recently; even though she can't see or hear her daughter anymore, Kitty and Maxie were usually able to communicate via notes, or with help from Mom, Melissa or me (the 3 M's, we actually don't call ourselves).

"She's *fine*. Don't call her! Please?" Maxie started circling the ceiling, which is what she does when she's agitated. If someone could find a way to prescribe Ritalin for those beyond the grave, Maxie would be a regular customer.

"Then tell me what's going on with you. How come you've been going to see your mom every day? And why hasn't she come over here recently? She used to come here about once a week."

"You are not my commanding officer!" she yelled, and once again launched herself skyward and out of the room.

Oooookaaaaaay . . . Well, if nothing else, I guess I'd found a new and effective way to get rid of Maxie when I wanted to. In this case, it was unfortunate, because I'd wanted to ask her to do some research on Detective Ferry, to see if there was any indication he'd been anything but an upstanding, honorable peace officer during his years on the force. I'd have to ask her later. I hadn't actually said she could have the morning off—she'd gotten that, right?

Melissa and Wendy, sleepy eyed from having stayed up late talking, dragged themselves into the kitchen not long after. Liss was stretching her arms over her head, and Wendy smiled, because she always smiles.

"Good morning, Alison," Wendy said. Kids think it's amazing to call grown-ups by their first names. I had no problem with it because I knew Wendy wasn't being disrespectful.

"Morning, Wendy. Who's that you have with you?"

She looked startled. "You mean Melissa?"

I pretended to look more closely. "It is? Wow. That must be what she looks like when she doesn't get any sleep because she's been up giggling all night, huh?"

Liss regarded me with something like disgust, but no less enthusiastic. "Where's coffee?" she rasped.

"If I'd wanted to have conversations like this, I could have stayed married to your father," I told her. "You know where the coffee is."

Wendy, astounded that Melissa actually drinks coffee now, followed her out to the den, where the urn and coffee accessories were currently available, and made sure there was plenty of milk, because my daughter's coffee-to-milk ratio is pretty skewed toward the milk. I chuckled to myself. Liss tried so hard to be an adult, but she was incurably eleven. For a few more months.

It sounded like one of my remaining two guests was ambling down from one of the rooms, so I headed to the den.

Joe Guglielmelli, a single gentleman who had booked his trip through Senior Plus "despite all this silly ghost business," was a widower in his seventies, a nonbeliever in the spirits and a jovial presence at the spook shows, constantly pointing out to the other guests and me exactly how he believed "the tricks" were done. Normally that kind of thing would get on my nerves, but Joe—he insisted—was so genial and engaged that he seemed like a little boy trying to understand how the magician made the dove appear.

He looked up from his glass of orange juice and smiled when I walked in. "Any new tricks from the 'ghosts' today, Alison?" he asked. He mimed the quotes around "ghosts."

"You'll just have to wait and see, Joe," I said with a wink. "Watch really closely."

"Can't wait," he said.

I was about to reply when my phone buzzed. I begged off for a moment, saying I'd be right back and apologizing for my technology-driven rudeness. Joe waved a hand to declare the infraction minor, so I walked to the other side of the room and checked my phone.

The message was from Lieutenant McElone: "Can you meet?"

With less than ninety minutes before the next ghostly spectacle, I couldn't leave my house right now. So I sent back: "Here until 10:30. Want to come over, or wait?" There was a time when this sort of negotiation could have been done quickly and efficiently in a fraction of the time with actual conversation between the two parties, but technology had now advanced us to a point where a simple exchange could take a half hour.

My last guest, Bonnie Claeson, had not yet emerged from her room, but I'd discovered during the past few days that Bonnie liked to sleep in, and our motto is: Do What You Like.

McElone texted back: "Come here by 11?"

I sent back: "Yes, but need to be back here at noon."

Jeannie and Tony were bringing Oliver in time for lunch. Melissa could easily handle him if I was gone, but I knew it would look so negligent in Jeannie's eyes that she might be unwilling to leave Oliver with us, and then Tony would probably kill me for ruining his anniversary vacation, and what good would that do anyone? Then *I* might become a ghost, and the whole thing would just get more complicated.

It's a slippery slope once you've met your first dead person.

There wasn't going to be much for me to tell McElone anyway. Paul hadn't been able to contact Detective Ferry yet, and what he had been told was both disturbing and unconfirmed. I wasn't going to upset the lieutenant, who was mourning her friend, with unsubstantiated allegations that he'd been a dirty cop.

Perhaps the best thing to do would be to find out if those allegations could be substantiated. *Hoping* they were false wasn't quite enough. If I could get information that cleared the detective, I could at least feel better about not mentioning them to McElone.

I needed Maxie. She does the serious online research work when we have an investigation going. Maxie apparently never knew it in life, but she has mad computer skills. Apparently, one *is* never really finished learning.

I walked over to Melissa, who was trying very hard not to laugh at Joe's assertion that the ghost effects were "all done with wires."

"My mom's good with tools, but she's not *that* good," she told him.

"Excuse me," I said, taking Liss gently by the arm. "I need to borrow my daughter for a moment."

"Of course," Joe said, and he headed for the front room.

"Find Maxie," I told Melissa.

Wendy appeared at Melissa's side. "Is this a ghost thing?" she asked.

Liss nodded. "What do you need Maxie to research?" she asked me. We could speak freely because Wendy knew all about the ghosts. The whole town, and those sections of central New Jersey served by the *Harbor Haven Chronicle* and its affiliated website, knew all about us, too. Whether they believed it or, like Joe, thought I was a genius with special effects was irrelevant. I'd given up any pretense that the place was normal.

My daughter looked concerned. "What's wrong?"

"Nothing's wrong, but I need her to do some research, and I don't think she'll come if I ask. She'd never ignore you, no matter what." Maxie absolutely adores Melissa and considers my daughter her "roommate." So asking Liss to find Maxie was a strategic move. Besides, Joe wanted to see a ghost show, and that meant I needed ghosts.

"I told you what Lieutenant McElone was here about yesterday, right? I need Maxie to find out everything she can about Detective Martin Ferry. Fast."

"Anything in particular?" Her eyes narrowed.

I didn't want to prejudice the investigation; it's something Paul has taught me. "No. Just whatever she can find out, and tell her to go beyond Google. I want deep stuff, okay?"

"Got it," Melissa said, but her expression was suspicious. "I'll call her. Better go up to my room. She might be there already, and if she's not, I'll have to yell pretty loud." Wise beyond her years, that one. She and her BFF were on the staircase in a blink.

Now that I had time to think about it, I wondered why I hadn't seen Paul yet this morning. Maxie was *never* out and about before him. The ghosts don't exactly sleep—they have no need to restore their bodies—but they do go off sometimes to be by themselves and to "rest our minds," Paul liked to say. It was odd he wasn't around.

I started calling for him quietly. "Paul," I said in a conversational tone. That's often enough to reach him; maybe he gets vibrations or something when his name is spoken. But this time, as I walked back toward the former game room to do some work on the walls, there was no response.

"Paul," I said more forcefully. I was dressed for stripping paint, certainly, in a pair of cargo shorts and a T-shirt that, while clean, was not entirely in mint condition. I got the paint stripper out of the closet—something that sounds a lot dirtier than it is—and used a paint-can opener to get the lid off after I'd shaken it sufficiently. Then I opened the nearest window to dispel some fumes.

Still no Paul. And while I can't say I was officially worried, I was certainly confused by this development. It's the rare moment when I call for him and he doesn't appear.

What the hell; everybody in a ten-mile radius knew I had a ghost infestation. Why play coy? "Paul!" I shouted. And was indeed a little relieved when I heard a rustling near the archway that served as an entrance from the hallway. I looked over.

Melissa and Wendy were standing there, looking just a tiny bit puzzled.

"What's wrong?" I asked.

"I can't find Maxie," Liss said.

"That's funny," I answered, although I didn't much feel like laughing. "I can't find Paul, either."

Six

A thorough search of the house, from attic to basement, turned up no sign of either ghost. It was possible that they were down near the beach or in the large backyard, but a quick glance out through the beach doors turned up Rita and Stephanie and no one else.

In Maxie's case, that wasn't entirely unexpected—unlike Paul, she can leave the property, and she had said (however unreasonably) that she was going to take the morning off and go visit her mother. Paul's absence was more troubling. He didn't have the ability to leave my property and didn't spend much time outside. I knew that his inability to move freely bothered him. Paul had come to New Jersey (when he was alive) by way of Toronto, Canada, but had been born in England and had something of a restless spirit. Or *was* something of a restless spirit.

"I'm worried," Melissa said. "There's no place Paul could have gone, but he isn't anywhere."

"Paul's fine," I said, completely unsure of whether I meant it. "He's probably just gone into hiding somewhere."

Wendy, the very soul of optimism, suggested that we might have been looking in one room while Paul was in another. The fact that Wendy couldn't have seen Paul even if he were standing a foot away from her was not brought up.

"There's only one thing to do," I told the two girls. They didn't ask what that thing was, which was good, because my thought process being what it was, I would have come across as seeming far too self-involved and not concerned enough about our friend. But the question remained: Once you're dead, can something really bad happen to you anymore?

Without considering that too deeply, I put my only course of action in play: I went over to Joe to inform him that, unfortunately, the morning spook show had to be canceled. "Don't worry," I told him. "The one this afternoon will be that much more spectacular." He nodded with a sly look and said he understood; Joe was an understanding if skeptical guy.

Since I had unexpectedly freed up some time, I got in touch with Lieutenant McElone and told her I'd be on my way. I did not tell her that I'd be bringing two eleven-year-old guests, since she might object, but I didn't have a babysitter on standby at the moment. It is illegal in the state of New Jersey to leave a person under the age of twelve alone and unsupervised.

On the way to the police station, though, I did ask Melissa to call my mother to see if she could meet us back at the house by eleven thirty. For one thing, that would free me up for whatever activity McElone might have in mind (if any) or to drive over to Kitty Malone's house to locate Maxie for the afternoon ghostfest and perhaps for a line on where to find Paul.

Wendy packed up what little overnight stuff she had—since she hadn't expected to stay over, it wasn't much—and called Barbara, who agreed to meet us at the Stud

Muffin after our visit to the police station. She couldn't get there *before* the visit, and that was actually fine with me. I like to bring other people with me when I visit Lieutenant McElone. There is strength in numbers.

We arrived at the Harbor Haven Police Department a little before nine thirty. I found an actual parking space around the corner and was careful to feed the meter to its time limit. The one place you're sure to get ticketed for illegal parking is around the corner from a police station.

McElone was not outwardly thrilled to see the two girls with me when the dispatcher in the reception area buzzed us through to the bullpen, where she has a cubicle. But being a mother of three (the only pictures she displayed on her disgustingly neat desk), she did not grouse about it, as she would about virtually anything else. In fact, she welcomed the girls, told them that she and I had to discuss some business that she preferred they not hear about—I respect people who speak honestly to children—and asked them to sit in a waiting area nearby, still visible but not within earshot.

I could see Melissa bristle a little at the move, because she believes herself to be a valuable and helpful asset to an investigation, which is indeed true. But Melissa also knew she had no chance of winning an argument with the lieutenant, so she led Wendy to the waiting area. It was quiet in the bullpen, and no one paid much attention to the girls.

McElone made sure to keep her gaze trained on them. "Did you really think it was a good idea to bring a couple of fifth-graders in to consult?" she asked once the girls couldn't hear.

"What did you want me to do, leave them home with the ghosts?" I can usually use Paul and Maxie as a deterrent to any argument the lieutenant might make. She doesn't have enough ghost knowledge to contradict me. "Enough, anyway; they're here. So what's the emergency you called me in to discuss? I told you I haven't been able to contact Detective Ferry yet. It might still be a couple of

days." I didn't reiterate that it might be never; I knew Mc-
Elone would remember me saying that.

She did, however, look around with a slightly concerned
expression. Her voice dropped down to a murmur. "Let's not
broadcast that," she said urgently. "Remember, this is not
official police business, especially not in Harbor Haven."

I understood that she was right, and nodded. "Sorry.
What can I do to help, Lieutenant?"

McElone made a sound that was somewhere between
frustration and exasperation. "I've been told by the Seaside
Heights department that the investigation into Martin's
death is being ended. They're ruling it an accident and closing the file."

That wasn't good news. But I was also baffled as to how
that required my presence here. All McElone wanted me to
do was contact Ferry if he showed up on the Ghosternet.
Beyond that, if the department where Ferry had worked
was ending its investigation, that meant no one besides
McElone (and, in theory, me) was looking into his death.
More distressing was the idea that McElone would not be
able to draw on the work and the conclusions of the Seaside Heights police and would probably not be able to
access their files to help her in her investigation.

"I'm sorry to hear that, Lieutenant," I said. "So . . . what's
that got to do with me?" Tact. My middle name. Alison Tact
Kerby.

McElone didn't seem to notice. "I'm taking some vacation time from Harbor Haven," she said matter-of-factly, but
in a tone that indicated she wanted the conversation to stay
between us. I noticed a couple of uniformed cops a few cubi-
cles away, but they didn't seem to be paying any attention to
us. "I intend to use the time to find out who killed Martin. If
the Seaside Heights department isn't investigating because
they think they know what happened, I'm left to do it myself."

That was a little stunning, to tell the truth, but it didn't
answer my question. She'd get to my role in her own time.

I wasn't going to suggest that it would be one of an assistant investigator. The only thing worse than McElone condescending to me would be her laughing at me. I've been there.

"That means you won't be able to find me here," she continued. "When your . . . informants find out something about Martin, you'll need to call me on my personal cell." She gave me the number, and I dutifully entered it into my phone. "If you do call, don't tell me anything about the case over the phone. Just say that you have some information, and I'll tell you a place to meet. Okay?"

I nodded. "But you could have called me with this," I told her. "Why did you need to see me in person?" I looked over at Melissa and Wendy, who were deep in "conversation," although the exchange appeared to be taking place by text. These kids today, am I right?

"There's more," the lieutenant answered. "I need to give you something." She produced from her top drawer a thumb drive with the logo of the borough of Harbor Haven on it. No doubt they made great holiday gifts. "Take this and keep it safe. It's a backup of Martin's case file from the Seaside Heights PD. If I need it, I'll get in touch."

I took the drive from her hand and put it carefully in my hip pocket. "You act like you're going undercover with the mob for six years," I said. "Is all this cloak-and-dagger necessary?" I left out the part where I was honored that she'd chosen me to protect the case file. I was, but saying so would not be within the code of behavior McElone and I had established.

"It's precautionary," she answered. "I don't expect any problems, but I like to be prepared. And there's something else."

As I waited, Melissa walked over to me. "Okay if Wendy and I head outside for a minute?" she asked.

Before I could answer, McElone stood up. "Why don't we all go outside?" she asked.

That seemed telling, so I nodded, Liss turned back and

beckoned toward Wendy, and the four of us headed for the door.

Once outside, we started walking—slowly—toward the Stud Muffin. The girls pretended to be hanging back so McElone and I could talk freely, but I knew that Melissa could, and would, listen to every word we were saying.

"The truth is, I don't want you to know everything," McElone said. "That's partially because I don't *need* you to know everything. The ghost thing, well, I probably shouldn't have asked. I was emotional. I was upset. But it's out there, and it's too late to take it back."

"It can be helpful, Lieutenant," I said. "You can trust that any information I get for you will be accurate, I promise."

"Maybe. It still seems crazy, like one of those things that seems like a really good idea at three in the morning. I should have waited until I'd had a couple of cups of coffee before I decided to go ahead with it."

I could feel Melissa's eyes on my back; she is very serious about our ghost connections and impatient with those who treat it as a silly figment of our imaginations. But she wouldn't say anything, especially to the lieutenant. I'd have to hear her fury later, when we got home. It's all part of the service of being a mom.

"No turning back now," I told her. "What else is there that you want me to know?"

"The Seaside Heights department's decision doesn't feel right. It's too fast; it's too soon. It's like they wanted to get this out of the way as quickly as they possibly could." McElone was staring straight ahead again, in full detective mode. She is a very efficient cop and normally doesn't allow emotion to play a role in her process. This situation must have been extremely difficult for her.

After all, she was talking to me.

"I don't know anything about the personnel there," McElone went on. "I wasn't in constant touch with Martin after I left Seaside, and there has been some turnover since then."

"You two seemed friendly enough when I saw you together," I noted.

"Yeah, but even then he didn't tell me much of anything. The point is, Martin didn't gossip. He didn't complain about the other cops on the force. He just did his job, and did it well. And he pissed some people off because that was the kind of guy he was." I felt it was best not to pass along Paul's contention that the afterlife held at least one person who thought Detective Ferry had been working hand-in-glove with the local mob.

"I get it. You don't know the people in Seaside Heights, but you're concerned that they might be sweeping Detective Ferry's death under the rug." I heard Melissa quicken her step behind me so she could hear better. A thought struck me, and I almost stopped walking. "Do you think someone in the department he was working in might have killed Detective Ferry and covered it up?" I asked.

McElone's mouth might have twitched just a little in irritation; not with me, but with the suggestion. "I'm not saying anything like that. The point I'm making is that I don't know what the situation is here, or there. And that's why I'm not ever going to mention your name to anyone. That, and the fact that if they knew I was checking with a ghost person, they'd laugh me out of the job."

It took me a moment to decipher what she'd just said, and then I lowered my voice so that Melissa couldn't hear. "You think I might be in some danger?" I asked.

McElone gave me one of her patented sardonic sideways glances. "No," she said with emphasis. "I'm telling you this so that you'll use the proper caution, though I don't really believe there will be any reason whatsoever for you to put it into use. Understand?"

"Was that sarcasm?" Sometimes it's hard to tell. We're from New Jersey. I've heard people say hello sarcastically.

She shook her head. "I mean it sincerely. I'm giving you some backup folders because this case is not on the books.

I'm giving you my cell number so you can find me when I'm not at work. And I'm suggesting that you not mention any of this to people you don't know and trust because I still have no idea who killed Martin. Is that clear enough?"

"Crystal," I said.

"Good. Now forget everything except the being-careful part until you talk to some ghost who has a story to tell. Then you call me. Got that?"

Seven

After McElone turned around and walked away, no doubt to pack up the one stray paper clip on her impeccably neat desk and take her leave of absence, Melissa and I took Wendy to the Stud Muffin, where her mother, Barbara, reported a lovely evening out with her husband, and we reported a lovely evening spent in with Wendy.

The whole way back home, Melissa peppered me with questions about Detective Ferry, what McElone had told me when Melissa couldn't hear (I answered with something terrifically helpful like, "Oh, it was nothing important, honey") and what we were going to do to help.

"*I'm* going to do exactly what I promised the lieutenant I'd do," I told her. "Wait for Paul to get some information to pass along, and then pass it along. The rest of the time, I'm going to be a good innkeeper and a fabulous mother, just like always."

She didn't even chuckle at the "fabulous mother" crack. "But we can't find Paul," she said. "How can he report anything if we don't get to talk to him?"

Liss had a point, but I didn't want to hear it. "He'll be there when we get home," I said with some very shaky confidence in my voice. "You'll see." I made a mental deal with myself that if Maxie wasn't in the house either when we got back, I was going to call Kitty and ask if everything was all right. Let Maxie get mad at me when the phone rang at her mother's house. By the time she got home, she'd be in another mood entirely. Or so I told myself.

"Even if he is back, we need to be doing something more than waiting," Melissa protested. "The lieutenant is really upset, and she's our friend, so we should do whatever we can to help her." My daughter is without question a better person than I am, but she's eleven. She has lots of time to get worse.

"We are doing everything we can," I said. "We're keeping the lieutenant from having anything else to worry about. She wants us to stand on the sidelines, and that is precisely what we're going to do."

"But—"

"No. That's it. No wiggle room on this one, Liss. I agree with Lieutenant McElone. This is her thing to do, and she really does have the experience and the authority I don't have. She *is* hurting, and you're right to want to make her feel better, but all you and I can do is follow her instructions. I'm not discussing it beyond that. Clear?"

Liss seemed stunned that I was playing the mom card so forcefully. She sat back, folded her arms and didn't talk to me the rest of the ride home. I wasn't thrilled about that, but it indicated that she had at least heard my argument and would abide by it.

Oddly enough, I had been right about one thing: When we got back to the house, Paul was floating around the den looking serious, which is his default look. Melissa's face lit up when she saw him. "Paul!"

Bonnie Claeson, my sleepiest guest, was now awake and sitting in an armchair near the door of the den, reading a book. Bonnie seemed comfortable with the idea of ghosts in the house, but rather than interact with them, she seemed to simply want to spend most of her time quietly reading or walking on the beach.

My favorite kind of guest.

Now, Bonnie looked up, amused, at Liss, then went back to the book she was reading without so much as a word.

"What's wrong?" Paul asked, no doubt a little surprised by Melissa's oversized greeting.

"We couldn't find you," Liss said, moving to the far end of the room. Bonnie didn't seem to be listening to the conversation, but we didn't want to disturb her reading.

"Well, I was here," Paul said. "Don't worry." He seemed to be looking at the ceiling, which was odd. Paul was rarely evasive.

"We looked everywhere," Liss insisted.

"Clearly not *everywhere*," Paul told her. "I wasn't *nowhere*." It was worse than I thought; he was treating Melissa like a child, which he'd never done before. I began to wonder exactly what Paul could possibly be trying to hide.

I kept my voice low but conversational. "We really did search pretty thoroughly," I told him. "Have you seen Maxie?"

"Not recently," Paul said. "Is something wrong?"

"I need her to do some research," I explained. "Lieutenant McElone is taking some personal time to look for Ferry's killer on her own, and she wants us to sit around and do nothing until you can get in touch with the detective himself."

Paul's hand went to his goatee, but he didn't stroke it. Not yet. He needed more.

I reached into my pocket and pulled out the flash drive McElone had given me. "Take this and put it in your pocket," I told Paul.

"Clever, Mom," Melissa said, smiling. "That way nobody but us can ever get it back." That was the plan.

Very few people could see Paul, and even those of us who could wouldn't be able to get the tiny flash drive if he hid it in his clothing, since the ghosts can make objects "disappear" to the living by doing that. It helps them transport objects through walls and so forth. Maxie, for example, will often "put on" a bulky trench coat in order to move the laptop around.

"Exactly." I told Paul what was on the drive, and he looked impressed. He put it into the pocket of his jeans. "And don't give it to anybody but me, Liss or my mother."

"Of course," Paul answered somberly. His British/Canadian upbringing meant he could do serious like few others. "Now, what's this about Maxie?"

Maxie. *Remember her?* "I need to call her mother," I told Paul, reaching for my phone. "Maxie keeps going over there, supposedly to visit Kitty, but she gets really defensive about it. I'm worried something's wrong."

Paul looked concerned. "Now that you bring it up, Maxie has been especially mercurial recently."

If Paul noticed a change in Maxie's mood, it could be serious. I got the impression my two resident ghosts didn't interact very much when we were not all meeting communally. It's not that they don't like each other; they just don't have much at all in common. So Paul isn't always Maxie's most meticulous observer. Seeing a change in her demeanor meant the change was not subtle; but then, nothing about Maxie is subtle.

"That's it," I said. "I'm calling Kitty."

"Why?" came a voice from behind me. My father, floating a foot or so off the floor, was suddenly there, a habit he's picked up since passing away, and one that is not my very favorite of all time. I adore my dad, but it was so much more convenient when you could hear his shoes on the floor.

"Hi, Grampa!" Melissa always brightens up when her grandfather is in the room. They have a special bond.

"Hello, peanut," he said to my daughter. "How's tricks?"

"Tricky," she answered. A private joke. My own grand-father once told me that grandparents and grandchildren always get along well because they have a common enemy. Now that I was on the other side of that, I chose not to believe it.

"Hi, Dad," I said. "I take it Mom is here?"

"Coming in from the car," he answered. "She brought dinner. It's not cooked yet, but she brought it."

Sure enough, there was a sound coming from the kitchen, as Mom, no doubt weighted down by the fifth-grader's backpack she uses in place of a purse, had stuffed more supplies to prepare a meal than you'd swear could fit into the backpack. The woman can cook, and she can pack. Both skills must have skipped a generation, because I don't have them. Melissa is still in the development stage, but already she's surpassed me in cuisine.

I opened the kitchen door. "Mom? Need help?"

"Nah," came the reply. "I just put the whole backpack in the fridge. So my driver's license will be a little chilly. In this weather, that's not a bad thing."

"There was room in the fridge?" I asked, mostly talking to myself.

"The carrot didn't take up much room." Mom never actually runs me down—even when she should—but the no-cooking thing is a sore point with her. She thinks I'm forsaking a wonderful talent I surely possess yet am refus-ing to put to use. She's wrong.

As Mom joined the group in the den, Bonnie Claeson greeted her (obviously, she couldn't see Dad), then said she was going up to her room for a bit. I made a mental note to ask Bonnie if she had any relatives who might want to come stay with us for a while, too. Having her here was like hosting no guests, but I got money.

As Bonnie headed up the stairs, the rest of us turned our attention to Paul, as if it had been previously agreed that we would do so. He watched after Bonnie for a moment, then looked back down at us and started. "What?" he said, see-ing our expectant faces.

"I don't know," I said. "You usually have a plan of some kind."

Paul shrugged. "I got nothin'." He puts on what he thinks is a Jersey accent when he's trying to be a regular guy. It doesn't work.

"Why are you calling Maxine's mother?" my dad asked again. Mom walked in behind him, and he turned to smile at her. They have a great marriage, despite her being widowed.

"Maxie's been acting strange, and Mom thinks maybe Kitty is sick or something," Melissa helpfully reported.

"Oh, my," Mom said. "Is it serious?"

"I don't even know if there's an 'it' yet, Mom. It's just that Maxie has been visiting her mom a lot, and she's being touchy about it. That's all I know for sure."

"You should call Kitty," Dad suggested.

"I will," I said, and got out my phone. I saw I had a new text message from McElone, asking if I'd secured the flash drive she'd given me. I looked up at Paul and smiled before texting back that the information was more secure than she could imagine. Then I looked at Melissa. "What she really wanted was an update, and we saw her just over an hour ago. She's more demanding than almost any client we've ever had."

Melissa shook her head. "Not as bad as Mrs. Murphy," she said. My client on Everett Sandheim's murder. Everett, a sweet bear of a man once you knew him, had been consider-ably easier to get along with than the client, even when con-fronted with his death in a public restroom. I liked Everett. He was no longer the mountain of a homeless man I'd known when he was alive. As a ghost, he'd reverted to a younger, trimmer form, that of the military man he'd been years before.

"What client is this?" Dad asked. "You out there gum-shoeing again?"

We brought my parents up to speed on the Detective Ferry investigation, which horrified my mother and got my father looking worried. "You be careful, baby girl," he said to me when I was done.

"Me? All I have to do is wait around. Paul's carrying the dangerous information, and there's nothing much that anybody can do to him."

"Detective Ferry was the lieutenant's friend," Liss said. "She feels bad, and she wants to do something."

"Just like you should do for Maxine and Kitty," Mom reminded me, and once again I reached for my phone.

Clearly, the call was simply not meant to be. A considerable tumult came from the front room, and moments later, Jeannie, Tony and Oliver appeared, Tony's arms loaded with supplies that appeared to range from stuffed animals to frozen containers of food, and Jeannie's loaded with Oliver, who was crying on her shoulder.

"He's been cranky all day," Tony said, putting down a suitcase, a blanket, what appeared to be a quart of carrot juice and a box of flash cards. "I'll be right back." He turned and headed back toward the front door.

"Where are you going?" Melissa asked.

"To get the next load."

"He's not cranky," Jeannie said. "He's dealing with abandonment issues."

I walked over to try to take Oliver from her, but Jeannie was holding on like Montgomery Burns to his last animated billion. "Abandonment?" I said. "You're still here."

"He's seen the luggage," she answered. "He's very intelligent."

"He's eleven months old, and you've never gone away before."

"He's intuitive."

"He's spoiled," Dad volunteered, but luckily Jeannie couldn't hear him. Of course, even if Jeannie *could* hear him, she'd decide Dad's comment was really just the wind blowing or a seagull honking as it flew by. Jeannie was a master of seeing and hearing only what she wanted to. That applied to babies as well as ghosts, apparently.

Paul simply looked mildly irritated. He is a lovely man, but hardly warm and fuzzy with children. They interrupt his investigative process.

"Jeannie, he'll be fine," I said. Melissa came around to get into Oliver's line of sight—he usually responds to her with a big grin. But he wasn't looking at her this time, and kept crying.

Tony walked in with a portable playpen under one arm, a yellow plastic bucket on his head (almost covering his eyes, which made his gait unsteady) and a beach ball, inflated, under his other arm. In his hands were a large box of raisins and a small tom-tom.

"We had less stuff than this in our whole house when Alison was that age," my father said. Mom covered her mouth and pretended to cough. Luckily Jeannie didn't notice, or she would have had my mother disinfected and put Oliver in a hazmat suit.

"It's okay, Oliver," Melissa cooed at the baby. He heard her and looked over. The crying didn't exactly stop, but it did lose some intensity as Oliver seemed to remember that person with the lilting voice. "Aw, it's okay." Melissa reached up and tried to take Oliver from Jeannie. The baby held out his hands for a moment, but Jeannie, not seeing that gesture (I'm being diplomatic), turned the other way and walked a few steps toward the pile of baby accoutrements in the center of the room.

Tony was already on his way out the door for load number three. I remembered he had a rather large pickup truck he used for his contracting business and was suddenly glad I had a spare guest room where I could dump all of this junk (except what Oliver really appeared to want or need) once his parents were out the door and on their way to Bermuda.

"Why wasn't I told about this?" Paul asked, looking impatient. Had I not mentioned Oliver's visit to him? Was I actually obligated to do so? I mean, it was still my name on the mortgage, right?

"Don't you like kids, Paul?" My father was a fine handyman and a good businessman when he was alive, but he always said the most important role he'd ever had was being a dad.

Paul looked embarrassed. "I just . . . I don't have any particular difficulty . . . I'm concerned it will hinder our investigation." I didn't see how having Oliver around would do much to slow down our investigation, or at least our role in the investigation, which was to wait until Paul could Ghosternet with Martin Ferry, if it ever became possible.

By the time Tony had arrived with the third load of baby gear (which included actual necessities, like a stroller and car seat), it finally occurred to me that we'd let him out into the inferno to do manual labor alone. "Melissa and I will help you with the rest," I volunteered.

"The rest?" Jeannie scoffed, patting Oliver on the back although he'd stopped crying entirely and was eyeing Melissa over Jeannie's shoulder. "How much did you think we brought for a five-day stay?"

"Of course. How silly of me."

What followed was a seventeen-minute tutorial on the care and feeding (particularly the feeding) of Oliver Rogers Mandorisi, who was still attached as if by Krazy Glue to his mother's left shoulder. Eleven-month-old children are not tiny infants, and you'd think Jeannie's arm at least would be a little tired, but she would not budge. Not even as she showed me how to open and close the stroller, reinforcing the impression that she was leaving her darling child with a woman who had never seen a baby before, let alone raised one to the verge of adolescence.

I let Jeannie school me because I knew it would make her

feel better. And because she'd leave sooner if I didn't offer any resistance. My technique nearly backfired, though, when she finished her shpiel, gave me a sharp look and said, "You haven't asked any questions."

"That's because you've been so thorough, dear," my mother offered ahead of the emotional tirade I'd been planning. "There's no subject you haven't covered perfectly." Was Mom this duplicitous every time she'd told me what a swell job I was doing? Best not to think about that.

Tony had taken time during the floor show to excuse himself and check out my handiwork in the soon-to-be home theater. "It's going well," he reported when he returned. "The paint stripper is doing its job. You should be able to stain the paneling in a day or two."

"Paint stripper?" Jeannie repeated, her eyes suddenly wide. "Are there going to be fumes in the house?"

I shot Tony an accusatory glare and then turned to his wife. "Don't worry," I said. "Oliver won't ever be in the room when I'm working on the walls."

"You're going to leave him by himself?" I love Jeannie, but since she had a baby, I have occasionally fought the urge to slap her upside the head.

"No," Melissa said, coming to my rescue. "She's going to let me take care of Ollie sometimes." She waggled a finger at the baby. "Right, Ollie? Right?"

Oliver, perhaps wisely, did not answer.

"And sometimes I'll be here," Mom added, not noting that Dad would undoubtedly join her because . . . well, what's the point?

"Jean," I said in my calmest, coolest voice, "you have to be able to trust us. Oliver is going to be very well cared for while you're gone. But *like we talked about on the phone*, you have to let us vary—just a little bit—from what he's been used to. It'll be good for him, and it'll be good for you. Now hand over your baby and scram."

Jeannie looked stunned, but then a smile developed

slowly on her face. She put Oliver down, and he immediately started crawling toward Liss, who sat down next to him and started to tickle his chin. Oliver laughed his baby laugh.

Tony seized the opportunity and said to his wife, "Let's go while we can."

Jeannie's smile left, and her eyes got a little moist. "Now?"

"Now." Gently.

She started toward her son, her arms spreading for a hug that would probably last until after they were scheduled to return from the cruise. "Jeannie," Tony said, "just say good-bye." He got down on the floor and looked at Oliver. "Bye-bye, Ollie. We'll see you soon."

Oliver, at the sound of his name, turned his attention from Melissa to his father. "Da." Then he looked back at Melissa and smiled.

Tony stood up and turned toward Jeannie. "See?" he said.

Jeannie, her heart ripped from her chest despite being about to go on a cruise to a lovely island with her adoring husband, bit her lower lip and sniffed. She sat down next to Oliver and Melissa.

"Bye-bye, baby. Mommy's going to come back real soon. Okay? Promise."

Oliver looked at her with a confused expression. Those were a lot of words to take in.

"Bye-bye, honey," Jeannie repeated.

Oliver seemed to consider that, then smiled. "Bah," he said.

"That's 'bye,'" Tony translated for us, like we didn't already know.

"Bye-bye," Jeannie repeated. She sniffed again. Then she swooped down, clutched her son (who looked astonished) into her arms and kissed his forehead until I thought there might be a permanent indentation of her lips.

I took her by the arm and helped her up off the floor. Then, still holding her arm, I led her to Tony, who took her hand and headed toward the door, Jeannie still twisted to look at Oliver. "Bye-bye, sweetie," she said once again.

Oliver looked at Melissa and said, "Bah." Then he reached for an Oscar the Grouch puppet lying near him. He held it out to Melissa, who put it on her hand.

She took on a deep voice and said, "Bye-bye, Mommy."

"Bah," Oliver noted.

Tony managed to get Jeannie out of the room before she dissolved into what I was sure would be a flood of tears. I hoped he would manage to get her to stop while the ship was still at least north of Virginia.

Everybody who could breathe gave a sigh of relief when we heard the truck pull out of the driveway. Oliver, although he'd been here many times before, decided to case the joint, and started crawling around the perimeter of the den. Since it is the largest room in the house, that promised to take a while, which was fine with me.

Liss said she'd watch Oliver, and Dad decided to stay with her as a messenger (if needed) while Mom and I sorted Mt. Baby Stuff and stored the unessential items (i.e., ninety percent of the cache) in an unused guest room on the second floor. Paul followed behind us.

"Why didn't you tell me the child would be staying with us?" he asked again. "A little advance notice might have been helpful, that's all."

"Paul, you're not going to get anywhere sounding like my ex-husband," I told him. "Can you think of anything else we should be doing for Lieutenant McElone? In particular, things that aren't the least bit dangerous?"

"Once Maxie can research the claims I heard . . ." Paul hovered in the air for a moment. Oh, yeah. Maxie.

I reached for my phone. "I'm calling Kitty right now," I said.

From above and behind me, a shrill, piercing voice.

"You promised you *wouldn't*!" I hadn't promised anything, actually, but Maxie had asked me not to call her mother. To Maxie, her asking was the same as me promising.

Everybody turned, and sure enough, there was Maxie, just below the ten-foot ceiling, wearing her trademark sprayed-on jeans and a black T-shirt with the legend "Don't You Wish" emblazoned on the front. We stared at her for a good few seconds. Maxie stared right back.

"What?" she asked.

Eight

There wasn't time to argue with Maxie, which was just as well; it's a frustrating waste of time that usually gives me a headache. Besides, I'd already gone through the routine of "what's with your mom" followed by Maxie leaving in a huff twice. They say third time's the charm, but Melissa would miss Maxie if she left and didn't come back.

I probably would, too. After a couple of years.

Luckily (depending on one's point of view), we had work to discuss. I shrugged off any concerns about Maxie's mother—for now—and took advantage of the fact that our chief research specialist had returned. "We need you to do some work," I told Maxie. "Lieutenant McElone needs us to help her."

"I don't know," Maxie said, playing with her hair and spinning in a small circle near the ceiling. "I don't think the lady cop likes me."

"She doesn't believe you exist," I pointed out.

"Still."

"The lieutenant has hired us to help her on a case," Paul

told his ghostly counterpart. "Whether she likes you is irrelevant." Paul is a very nice man and an intelligent one, but his reliance on logic and the call of duty when talking to Maxie (or me, for that matter) is usually ill advised. Neither of us signed on willingly to be in the detective business.

"Roger that," Maxie said. She floated up into the ceiling, presumably in search of the stone-knives-and-bearskins-era MacBook I'd inadvertently donated to her. McElone had confiscated Maxie's much cooler laptop as evidence and then never given it back, seeing as how it was evidence in two murders. Kitty, after Maxie had prevailed upon her, had requested the return of her daughter's property, and had been entangled in red tape (something about possible appeals by the killer) for two years now.

I blinked a few times, stunned by Maxie's quick decision to be reasonable, since being reasonable is usually her seventh course of action. "Did you see that?" I asked Paul. "She just said, 'Okay,' and went off to help."

Paul's eyes registered wonder. "She didn't say, 'Okay.' She said, 'Roger that.'"

My mother looked at me and shook her head. "You know, sometimes you don't give that girl enough credit," she said. "Maxine has a good heart."

"Maybe so, but it's still attached to her mouth," I said. "Which one of us is your daughter, anyway?"

"You are," Mom agreed. "But it's not a competition."

"That's what you think."

Paul was (intelligently) ignoring this exchange, but he stared up into the ceiling with a puzzled expression on his face. "Odd," he said, probably not meaning for us to hear it.

"What's odd?"

He took a moment, then looked down at me, as he had risen very close to the ceiling himself. "Where's Maxie?"

I felt my eyes narrow. "What do you mean? You saw her go," I reminded him. "You heard her agree to help."

"Agreed, but we never told her what it was she needed to research."

That was true. Mom and I exchanged a look, and then Mom said, "I'm not braving that dumbwaiter. You go. I'll check on Melissa and Oliver." And before I could reply, she was on her way back down the stairs.

"I guess we're headed up," I told Paul.

"Meet you there. I'm making a stop."

I nodded my acknowledgment and headed toward the pull-down stairs to the attic, which Tony and I had renovated into a spacious bedroom for Melissa. It both kept her out of the guest traffic and gave her a bigger, more personal space than she'd had when we first moved in.

Tony had later rigged up a dumbwaiter for Liss to get in and out of her room without climbing another set of rickety stairs, but I don't like to use it. I feel like that's Liss's space, so the pull-down stairs, which lock on the inside and out for security, are my preferred route to her room.

When I'd gotten to the point above the floor where just my eyes were high enough to be considered inside the room, I stopped on the stairs, flabbergasted at what I saw.

Maxie, dressed in a sensible (even for someone who was *not* Maxie) but beautiful navy blue dress, floated in front of the full-length mirror I'd hung on a far wall. Maxie swirled in midair, turning her head each time in an apparent effort to see how the dress looked in the back. She was studying the mirror intently, but there was no reflection in the glass.

"It looks lovely," I said as I climbed up the last couple of stairs. "Even in the back."

Maxie jumped at the sound of my voice. And when Maxie jumps, she travels. Her top half ended up outside the house on the roof, so I couldn't see her face until she descended a few moments later looking embarrassed.

"You never heard of knocking?" she demanded.

"You really are stuck at the emotional age of sixteen, aren't you?" I asked. Maxie was twenty-eight when she died but still had some growing up to do. "What's the problem? I said the dress was lovely, and you look good in it."

Maxie immediately changed back into her standard jeans and black T-shirt. This one read, "Don't Go Away Mad. Just Go Away." "You scared me," she said, though she kept twirling.

"That's a role reversal. What's up?"

"Up? Nothing's up. What makes you think something's up? What's up with *you* all of a sudden?" I'd seen Maxie in a lot of moods, most of which I found annoying. But I'd never seen her jumpy before. I wasn't sure what to make of it.

"Sorry. I've just never seen you in a dress before."

"Well, I'm *allowed.*"

"Nobody's saying otherwise. You looked nice."

She stopped twirling and looked at me. "You really think so?"

"Definitely. I didn't mean to startle you."

Paul chose that moment to rise up through the floor. He wasn't looking at either Maxie or me; as soon as he could reach into his pocket, he turned his attention to the object he pulled out.

It was the bare-bones prepaid cellular phone I'd gotten him for the times when I'm out of the house and he needs to communicate with me for a case. He can't be heard on the phone, but he is able to text. He stared at it with serious concentration. His fine motor skills are much better than when we first met, but he still needs to think about what he's doing in order to work with objects in the material world.

"Your mother says Oliver is taking a nap," he told me without looking up. "Melissa is watching him sleep."

"Thanks. What are you doing? Returning phone calls?" I caught myself. "Sorry."

Paul looked up. "Why?"

"Forget it."

Maxie, who normally would've leapt on the opportunity to point out my rudeness, had now changed into another dress, a black, tight, short number that, if she were visible to the general public, might cause cardiac problems in some more vulnerable men. She was back at the mirror looking at nothing.

"I'm texting you, Alison. See if you receive what I'm sending," Paul said, punching some more keys on the phone. It wasn't painful to watch him interact with physical objects like it used to be, but he was definitely not in Melissa's weight class when it came to texting. My daughter could send the complete text of *The Brothers Karamazov* in less time than it took you to read this paragraph.

Soon enough, my phone buzzed. I pulled it out of my pocket and checked for Paul's text, which read, astoundingly, "Text."

"Wow," I said. "That's impressive. Next you'll tell me I can send my voice through this magic box as well."

"That's very amusing," he said. "Now consider that my phone has no battery in it."

That was strange. "Did you lose the battery?" I asked.

"No. You're missing the point. I was able to generate the power needed to send that text message myself. I sent you a text from a *dead* cell phone."

Ignoring the irony of a dead man using a dead phone, I started to see the point he was trying to make. "How is that possible?" I said.

"I have a theory," Paul said, as Maxie changed into an off-the-shoulder number in cobalt blue. "It has long been observed that it is impossible to destroy energy. The physical body might deteriorate, even disintegrate, but energy is not destructible. Many people believe that the essence of a living being, the soul, is composed of energy."

"So even though you're dead, your energy lives on, is that it?"

He pointed at me like a teacher whose student is starting to catch on. "I've been working with the proposition that our bodies, those of Maxie and me and other people like us, are actually made of the energy that we carried with us when we were alive. Our physical bodies are gone, but the energy remains in a purer form. So I can send a text message without a battery because I am, essentially, made of energy."

That was as far as my mind could go; I had to ask, "So what's that got to do with Detective Ferry and his murder?"

Paul had a confused expression. "Nothing. What made you think it was related?"

"When we're on a case, you almost never think about anything else," I noted. "What's gotten you on this energy stuff all of a sudden, when there's a crime to be solved?"

Paul frowned. "Until Detective Ferry does or does not materialize in some form, there's nothing I can do about his case," he said. "However, the implications of this theory are enormous."

"How so?"

"Don't you see? If I can find a way to harness and control my energy, I might be able to evolve past this existence and on to the next level."

That knocked me for a loop. While I knew that Paul and Maxie were intrigued by the idea of other planes of existence, especially when we'd witnessed some other ghosts presumably advance to . . . whatever comes next, without any of us really understanding what was happening, and I recognized that Paul seemed mildly envious of those other ghosts, I'd thought we'd settled into a comfortable setup in the guest-house. "You mean you want to leave?" My voice sounded a little squeaky.

Paul looked up from the cell phone and examined my face. "Well, certainly," he said. "I don't mean to offend you, Alison, but becoming the next . . . thing is natural. It seems like what we *should* want, don't you think?"

"I don't want to go anywhere," Maxie chipped in, now back to wearing her more typical ensemble of jeans and a T-shirt, this one currently reading "Restore the Shore." "Things are good here." She looked at me. "Which dress did I look best in?"

"The first one. See?" I turned toward Paul. "Things are good here. Why do you want to go?" This was suddenly becoming a very disturbing conversation for me.

Paul's eyes indicated he was talking to a crazy lady. "I don't sincerely believe anything is going to happen very soon, Alison. There's no need to be upset."

And yet for reasons I couldn't adequately understand, I *was* upset. Paul had become such a stable and reliable presence in the house over the two years I'd lived here, I couldn't imagine what it would be like without him to confer with.

"Is it so bad staying here?" I asked. Yeah, I was being selfish. News of the day: I'm not perfect.

Paul looked at me carefully and curled his lip. "Yeah. It's a misery," he said. "I hate every minute of it."

I was devastated. I couldn't think. "Really?"

"Of course not!" Paul replied hurriedly. "I was being sarcastic."

"You're not from New Jersey, Paul," I informed him. "You don't pull off sarcasm successfully."

Paul, perhaps trying to shift the mood, looked over at Maxie. "What have you found out?" he asked her.

Maxie stared at him blankly. "What are you talking about?" she said. Maxie's a lot of things—I could give you a list—but clueless isn't normally one of them.

"You came up here to do research on Detective Ferry," he reminded her. "Then Alison came up to give you specific areas in which we need questions answered." His voice betrayed some bewilderment; surely Maxie knew all this already.

I didn't mention that in my astonishment at finding Maxie acting like she was on *Say Yes to the Dress*, I had forgotten to pass on the instructions.

"Oh," Maxie said. "Yeah. I'll get right on that." She looked at me. "What was I looking for, again?"

Paul's eyes, usually on the smallish side, widened to the

size of half dollars, or whatever the equivalent currency is in Canada. "You *haven't* been researching the case?" he asked incredulously. "What have you been doing up here?"

I decided to talk over him to defuse any situation that might have otherwise arisen. "You know how the ghost Paul talked to earlier said Detective Ferry was a dirty cop working for the local mob?" I said, condensing madly. "We want to see if there's any evidence—bank records, incriminating e-mails, notes in his personnel file, for example—that can confirm or deny that."

Maxie immediately had the laptop in her hands, but as she began clacking away and looking industrious, Paul got a very odd look on his face. Suddenly, he seemed to be either horribly surprised or sick to his stomach. I knew the latter wasn't possible (at least, I was pretty sure it wasn't), so I guessed it was the former.

"You okay?" I asked him.

"Something's happening," he said, choking out the words.

A hollow feeling hit my stomach. Was Paul already moving to the next plane of existence? "Paul?" I said.

Maxie looked up, then looked back at the screen.

"I'll be right back," Paul said, and started to descend into the floor.

"No!" I yelled on an impulse. "Don't go! What's happening?"

He continued to slowly melt into the carpet. "I believe I'm getting a message from Detective Ferry," he said.

Oh. That.

Nine

"What is that?" Lieutenant Anita McElone asked me.

I looked over at Oliver, who was playing with a set of colored rings that stacked on a plastic post. He didn't seem to be all that difficult to identify.

"It's a baby," I said. "As I recall, you've had some yourself."

I'd called McElone as soon as Paul had reported back from his "conversation" with Ferry, who was still emerging from his stasis and barely cognizant of his new ghostly status. Ferry's message to Paul was that he was at his apartment and couldn't leave. That's not at all unusual, especially when the ghost is just becoming a ghost. Beyond that, Paul said, Ferry "wasn't especially conversant."

Happy to have some progress to report, I'd let McElone know, and she'd suggested that we meet at Ferry's apartment. Personally, I'd have preferred to go see Ferry alone. I didn't think McElone had taken my news seriously, but she said any chance was better than none, then reiterated that it was imperative I tell no one I was involved in the investigation.

I'd just put Ollie down on the floor of Martin Ferry's Seaside Heights apartment. The place, no longer classified a crime scene, wasn't incredibly child friendly, but it wasn't exactly a danger zone, beyond a lack of covered outlets, something people of my generation had survived well enough.

Mom had offered to watch Ollie while I was at Detective Ferry's apartment, but I knew she had a beauty-salon appointment, and besides, I saw no reason McElone could object. It was possible I'd miscalculated that one. I did ask Mom to take Liss with her to the salon, which was next door to a bookstore. Liss would browse the aisles while my mother became more gorgeous.

"Yes, and my babies are very nice, polite people now," McElone answered. "But I still don't bring them with me to crime scenes."

"I'm watching Oliver for my friend until Sunday," I said now. "You want me, you get him."

McElone didn't say anything, but she made a face indicating just how unprofessional I was, which didn't bother me in the least. Professionally, I was an innkeeper. Talking to ghosts for police detectives was just a sideline.

My phone buzzed, so I took it out of my pocket. It was a text from Josh Kaplan, whom I'd been seeing now for long enough that I supposed I ought to call him my boyfriend. The word sounded weird, since we were both adults, but I'd actually known Josh when he *was* a boy—we'd met at his grandfather's paint store as tweens, then lost touch until a little less than a year ago.

The text read: "Dinner tonight?" I texted back in the affirmative. This relationship was getting easier, especially since I'd told Josh all about Paul and Maxie and didn't have to worry about what I could or couldn't say in front of him anymore. One thing a single mother learns on the dating scene: There aren't a lot of guys you can tell about your resident ghosts.

Ollie continued to play with the rings, which were in vivid colors. The orange one, I noticed, was most often used as something to chew on. Luckily, it was far too large for Ollie to get it all the way into his mouth.

"Easy, Ollie," I said, putting the largest ring on the post first, hoping to get him interested in something other than the flavor of the orange ring. "Which ring goes next?" Oliver looked at me with wonder in his eyes.

"Gah," he said.

"That's right," I agreed.

McElone let out a guttural sound. "Okay. Where's Martin?"

It was a good question; as far as I could tell, the detective's ghost was nowhere to be seen in this room. But since Oliver and I had just arrived, we hadn't had a chance to look elsewhere.

This wasn't a very ghosty area, I'd noticed on the drive here. There were plenty of tourists—Seaside Heights is one of the bigger draws down the Shore—but the ghost population was fairly small. I guessed people didn't die near amusement piers as frequently as they did in other shore resort towns. And the neighborhood was still in recovery; now, rebuilding after a flood *and* a fire, Seaside was no doubt anticipating the appearance of locusts.

The apartment wasn't large. It was a two-bedroom apartment on the second floor, a single man's undecorated residence, with a front room (where Oliver and I now sat on the floor), a galley kitchen back and to the right, and a corridor leading off the main section, where I could see three doors leading to other rooms.

"Not here," I told McElone. "Let me take a look." The lieutenant was already examining the room, which had been cleared of any evidence, no doubt trying to determine if there was something the Seaside Heights detectives had missed.

I stood to pick up Oliver, and he immediately began to protest. He had been happy on the floor playing with the rings; he had no interest in finding a dead detective he wouldn't be able to see or hear anyway. He squawked loudly.

My options were limited; I looked at McElone. "Do you mind?" I asked.

"Mind what?"

"Watching Ollie while I check out the rest of the apartment. He doesn't want to give up the game he's playing." To cement my case, I put Ollie back down, and he went happily back to what he'd been doing.

McElone rolled her eyes. "You want me to babysit in the middle of a murder investigation." It wasn't a question. "I should have my head examined for talking to you about this at all."

"You won't say that when we get the straight poop from Detective Ferry," I reminded her.

"Don't say 'poop' in front of the baby."

"I'll be right back." I walked toward the corridor. "Detective Ferry?" I called. "Are you here in the apartment now?"

I caught a glimpse of McElone shaking her head as I walked away.

There were three doors, plain pine with a light coat of sealer but no stain, the sign of a housing company that offered a roof over your head and not much beyond that. The one at the end of the hallway was clearly the bathroom; the door was open, and cheap porcelain tile was visible.

The second door led to the bedroom, which was empty, or at least devoid of any ghosts. The room held a bed, a dresser and a nightstand. A closet with sliding mirrored doors was half-filled with clothing, mostly cheap suits and some jeans and casual shirts, but no T-shirts. Despite living so close to the beach, Detective Ferry had dressed mostly for work, it seemed.

I went back out into the hallway to the third and last door. I almost knocked, but that seemed silly. I opened the door.

Detective Martin Ferry, or what survived of him, was hovering near a desk on which a laptop computer was sitting, turned off. He was wearing a relatively cheap blue pinstriped suit. Luckily for me, there was no evidence of the gunshot wound that had taken his life. He looked like an average middle-aged, somewhat paunchy man. If not for the being-able-to-see-through-him, you'd never give him a second look.

The room also held a daybed, a stationary bicycle and the desk chair Ferry would have been using if he hadn't been floating two feet above the floor. He was trying to press keys on the computer keyboard, but his hand kept going through the keyboard and the desk, creating a sort of hacking motion that made it look like Ferry was attempting to beat up the keyboard. His face showed frustration.

"Detective," I said. He turned and looked at me.

"My hand doesn't work," he said.

"The baby is trying to eat the coffee table!" McElone called from the living room.

I looked at Ferry. "Your hand will probably get better over time," I said. "But in the beginning, that's the way it is for most people like you."

He squinted to get a better look at me and hovered over a little closer. "I remember you," he said. "You were that nut who thought she could see ghosts."

I nodded. "Alison Kerby."

"And I'm . . . a ghost?" Ferry said. "I'm a ghost. What's going on, Kerby?"

"Paul Harrison sent me. Come on into the living room," I said. "I brought a friend of yours."

"Paul Harrison," he said, thinking hard. "I got a . . . there was some question in my head from a guy named Harrison. How does that work?"

Thinking it was best not to get into technical details I

didn't understand, I shrugged, then led Ferry into his living room, where I found McElone holding Oliver on her shoulder and bouncing him a little. He looked amused.

"Anita," Ferry said. "Anita, what's going on?"

Of course McElone did not answer.

"She can't hear you," I told him.

McElone turned to look at me. "You're saying Martin's here now?" she asked, looking up and over my shoulder suspiciously. People who can't see ghosts always look up, though the ghosts aren't always up.

McElone put Ollie down, and he crawled to the coffee table, where there was a bowl with some large round glass spheres in it for decoration. I sized them up, decided that he couldn't get one entirely into his mouth and let him go for it. Somewhere on the Atlantic Ocean, Jeannie probably felt a chill up her spine. Ollie pulled himself up to an almost-standing position via the coffee table, from which he could just touch the purple orb but couldn't move it.

"Anita can't see me, either?" Ferry asked.

I shook my head, since talking to him directly would probably make McElone uncomfortable. "Yes, he's here, Lieutenant."

Her eyes narrowed. "How do I know it's him?" she asked.

That hurt. "You don't trust me?" I said. "I'm here doing this favor because you asked me to, and you still think I'm the crazy ghost lady?"

McElone's mouth flattened out, but she didn't say anything. Ferry, however, shook his head. "She's a cop," he told me. "She doesn't trust anything she can't prove herself."

I thought for a moment. I couldn't ask Ferry to move something or float it around the room; his physical skills weren't developed enough yet. "Ask him something only he would know," I said. "Something I couldn't possibly figure out on my own."

But Ferry beat me to it. "Handcuffs," he said. "Tell her 'wet handcuffs.'"

McElone was about to speak, but I stopped her. "He says to say 'wet handcuffs,'" I said.

A laugh like nothing I'd ever heard from McElone came out. Then her eyes widened. "It *is* Martin," she said.

I felt like saying, "Yeah, I already told you that," but I had resolved in the past seven seconds to try responding to things in a more mature manner than Maxie might employ. It was a new strategy, but one worth trying. "Yes, it is," I said. "Now, what can he tell you that you need to know?"

McElone's cop face came back on; she looked as serious as Hurricane Sandy, and in my world, that's serious. "Okay, tell him this *exactly* the way I say it," she began.

"I don't have to say it," I explained, pointing toward what she saw as empty space. "He can hear you."

Ferry had, in fact, floated down from his spot, which hadn't been that high up to begin with, and was looking McElone deep in the eye from maybe six inches away, as if she were a favorite celebrity he'd encountered unexpectedly, or an especially intricate museum exhibit. "Anita," he said quietly.

McElone, however, was still staring up at a spot her former partner had not inhabited to begin with. "Martin?" she said much more loudly than he had spoken. "Martin, are you there?"

Ferry, shouted out of his reverie, gave me a look. "Yes, he's there," I reiterated. "What can he tell you that will help?"

Oliver, I suddenly noticed, had stopped playing with the purple ball, which he hadn't been able to lift, and was staring up into the room.

Directly at Martin Ferry.

I stored that information away for another time (maybe *all* babies can see ghosts? Ollie had looked up vaguely in

Paul and Maxie's direction before) and concentrated back on the conversation.

"What can he tell me about who . . . about what happened to him?" McElone asked the air.

"She means how I ended up like this?" Ferry asked. I nodded. "I'm a little fuzzy on that."

"He says he doesn't remember everything clearly yet," I translated. "That's not uncommon. I've never gotten a full story out of a ghost who just made the leap."

Ferry blinked a few times and made three popping noises with his mouth, which definitely attracted Oliver's attention.

McElone pursed her lips. "Martin," she said. "Think about this. They're saying you shot yourself by accident. I know you didn't do that. So tell me about your weapon, and where it was when this happened to you."

Ferry looked surprised. No, astonished. "They think I was careless with my service weapon?" he said, not to anyone in particular. "I might not be the neatest guy on the planet, but that gun is *never* loaded unless I'm on duty. They're wrong."

I relayed that to McElone, who nodded. "I know that, Martin. But I need to know who else was here when this happened. Who could have gotten their hands on your gun, maybe when you were out of the room or something?"

Ollie gave up on the large, heavy glass balls, which looked pretty but weren't all that interesting to play with. He let himself down onto the rug and crawled toward Ferry, looking up.

Ferry's hand went to his forehead, as if he had a mild headache. He closed his eyes. "Honestly, I don't know. Ask me about the wet handcuffs, and I'll remember. But ask me about today . . ."

"It happened about three days ago," I told him. Let him get perspective.

"Really?" He stopped and stared forward, stunned by all the information he was getting in one gulp. Meanwhile,

I was wondering about those wet handcuffs these two thought were so hugely hilarious. Oliver lay down flat on his back on the floor to get a better view of Ferry. With any luck, he'd be asleep in a few minutes.

"What was three days ago?" McElone asked.

"This'll go a lot faster if you don't ask about everything I say to Detective Ferry," I told her. "Anything relevant I'm going to say just as he says it or explain it immediately. I promise."

McElone's face closed up again. "I'd still feel better if I could see him."

It was harder to feel sympathetic toward her when the person she was mourning was there in the room talking to me. I sort of rolled my eyes. No. I completely rolled my eyes.

"What more do you want me to do?" I said. "Throw a blanket over him so you can see that he's there? It doesn't work like that." It actually could sometimes sort of work like that, but I was making a point.

She cocked an eyebrow as Ferry folded his arms, seemingly trying to figure out what to do in such a situation. "Every time I question this dippy visit, you tell me that's not the way it works. It sounds like you're trying to dodge the questions."

"*You* called me in on this," I reminded her. "I can leave anytime you think I'm lying to you. Why would I do that?" I walked over toward Oliver, who was not at all asleep, but gurgling and waving his arms toward Ferry. "We're out of here, Ollie," I told him, and went to put my hands under his arms, the most wiggleproof method of lifting a contrary almost-toddler. I didn't look at McElone, but she certainly wasn't trying very hard to stop me.

"Hold it," Ferry said. "You can't go!"

I looked up at Ferry, not caring what McElone thought. "Why not?" I asked. "Your pal over there thinks I'm lying to her. She doesn't want me involved. I'm doing what she wants me to do; I'm leaving."

"Pretending to have an argument with Martin and making me the bad guy isn't going to help," McElone said.

I turned to face her. "Listen, if you don't believe me, why did you ask me to do this?"

She shook her head. "I wasn't thinking straight. I was desperate. I'm sorry. I thought if there was even a chance you could talk to Martin . . ."

I opened my mouth to answer, but Ferry beat me to it. "Tell her I did what I always do with my weapon—I unloaded it and locked it away. I don't know how I got shot."

But McElone's lip curled when I repeated her ex-partner's message. "I told you all that," she said. "You already knew it."

"I didn't know about wet handcuffs," I pointed out. "In fact, I *still* don't know about wet handcuffs."

Ollie, having had enough of grown-ups not paying attention to him, started to fuss and sat up. There wasn't anything for him to pull up on so he could stand, so he crawled toward me.

But I couldn't give him my undivided attention at the moment. "That's true," McElone said. "You couldn't have known about that."

"So you realize the only way I could have said those words would be if Detective Ferry was here telling me to say them," I told her.

McElone studied the carpet. "Ask him who was here," she mumbled.

"Ask him yourself." I needed her to accept that Ferry was here, to trust that what I told her was from his mouth.

Her eyes glared, but she looked up. "Where is he?" she asked. I pointed in the proper direction, and she made eye contact—sort of; she was actually looking at his neck—with Ferry. "Martin. Tell me who was here the last you can remember. Who can I talk to?"

Ferry looked into McElone's eyes.

"I don't know," he said sadly.

I waited, thinking there'd be more. But there wasn't, so I passed that along to McElone, and the information didn't help. However, I could see her eyes looking around the room, meaning she was thinking. "What's the last thing you do remember clearly?" she asked, now fully engaged as a detective.

Ferry squinted, trying to look into his past. Hopefully, his very recent past. He took a good few moments, during which Oliver managed to pull himself up by grabbing onto the shorts I was wearing, which would have been really risky if I hadn't been wearing a belt. He stood, shakily, holding on hard to my leg.

"I remember coming home, and putting the gun away," Ferry started. "And going into the kitchen to get a beer or . . . something . . . when the doorbell rang."

"Who was at the door?" I asked on my own.

Slowly, he shook his head. "I can't remember. That's when the world changed. There's nothing I remember after that."

McElone listened to me repeat Ferry's words, then chewed on the inside of her lip. "Were you expecting anybody?" she asked. She had started looking at Oliver, no longer willing to simulate a real conversation with Ferry.

"No," Ferry answered. "I remember being surprised when the bell rang."

McElone absorbed that. "The gun was locked in the drawer like always?" she asked.

"I can remember that clearly," said Ferry. "I'm sure of it."

"Where was the key?"

"In my jacket pocket. I hadn't had time to change out of my suit yet."

"Any reason somebody would want you dead?" the lieutenant asked.

"Besides the usual?"

McElone and Ferry shared a chuckle, but she didn't

hear any except her own. "It *is* Martin, isn't it?" she sort of asked me.

"What have I been saying?"

The smile dimmed on McElone's face, and she tried to look in Ferry's direction. "Martin," she said. "Have you heard from Elise lately?"

Ferry, who hadn't exactly looked cheery to begin with, took on an even gloomier expression. "It wasn't Elise," he said.

McElone waited for my reiteration of the response, then said, "Nonetheless. Have you heard from her?"

Ferry nodded, perhaps forgetting that only I (and apparently Oliver) could see him. "She started calling a couple of months ago," he told his colleague. "Said I was behind on Natasha's child support."

"What did you tell her?"

"To read the divorce decree. You know perfectly well I'd give my daughter the shirt off my back, but Elise just wanted me to pay her out of spite, for revenge."

McElone sighed. "I'm going to have to call her, you know. Just to ask a few things. Unofficially, you understand."

"Try to keep Nat out of it, will you?" Ferry asked.

"I will if I can, but I'm not promising. Is there anyone else I should be looking at? Who do you like for the murder?" Cops have their own jargon, and they have an interesting attitude: McElone was asking Ferry whom he suspected might have killed him, but they were both treating the question like a consultation on a case, and nothing else. It's a way to cope with what they see on a daily basis: people at their worst.

Ferry considered. He paced a little, a foot off the floor, and actually scratched his head at one point, which made Oliver laugh. Ferry looked down, saw the baby and smiled.

"Who's the kid?" You had to be newly dead to have missed Ollie until now, but Ferry was adjusting rapidly.

We had to make allowances for circumstance. He looked at me. "Yours?" Some allowances.

"I'm watching him for my friend until Sunday," I said. "My daughter's eleven."

"Watch out for her when she turns twelve," the dead detective said. "That's when they start getting mean." He grinned and waggled his finger at Oliver.

"Thanks," I said. (If you're reading this, Melissa, I said it with a sarcastic tone. I'm not worried about you. Much.)

"Martin." McElone rotated her hand in a "come on" motion. "Who else should I talk to?"

Ferry stopped trying to get Ollie to laugh, and his eyes unfocused, trying to remember. "You need to see Captain Stella at my department. He's not a bad guy, and didn't have anything to do with . . . this . . . but he knows the mood in the squad room. I know you'll be shocked, Anita, but I wasn't the most popular guy there."

McElone snorted lightly and shook her head when I relayed that info. "Imagine. Anyone else?"

"There's a drug dealer who works the boardwalk, not as much as before the storm, but he's still there. Calls himself Lay-Z. I was working on a case with him as a confidential informant. He might have gotten the wrong idea."

McElone took all that in. "Were you about to bust him?" she asked.

"No. But I heard just before . . . you know, *this* . . . that someone had found out he was my CI. He might have thought I ratted him out."

"How about the person you were really trying to bust?" McElone asked.

"Buster Hockney. Not a great big kingpin, but a guy doing damage with the locals and a few tourists. I wasn't that close to an arrest, but maybe Buster didn't know that. Buster might do something this crazy, though. He's not exactly what you'd call rational. Likes to hurt people."

"Where can I find your files on that?" the lieutenant said.

"I don't know what they did with my files," Ferry told her. "That's something else you'll want to ask the captain about. I can't seem to leave this apartment."

"That's not unusual for most ghosts," I told Ferry.

"I'm really a ghost?" The idea takes some getting used to, I'm told.

"You're you," I said. "Just not the same as you used to be."

"That sounds like something they'd say in a weight-loss ad," McElone butted in. "Martin, you tell me if you get any ideas. Get in touch through this one." She pointed at me. "I'm working your case."

Ferry's eyes narrowed. "Wait. Anita. I've been telling you all this, but you're not in the department anymore."

"For the next two weeks, I'm a private eye," McElone said, looking directly at me. "A *real* one."

"You're welcome," I said. "Come on, Ollie, let's go home."

"Gah," Ollie said.

Ten

"You think Oliver could see Detective Ferry?" Josh Kaplan asked. He looked down at Ollie, who was sitting on the floor with an Ernie bath toy, squeezing it to make it squeak and laughing every time it did. Babies are terrific audiences; they think the same joke is hilarious four thousand times in a row. The rest of us might have differing opinions.

It was good to have Josh there. He comes by a couple of times a week, knowing that I can't go out very often at night because I have guests. Since we'd rediscovered each other—we met as kids—I'd found him to be a calming, understanding presence. Josh accepts the weirdness in my house with a smile, and accepts me as . . . me.

"I'm not sure. Maybe all babies are more sensitive. Ollie has sort of reacted to Paul and Maxie a little bit before, but I've never been sure," I said. Josh can't see or hear my resident ghosts—or any others—but he trusts me enough to believe they're there when I say they're there.

Josh had arrived just as Mom and Melissa were getting

dinner started, no doubt with my father watching. They cook; Josh and I clean up. It works for us.

This might be the only time we'd spend alone all evening, if you consider having two ghosts and an eleven-month-old in the room with you "alone." At the guesthouse, things are relative.

"Oogie boogie," Maxie said to Ollie, testing my theory. But Ollie wasn't interested because Ernie was so darn much more fun. Squeeze. Squeak. Laugh. Seriously, how could you top that?

Paul, hovering at the far side of the soon-to-be movie room, looked uncomfortable. "Can we get past the baby talk and discuss the case?" he asked.

"*We* don't have a case," I reminded Paul. "Lieutenant McElone has a case. We're helping when we can. Right now, since there's nothing we can do to help, we're not doing anything."

Josh, used to this sort of one-sided (to him) conversation by now, smiled vaguely and tried to look where he thought Paul might be. Paul wasn't within ten feet of there, but I saw no reason to spoil Josh's attempt at camaraderie.

"But there's quite a bit we can do," Paul argued. "Maxie, what did you discover about Detective Ferry?"

Maxie stopped trying to get Oliver's attention and looked startled. "Huh?" Maxie doesn't cover for herself well.

"We asked you to research the rumors I heard about Detective Ferry. What have you found out?" Paul, because he thinks logically and acts accordingly, believes everyone else does, too, which is not actually a very logical way to think or act. So maybe Paul's not really so logical after all. Don't think about that too long. It'll make your head hurt.

"Roger that," Maxie said with an edge of "jeez" in her voice, and floated up through the ceiling, presumably to look for my MacBook, which was so old it was probably put together in Steve Jobs's garage.

Paul sputtered a bit at Maxie's behavior. "What is going on with her lately?" he asked.

"You've noticed it, too?" I asked.

"Noticed what?" Josh said. He at least likes to know what the topic of conversation is among the people in the room he can't see.

"Maxie's acting strange," I explained.

Josh's brow wrinkled a little; it was cute. "How can a ghost *not* act strange?"

Oliver decided that he shouldn't keep the blatant hilarity of his Ernie doll all to himself, so he stood, considered walking, remembered he didn't know how, dropped back down and crawled over to me. He held out the doll, and Josh, probably for want of something to do, took it. Ollie didn't mind getting a substitute when asking for my attention, as long as Ernie continued to make that hilarious noise. Squeeze. Squeak. Laughter.

"A ghost can act the same way any living person can act, emotionally," Paul said with a slight snippy tone in his voice. Paul has had, let's say, some issues with a few of the men I've dated. He doesn't mind Josh as much as my ex-husband, The Swine, but he still seems to think I'm better off when I'm on my own. My opinion differs from Paul's.

"Maxie is acting *uncharacteristically* strange," I told Josh.

"Ah," he answered. Squeeze. Squeak. Laugh. Being a baby seems like so much more fun than it probably is.

"Maxie," Paul reiterated. "Do you know why she's so flighty?"

"She won't tell me," I said. "I'll get Liss on the case. If Maxie will talk to anybody, it's her."

Maxie took that cue to come down through the ceiling dressed in a trench coat and her "work hat," which is what she calls a green visor she wears in the mistaken belief that it makes her look more professional. She looks like she should be dealing at a poker table with Oscar Madison and Felix Unger.

"Okay. Detective Ferry," she said to Paul. "What's his first name, again?"

I reminded her of the detective's name to avoid Paul's eyes actually springing out of their sockets with irritation. Josh sat down on the floor next to Oliver and squeezed Ernie again. Same sound, same uproar.

Maxie started clacking away on the keyboard. While she was toiling away, Paul ventured closer despite the presence of what he clearly believed was an infectious baby and looked down to deliver one of his periodic lectures on criminal investigation procedure.

"Alison, just because the lieutenant sees you strictly as a specialist in . . . communication with the victim does not mean that we can only sit idly by until I get another message from Detective Ferry. We can help her in ways that she hasn't thought of yet."

I looked at him. "Weren't you the one who was saying we should just wait and see what happened?" I asked. Josh, practiced at not looking surprised, didn't look surprised that I was talking to nothing.

"That was before you spoke to the victim," Paul countered.

"Do you mind if I do this for a minute?" I asked Josh, and gestured up into the air, where he knew the ghosts were.

"Nah. Ollie and I are considering what tint of wood stain to sell you when you're done stripping the paneling. We'll confer." Josh grinned, which is one of my favorite things for him to do.

I grinned back at him—a down payment on a later promise—and turned back toward Paul. "Look. I trust the lieutenant's judgment. She's taking charge of the investigation. It's not like Ferry's asking us to do anything else. We help when she asks us to. Doing anything else would be overstepping our boundaries."

Josh smiled. He thinks it's cute when I sound authoritative, as long as I'm not arguing with him. Paul didn't look annoyed or angry; he looked challenged, as if I'd slapped him with a glove and told him to contact my second for choice of weapon.

"We *can* help," he said. "We are not overstepping anything if we can offer the lieutenant something she could not find otherwise. And the faster we do so, the sooner this matter will be brought to an end." Now that part was odd; Paul rarely wanted to finish a case quickly.

It's not that I didn't want to help Lieutenant McElone. But even though she had been the one to approach me, she was clearly mortified at dealing with the possibility of ghosts, and I didn't want to seem even sillier than usual in her eyes.

So I decided to push Paul in the hope that he wouldn't be able to answer me. "Help her how?" I asked.

"Like this." It was Maxie, not Paul, who responded from way up near the ceiling. That probably meant she'd found something. She tends to float pretty high in the room when she's engrossed in computer research. "Here. I had to go into Detective Ferry's arrest records and the cases he was assigned, but you can see there's something there."

"I can't see anything without a six-foot ladder," I told her.

Maxie guffawed a little and lowered herself and the computer to an angle that was visible from where I was standing. She gets so cocky when she discovers something that you almost start to wish she wouldn't find anything. Or maybe that's just me.

"Look here," she began. "Ferry worked for two years on a case involving this guy Harry 'the Fish' Monroe."

"Harry '*the Fish*' Monroe?" I said. There really were guys with names like that? Josh looked at me and laughed. He saw the laptop floating around in the air and waved to Maxie, who waved back. The difference was, she could see him.

"So what happened with Detective Ferry and the Fish?" Might as well speed this along; dinner would be ready any minute.

"Well, that's what's interesting," Maxie said, regaining the attention of everyone in the room who could conceivably offer it. (Ollie thought Maxie was hilarious, assuming she was what he was looking at. Then Josh squeezed Ernie. Squeak. Hysterics.) "It seems Harry lives down the Shore, in Brick, at least part of the year. But Ferry thought he was bivouacked in Seaside Heights and dealing some nasty stuff."

"Bivouacked?" I said. I was roundly ignored. Josh picked up Oliver (and, by extension, Ernie) from the floor and carried him over to the wall I'd been working on earlier in the day. He got fairly close—enough so that Ollie could touch the wall—and examined it, no doubt listening to my end of the conversation but also employing his specialty.

"So Ferry catches the case, and he starts investigating right up to the day he died. He told at least one cop he was close to making the collar." Maxie tends to talk like she's in a nineteen forties gangster movie when she's doing research on crimes. No one has had the heart to tell her that people haven't actually spoken that way in decades, if they ever did.

"What happened?" Paul said. He seemed in a hurry, like he wanted to get on to some really important stuff he hadn't mentioned as soon as he could get this out of the way.

"That depends on who you talk to," Maxie said. "Two months ago, Ferry's captain's report says he expects to announce an arrest of the Fish in a few days."

As Maxie was speaking, there was a sound from the other side of the room, and then a light came on where it had been dark before.

I turned to see Paul floating near a table on which I'd put a lamp. He'd unplugged the lamp, then inserted the plug into his own transparent abdomen. The lightbulb, unattached to any visible source of power, was glowing brightly.

"I knew it!" Paul said. "My energy is increasing."

Maxie ignored him as I told Paul to put the lamp down and plug it back in. Josh watched the unplugged, lit lamp float around the room and looked very, very puzzled, which was frankly the only way to look under the circumstances.

Just as I was about to grab the lamp out of Paul's hand and return it to the table, Maxie said, "Detective Ferry's savings account went up thirty thousand dollars after the captain said he expected an arrest. There never was an arrest."

I swiveled to face her, wanting desperately not to believe what I'd just heard. Josh, maybe by reflex now, squeezed Ernie. Squeak.

Oliver started to cry.

Eleven

"Thirty thousand dollars?" Melissa said. "That's an awful lot, isn't it?"

Melissa had prepared (under Mom's careful supervision) a "summer dinner" of grilled turkey breast marinated in soy sauce and basil, with sides of creamed corn and Caesar salad. So my attention to the investigation talk might have been a little diffused. Melissa had already far surpassed me as a chef, and Mom (who admittedly was a little biased) told me she had an understanding of meal planning and cooking that would soon outpace her teacher.

As those of us living ate, we'd bandied around the information Maxie had found out about Detective Ferry without much conclusion. Paul's opinion, after he stopped being an electrical outlet, was that no conclusions could be drawn: "We don't have enough facts."

Maxie, of course, believed that the information she'd uncovered "solved the case," and would not be persuaded that we still had to figure out who had shot Martin Ferry.

Dad thought a light run with sandpaper over the paneling would help the stain bond better with the wood veneer. (It's not that Dad wasn't paying attention to our conversation—he was—but he believes his expertise is in the home-improvement area and offers advice only when he thinks he has something helpful to contribute. Dad is the anti-Maxie.)

I was struggling with the reality of *my* situation, which was that the next time I spoke with Lieutenant McElone, I would have to let her know what "I" had found out.

"It's a very big amount of money," I said. Melissa has a fluid vision of finances. In some areas, she's very savvy (she can always tell me which gas station has the lowest price, despite my always going to the Fuel Pit, in part to check in on our ghostly friend Everett, who died in the men's room there and is often still hanging around the station, if not the restroom), but in others, like the amount of my monthly mortgage payment, or by how much her father's child support check is often short, she has a foggier view. "The question is whether it was a payoff, or whether he might have gotten it from somewhere else," I explained.

"I only met Detective Ferry once," my mother said. "But he didn't dress like a man who was getting a lot of money from organized crime." Ferry had taken the "plain" in "plainclothes officer" pretty seriously.

Josh took a sip of beer—I always have some in the fridge—and looked thoughtfully toward the napkin I'd given Paul to hold so Josh would have a point of reference. "Does Maxie know if the thirty thousand was a one-time-only event, or was it a regular deposit?"

Maxie, who had not volunteered to hold an object, snorted. "Why does he have to ask Paul?" she wanted to know. I gave her a look. "No, as far as I can tell, the thirty grand was the only suspicious deposit. But there could have been smaller payments, or maybe accounts I don't know about. Yet."

Liss relayed Maxie's reply to Josh, who nodded and

looked at Oliver in the high chair next to me. Ollie wasn't watching either ghost at the moment, probably out of a sense of perversity. If he didn't watch them *all* the time, how could I know if he really saw them? I fed him a little of the creamed corn, which he appeared to like quite a bit. Jeannie hadn't *specifically* told me not to give him any. "Maw," he said.

This time, Josh's question really was for Paul. "Isn't it best, then, for Alison to relay the information to Lieutenant McElone and let her conduct the actual investigation?"

As much as I dreaded passing these allegations on to McElone, that was precisely what I thought had to be done, and I said so. But Paul, stroking his goatee in thought, wasn't in total agreement. "Not just yet. We *should* be taking some action. What we should do is question Detective Ferry without the lieutenant present."

I told Josh what Paul had said, and he must have read my face. "How does that make sense?" he asked me.

"Let me guess," I said. I looked up at Paul, who was slightly tilted to the left. When he's not paying attention to his positioning, he can list a little. "You think that Ferry will be more apt to speak freely without McElone there, even though she can't see or hear him?"

"Exactly," Paul said. "The lieutenant was his friend and once his partner. He does not want to appear dishonest or questionable to her. He does not know you very well at all, and might be quicker to acknowledge any possible discretions."

Josh thought that over. "Maybe so, but I don't think you should go to Detective Ferry alone," he said when he heard Paul's plan.

"I won't be alone," I said. There was no point in arguing with Paul on something like this. For one thing, he was always right. For another, I'd end up doing what he wanted me to do anyway. "I'll have Ollie with me. Won't I, Ollie?" A couple of kernels of corn emerged from Oliver's mouth, but he wasn't crying, and that was a definite plus.

"I was thinking of someone a little bigger than Ollie," Josh said. "I was thinking maybe I should go."

That was a line we'd discussed crossing, but had not done so. I wasn't sure I wanted Josh in on the detective stuff. For one thing, he had a store to run, and his grandfather Sy, though awfully spry for a man in his early nineties, could not handle Madison Paint all by himself. "You have work," I said. "And I'm not sure Ferry would talk so freely around you, either. How about Maxie?"

Maxie, who had been floating on her back, sat up. "What about Maxie?" she asked.

"How about coming with me to get some answers out of Detective Ferry?"

Maxie's face changed immediately into a picture of something two inches short of alarm. "When?" she asked.

"I'm thinking tomorrow."

"Tomorrow!" Maxie closed those two inches in a blink and was now in a full-on panic. "I can't! I have to go see my mom!"

"Okay, that's it," I said, standing up. Not that it helped much, because Maxie was already over my head, literally. "What is going on with your mother? Is there anything we can do to help?"

Maxie squeezed her eyes shut, and her head vibrated. *Shook* would have been too mild a word. She was about to either yell out something (possibly even the truth) or vanish into thin air again.

Until a knock came on the kitchen door. Everybody turned to look.

"Yes?" I called.

Stephanie Muldoon stuck her head through the swinging door. "Hi, Alison?" she began. Some guests believe that because I don't serve food, the kitchen is a verboten area at the guesthouse, although I never tell them anything like that. Most of the ghost conversations take place there, but I don't keep the room off-limits.

"Hi, Stephanie. What's up?" I gestured her in, and she walked toward Melissa, Oliver and me at the center island, where we were eating. "Something I can help with?" I asked. As I keep reminding everyone, my primary business *is* as innkeeper, not detective. There are times the line gets a little blurry, but it's never erased.

"There isn't a problem," Stephanie answered. She nodded to Mom, whom she'd met a couple of nights earlier, and then Josh and Melissa. "It's about the ghosts."

Paul and Maxie looked at each other. Dad looked at me.

I saw Paul's hand go to his head, like the last time he'd gotten a message from Martin Ferry, and he sank down through the floor into the basement, which I thought I might start calling "The Paulcave." The napkin he'd been holding as a signal to Josh floated down to the floor, unnoticed by Stephanie.

"It wasn't me," Maxie said.

"What about the ghosts?" I asked Stephanie.

"Well . . ." Stephanie looked up. I wasn't sure if she was trying to look for the ghosts or just thinking of how to phrase whatever was coming next. "I think Rita might be a little more nervous about being in a haunted house than we anticipated."

This is not unusual. Some people take on the haunted vacation with Senior Plus thinking it'll be a great adventure, or that they can face their fears, but then, no matter how benign the ghosts in my house act (and really, even Maxie would never hurt anyone), they convince themselves that they're in great danger. I've even had a few guests leave early, though I sincerely hoped Stephanie and Rita were not about to join that group.

"Then why not go and talk to her about it?" Melissa said.

"Maybe that would be best," Stephanie agreed. "I think she's a little . . . reluctant to come in here. She's heard you talking to the ghosts in this room."

We all filed out of the kitchen—I picked up Oliver, who would probably need a diaper change soon—with Josh, Melissa and Mom following behind me. I wasn't sure whether

Dad and Maxie were coming, but it was a decent bet. Dad for the support, and Maxie because there's nothing she enjoys more than seeing someone who isn't her be made to feel uncomfortable, especially if that someone's me.

Rita was in the den, sitting in an intentionally nonchalant pose in one of the overstuffed easy chairs. I set Oliver down on the floor and sat on the edge of the coffee table in front of her.

"Hi, Rita," I began conversationally. "So Stephanie tells me that you might be feeling a little anxious about being in a house that has ghosts in it." (*Haunted* is a word to avoid with the queasy.)

"Maybe a little," Rita allowed. "I mean, I don't think anything bad has happened or anything."

Oliver, who had crawled over to Josh and been picked up—his goal—was getting sleepy, and the need for that diaper change was getting more . . . noticeable. Josh bounced him a little, then carried Ollie out of the room to the kitchen, where the diaper bag was stashed.

"The man's a keeper," Dad said, pointing at Josh. Dad is on a campaign to get Josh and me married, despite our never once discussing the subject (me and Josh, that is; Dad's discussed the prospect with several people). I gave him a curt nod and looked back at Rita, whose attention was concentrated on Stephanie, who stood to her side. Rita seemed to be asking for strength from her wife, and getting it.

"So what is it that bothers you, then? Is it just the idea of them?" Mom, being direct, sounded a little more like a district attorney; that might have been her intention.

"I guess." I could tell that Rita wasn't being intentionally evasive; she honestly didn't seem like she could quite put her finger on what was bothering her. "I'm sure the ghosts in your house are very nice. I'm not afraid in the house."

Okay, that was odd. "You're anxious outside?" I said. "Has that happened before you came here?"

"No." Rita shook her head. "But I saw something outside I wasn't expecting, and it shook me up a little."

"What did you see?" Liss asked. It must have been something pretty gruesome, I figured, to be an issue. Too late, I wondered if my eleven-year-old should be listening, let alone leading the interrogation.

"A hat."

"A hat?" I said. Well, at least that seemed pretty PG. "You saw a hat?"

Stephanie sat down next to her wife and took her hand. "Rita said she saw a hat floating right on the edge of the ocean, and she thought that meant there was a ghost out there."

"And you didn't see this hat?" I asked Stephanie.

She looked embarrassed. "I was in the ladies' room."

"Couldn't it just have been blowing in the wind?" Mom asked, unintentionally setting Bob Dylan on a continuous loop in my head. "Someone's hat got away from them? It gets pretty breezy by the water."

Again, Rita shook her head negatively. "It was floating there. Steady. At one point, it looked like it was floating back and forth, like the ghost was moving his head around for no reason. Somehow that image just made me a little . . ." Her voice trailed off.

"What kind of hat was it, exactly?"

"A cap," Rita answered. "Kind of uniform-looking, like a cop or a soldier or something."

Maxie was staring out the glass doors in the back of the room at the beach, which was still visible even as the sun was going down. I couldn't tell if her expression was one of puzzlement or worry. Did she know something about this hat-wearing ghost? Was she thinking about her mother? Either way, her reaction was odd.

Paul rose up through the floor looking serious, which was not at all odd. Paul would look serious at a Mel Brooks film festival. He has a sense of humor, but there are times I think he left it in Toronto when he moved to New Jersey to start his career as an investigator.

"I think I can allay your fears," I told Rita. "If you saw a hat by itself, you didn't see a ghost." I was stretching the truth a little. Paul or Maxie could hold up objects seen by living people—that was the basis of what they did during the "spook shows," anyway—but I wanted to make Rita feel more secure.

Stephanie and Rita exchanged another look; Rita seemed edgy, Stephanie indulgent. I got the impression that Stephanie thought Rita had just been out in the sun a little too long.

"I didn't?" Rita said.

"No. The clothes the ghosts have on are not visible. If there had been a ghost wearing that hat, you wouldn't have seen it." Again, I was fudging in an attempt to make Rita feel better.

It seemed to work: Rita visibly relaxed. She turned to Mom. "So maybe you were right, it was just blowing around." But she still didn't seem convinced. "It sure didn't look that way, though."

"Don't worry," I said, glad that I wouldn't have to refund any of their week's booking. "But if you see something like that again, you let me know, okay?"

"Okay," Rita said. She and Stephanie stood up, and Stephanie said they were going to go out on the porch to enjoy the night breeze a little, although I think she might have found that a more appealing prospect than Rita did.

Josh walked back in from the kitchen carrying Oliver, now in his pajamas and fast asleep in his arms. Maybe Dad was right; Josh *was* a keeper. He motioned with his chin that he'd take the baby to my bedroom, where Ollie's travel crib was set up, and kept on walking. Everyone stayed quiet as they passed. A sleeping baby is an easy baby. And something of a miracle.

"Gotta go," Maxie jumped in. "I'll see you later."

"Hold on," I started to say, but she was through the ceiling and presumably out of the house before I could get to the *l* in *hold*. I looked at Paul.

He shrugged. "I don't know."

I looked at Melissa. "Do you have any idea what's going on with Maxie lately?"

Liss seemed surprised I'd asked. "I figured it was a grown-up thing."

"Grown-up? It's Maxie."

"Alison," my mother admonished.

I asked Liss if she could perhaps probe Maxie—gently—the next time they were alone and see if she could discover what was up, and whether there was anything we could do to help with whatever difficulty Maxie or Kitty was having. My daughter, who is among the most responsible people I have ever met, agreed to report back any findings she might, you know, find.

Dad excused himself, as if he needed to, to do some more work on the movie-room walls. The guests had been warned that it was a construction area, so they were steering clear, and besides, the ghost-lovers among them would probably be tickled to come across a brush and rag stripping paint off a wall by themselves.

"There is more news to report," Paul said, and everyone turned to look at him.

"I saw you go downstairs," I said to him. "Did you hear from Detective Ferry again?"

"No," Paul said. "It's more interesting than that."

More interesting? Who'd he hear from, Abraham Lincoln? Technically, it was possible. But let's be clear: Lincoln definitely did not die in New Jersey; you can't blame us for that one. "How so?" I asked.

"I got a message." He looked at me with a raised eyebrow. "From Harry 'the Fish' Monroe."

Twelve

I digested that little bit of information for a moment. "Harry 'the Fish' Monroe? I didn't know he was dead."

Paul flinched a little, but just a little. He doesn't like the *D* word. "He wasn't, until just a few days ago."

"When did he pass away?"

"The same night as Martin Ferry," Paul answered. "He must have picked up on the message I'd sent looking for the detective, and answered me back himself."

"What did Mr. Fish say?" I asked.

"Mr. *the* Fish," Paul deadpanned.

Mom was sitting on the sofa, which gave her a view of the hallway to the movie room. She likes to keep an eye on Dad, mostly because she likes to see him. They have a great marriage, even now, years after my father died. "What happened?" Mom asked. "Did Mr. Monroe get shot like the detective?" Even an (alleged) gangster like Harry the Fish got respect from my mother.

"He's not sure," Paul said. "You know how these things work. If Maxie were here, she could find out."

Melissa gave Paul a "duh" face. "This is an easy one. We don't need Maxie." She went to the stairway, no doubt to get her own laptop.

"And you have to understand that this wasn't a very detailed conversation. I receive messages and I send them, but questions and answers are a little more complicated. He's not happy right now."

"Well, he's had a pretty serious blow," Mom said. "After all, he was alive last weekend."

"Did you get anything, Paul?" I asked. "Impressions, feelings, something?"

Paul stood (floated) and pondered that. "Mostly anger, with a tinge of sadness. And shock. I very distinctly got the impression that Harry was not interested in discussing anything other than his demise, which he seemed to believe was not of natural causes. That's where I'm getting the idea that this was not a lingering illness or something anticipated."

"Did you mention Detective Ferry?" I saw Melissa walking down the stairs carrying her laptop.

"I tried, but I have not received an answer to that message yet. Keep in mind that like Detective Ferry, Monroe is new to this state of being, and might not be at full energy just yet." Paul was all about energy these days. It was a small surprise that he didn't try to plug Melissa's MacBook into his left leg to see if it would charge.

"Harry 'the Fish' Monroe," Liss said, clearly reading from the screen, "a reputed gangster allegedly tied to organized crime in New Jersey shore towns, was found dead in his car, parked at a Walmart in Brick Township, yesterday." She looked up. "Based on when this article was written, that would be the same day Detective Ferry died." Back to reading the article. "Brick police said Monroe was found in the driver's seat of his Lexus with no outward signs of violence. While no official cause of death was announced, a police source who asked not to be named because he has no authorization to speak on the subject said Monroe appeared to have died from natural causes."

"Harry doesn't think so," Paul suggested.

"Well, it could've been a heart attack or stroke, some sort of sudden health problem," I pointed out. "The cops seem to think it was something along those lines."

"Don't you think it's a very glaring coincidence that the detective and the man he was investigating died suddenly on the same day?" Paul countered. "I am not prepared to accept that on face value without a good deal more data."

A thought struck me. "McElone must have heard about this," I said. "It's weird that she didn't say anything." I rescued my cell phone from the pocket of my jeans and called McElone's private number. The call went directly to voice mail, so I hung up assuming McElone would see the missed call and get back to me.

"I think it's important that we try to locate Monroe and talk to Detective Ferry again," Paul said when I hung up.

"Doesn't Mr. Monroe know where he is?" Melissa asked. She had not looked up from her screen and was no doubt trying to find more about the Fish.

"He wasn't clear on that, either," Paul said. "I doubt he's still in the Walmart parking lot, because he mentioned something about being wet."

"Well, he *is* a fish," Mom suggested.

"The cops had to take him out of his car, certainly," I said, thinking aloud. "You have to figure he's in the county morgue or a funeral home by now."

"That's where his body is," Paul answered. "His spirit, as you know, could be anywhere. My body is not actually located near this house, and yet here I am." It really did bother Paul that he couldn't travel around freely.

On the other hand, he'd been experimenting with electricity so he could move on to another plane of existence, and didn't seem the least bit squeamish about trumpeting his delight at the prospect. Was I hurt? Me?

Yeah, I was a little hurt. It wasn't rational, but I was.

"Maybe Phyllis Coates can help," Melissa said.

Phyllis is the editor, publisher and entire staff of the *Harbor Haven Chronicle*, the town's only legitimate source of news specific to the area. She's a twenty-year veteran of the *New York Daily News* and has been a friend and mentor of mine since I started delivering papers for her when I was thirteen years old. These days, Phyllis's circulation for the physical paper is a little smaller, but she's transitioning to an online presence and is still making enough money through advertising to keep the enterprise going. So the next time an online ad annoys you, think about how it's keeping publications like the *Chronicle* alive. Maybe it'll help.

She also has a special source of information in the county medical examiner's office and can sometimes get autopsy reports before anyone else.

Melissa was right; Phyllis almost certainly would know something more about Harry Monroe. I looked at Paul, who seemed expectant. So I dialed Phyllis's number.

Unlike McElone, Phyllis, at least, answered.

"Harry the Fish?" she asked with a tone of amusement. "Yeah, they're going over that one with a fine-tooth comb. After all the violence that guy caused, to see him go from a heart problem is just a little too neat."

I told her about Martin Ferry, a rare bit of area information Phyllis seemed not to already know about, and mentioned that the detective had died the same day as the gangster he'd once investigated.

"Interesting," she said. "Maybe I should do a little digging on that myself." I had left out the part about McElone's involvement; like the guy in the online story Melissa had found, I had not gotten authorization to speak on that subject.

"Has the autopsy been done yet?" I asked.

"Oh, yeah, they did it right away, but the results haven't come back, and I'll bet it's not just the cops being cautious. I think they really don't know what they're looking at yet. It's just way too coincidental." I immediately gave up on the idea of a strange cosmic joke causing a situation that made things look, please pardon the expression, fishy. If both Phyllis and Paul tell you you're sick, lie down.

"The only other time I saw a heart attack that wasn't a heart attack, it was an electrocution," I told her. "That doesn't seem likely in a car."

Phyllis agreed. "No, I'm putting my money on poison, if I have to make a guess. Although that's a more genteel way of getting rid of somebody than Harry and his pals usually employ."

I was getting just a little queasy. It was one thing to help McElone with the ghost end of her investigation. This was starting to feel more like I would actually have to try to find out who killed two men, the type of thing I generally try to avoid whenever possible.

Paul, now hovering lower, clearly wanted to know what Phyllis was saying. I could have hit the speakerphone button, but decided that would sound too weird. Phyllis has seen things happen in my house and has heard me say that there are ghosts inhabiting the place full time, but she and I have never had the "ghost conversation." Even when she has interviewed me for the *Chronicle* after some very questionable events, she avoided asking. I respect that. Phyllis is a journalist. She believes in what she can prove. She can make a logical assumption that there are ghosts in my house based on her own observations and common sense, but that's not the same thing as having hard facts. She avoids drawing conclusions.

It's a shame. In many ways, I expect Phyllis and Paul would've been incredibly fast friends. They think alike.

Anyway, I decided I'd tell Paul about the conversation after it was over. "Is there any way to find out how he died before the report comes out? It could be weeks." I was implying, delicately, that Phyllis might want to check with her "special friend" at the ME's office.

"No dice, honey," she answered. "My friend works for the wrong county this time. He's not doing the autopsy. Won't even see the report himself."

"So how are you covering the story?" I asked. Sometimes I can get ideas for an investigation by watching to see which direction Phyllis heads. If she has an idea, I can often "borrow" it and end up with good results.

"Story? I'm not doing a story on Harry 'the Fish' Monroe," Phyllis said with a chuckle. "Not interested. Didn't happen in Harbor Haven, and that's my readership."

"But you've already made phone calls. You said you'd have to do some digging."

"I'm a snoop," she said. "It's not just professional. I'm nosy personally, too."

"You're being coy," I told her so Paul and Mom could hear. "What have you got?"

"I'm sure I have no idea what you're talking about," she said in an especially affected tone. Then she became Phyllis again. "You brought it up yourself, the thing with the Seaside Heights detective."

"Yeah, and you acted like you didn't know about it."

"Well, I wanted to see what you knew first." Being Phyllis's friend requires a certain touch. She's a reporter more than anything else, and if she has to do some manipulation to get the information she needs, she doesn't think twice about it. Phyllis is, you should know, a joy and a dear, but she'll quote you on anything you don't declare off the record. "From what I hear, these two deaths are not completely random. These two guys knew each other."

Of course they knew each other; Ferry had been investigating Harry the Fish, according to Paul's ghost source and the Seaside Heights files. But from Phyllis's tone, I was getting a vibe I didn't like. If Phyllis believed that

Martin Ferry was on the Fish's payroll, it was going to turn out to be true. And I'd have to tell McElone. And that meant . . . I'm not sure, maybe that I'd have to sell the guesthouse and leave town so I wouldn't ever have to talk to the lieutenant again, because she'd certainly never want to see my face again.

"Martin Ferry," I said, and Paul's eyebrows went up.

"I hear there was a connection between them," she said.

"A professional connection?" I said. Melissa actually looked upset. She's very sensitive and didn't want to believe that a friend of McElone's could've been working for the mob.

"Well, they didn't go out dancing together," Phyllis laughed. "What kind of a connection *would* a creep like Harry the Fish and a cop have?"

"You think their two deaths are connected, too?" I asked. Maybe I could change the subject just enough so that I could avoid having Phyllis say the words I didn't want to hear. If she didn't say it, I didn't have to believe it was true, and I wouldn't have to report it to McElone.

I'm not proud of the plan, but it was a plan.

"Remember what I said about coincidences? This one would be a whopper." She was practically giggling; reporters are nuts.

"So what does it mean?"

"A damn good question. You should have been a reporter, sweetie. Where did you go wrong?"

That one made me laugh despite myself. "In so many places it would be impossible to count," I said before hanging up.

I brought the rest of the room up to date on the conversation, and Paul began to stroke his goatee at about the second sentence. Mom looked unusually determined, moving her mouth back and forth like she was thinking. "Excuse me," she said, and without hesitation got up to walk toward the movie room. No doubt she wanted to confer with Dad; they're like one person who is split into two bodies for the purpose of mobility or convenience. They have the same mind and express it differently. Mom will ask Dad about any thought she has that she thinks is unconventional. Dad will ask Mom about anything when he thinks he might set a foot wrong and upset her. Upsetting Mom is Dad's idea of hell.

Melissa was also clearly thinking very hard. She wanted to find a way that Martin Ferry *wasn't* working with Harry Monroe. It was exactly what I was trying to do, but the eleven-year-old version.

"There has to be something wrong," she said finally. "Lieutenant McElone really believes Detective Ferry was a good officer. She's never wrong about things like that." Liss was right. In fact, it was rare that McElone was wrong about anything. She's very prepared and professional, and doesn't speak when she doesn't know what she's talking about.

Don't tell her I said that.

Josh walked back in, and I kissed him in thanks for putting Oliver to bed. He didn't ask what was going on. He knew I'd tell him when I could.

Paul, pacing furiously in thin air now, looked over at Melissa. "The lieutenant might not be thinking rationally about the case," he told her. "She is seeing her friend, not the man who might have done some things wrong." Paul is good at talking to Liss; that is, he doesn't treat her like an idiot just because she hasn't had the good sense to live past the age of majority yet.

But Liss shook her head. "I don't know. It doesn't really add up."

I checked my phone again; no message from McElone. She must have been on to something fairly serious. I'd try her again tomorrow. There was, however, a missed call from Jeannie. Her, I'd have to get back to and let her know Oliver was okay, or she might dive off the ship and swim back to Port Elizabeth, New Jersey, in a panic.

Nobody spoke for a while; we were all lost in our thoughts and unable (based on the silence) to come up with much that was useful. I got Josh up to speed on the situation with some help from Melissa. Paul was listening closely, which he does to help him get perspective. He says hearing the facts from someone else's mouth makes him consider them from all sides.

"Well," Josh said. "It seems like you really need to see Detective Ferry tomorrow. Are you sure you don't want me to come along?"

"No. You need to keep your business going. Don't worry, there's no danger involved."

"I'll go," Liss said.

"The heck you will."

"I would if I could," Paul told me. "We should talk to Maxie again."

"Maxie's not interested," I said. "She made that clear. Everybody needs to stop trying to protect me from something that isn't dangerous. I'll go alone."

Thirteen

"Have I met Detective Ferry before?" my mother asked.

Don't ask how Mom got involved in the trip to Ferry's apartment. Let's just say she's my mom, she's a force of nature and there isn't much one can do when she decides she's going to take part in something.

We'd come by way of the Fuel Pit, where I'd gassed up my centuries-old Volvo station wagon (actually Marv Winderbrook, who owns the station, gassed up the Volvo—Jersey girls don't pump gas, by law) and looked around for Everett Sandheim, eventually finding him hovering just beyond the gas pumps.

"I've been able to go on maneuvers beyond my home base," he replied to the simple "How are things going?" I'd offered. "I am still adapting, but I'm more efficient than when you saw me last, Ghost Lady." I've given Everett permission to call me that, since that's how he remembers me from when he was alive.

"I'm so glad to hear it," I told him. "I was concerned

about you for a while." It was true: Everett's initial reaction
to the news he was a ghost (which I'd been present to witness) was very sad and fairly awful, so I'd made it a habit
to check in on him to see the slow but steady progress he'd
been making. "But I'm here to ask a favor."

Everett, already in a standing position, straightened as
if called to attention. "How can I help?" he asked.

"That's a nice man," Mom noted in approval at Everett's reply.

"Sooner or later, everybody in town comes through this
gas station," I said. "I'd like you to keep your eyes out for
someone named Buster Hockney. I don't know what this
guy looks like or who he'd be with, but it'll help if you can
give me a description and any information you can pick up.
Can you do that?" I didn't really think much would come
of this, but Maxie, who had been helping Everett navigate
his way out of the men's room, had told me a few weeks
earlier that Everett did best when "given a mission." So I
was giving him one.

He stopped short of saluting, but nodded vehemently.
"I'll keep my eyes peeled, Ghost Lady. You can rely on me."

Why more men can't be like that, I'll never understand.

Now, Mom and I were walking from my car to the front
door of Ferry's apartment building, and even in this heat,
Mom was primping her hair and smoothing out the shift
dress she was wearing to look nice. I was going to kid her
that Ferry wasn't her type, given that he was dead, but then
I remembered that Dad was, too, and that didn't seem to be
slowing the two of them down any.

Dad had begged off the trip, saying he'd go hang with his
painting buddies at Josh's store for the day. Which is what
he'd occasionally do when he was alive, too. Sometimes
Dad needs a little time off. Maxie had not been visible after
the morning spook show, when I'd left to pick up Mom, no
doubt off to see Kitty again. And I'd left Oliver at Wendy's
house with Melissa because Wendy's mom, Barbara, said

she was trying to talk her husband out of the idea of having another baby and thought Oliver could help.

"I think you might've met Ferry when we were asking about Big Bob," I reminded her. Mom thought for a second and then gave a nod. Ferry had visited the guesthouse late in the game on that case, and I think he and Mom ran into each other, but it's not like they struck up a close and important friendship.

This morning had gone like most mornings this week at the guesthouse: Don and Tammy Coburn had taken off early for another sightseeing trip (I could only hope the air-conditioning in their car was efficient); Joe Guglielmelli had been thrilled by the morning spook show, during which Maxie had covered her hand in chocolate syrup and flown through the den, pretending to try to grab him once or twice; Stephanie had stayed for the show and seemed to enjoy the hand thing, but Rita, no doubt still a little shaken by her encounter with a flying hat, had opted to get some breakfast in town instead.

As usual, Bonnie Claeson had slept in. Thank goodness for Bonnie Claeson.

"I should have worn something else," Mom said as we started up the stairs to the second floor (it was a three-story building with no elevator). Mom was walking slowly because of her knee but wasn't letting on that it was hurting. In turn, I was not letting on that I could tell, and I slowed down my pace a bit.

"You look fine," I said. "We're not here to flirt."

Mom took on a droll expression. "I'm not flirting, Alison," she said.

It had occurred to me that without a key, I had no way of getting into Martin Ferry's home. So before leaving the guesthouse, and after Maxie had agreed to do a little bit of online research before heading out on another mysterious visit to Kitty, I had called the number for the building's owner, who I figured would have probably listed the apartment as for rent by now.

Sure enough, there had been a "vacancy" sign outside the building when we'd arrived, and the real estate agent had agreed to meet us inside the apartment.

"Remember," I told Mom, "it's going to be your job to distract the real estate agent with questions about the apartment so I can talk to the detective about his . . . situation, okay?"

"Right, chief," Mom said. "This is a brilliant plan." She tends to see everything I do as brilliant, when I've actually only been brilliant perhaps three times in my life. Okay, twice that I can think of.

The agent, a downtrodden sort of woman named Alice, opened the door for us, smiling one of the least encouraging smiles I have ever seen. She looked like the truck bringing her lottery winnings had just run over her dog.

"I'm afraid the place isn't entirely cleaned and prepped," she said before we could even suggest that we had any interest in the apartment. "I'm required by law to tell you that someone passed away here recently, and that's why the apartment is now available."

"Oh, dear," Mom said, playing the less confident potential renter (unconvincingly, in my opinion). Our cover story was that Mom was thinking of taking the apartment to be closer to me and her grandchild, although we did not mention the fact that where Mom lived now was probably closer to our house in Harbor Haven than this apartment was. "I hope the poor person wasn't ill for very long."

"I don't know the exact details," Alice answered, "but there's no reason to think the apartment is at all unsafe for you. Before anyone else moves in, it will be cleaned and painted from top to bottom."

"Well . . ." Mom pretended to hesitate while I noticed Ferry sticking his head through his home-office door. I moved toward his location.

"Those are the bedrooms," Alice told me when she saw my direction. "We'll take a look at those in a minute, okay?"

"Um . . ."

Mom pointed at a cabinet over the refrigerator. "Can you fit something in there, or is it just for show?" she asked.

Alice turned her attention back to Mom, and I hustled into the spare bedroom, where Ferry was hovering, standing straight up, near the window. The light from outside shone through his midsection and made him more transparent than he would have otherwise been, so he looked eerily like a head and shoulders floating over calves and feet.

"Where's Anita?" he asked as I walked in.

"Nice to see you, too, Detective," I said. "The lieutenant isn't here."

"So who's the older lady you brought with you? Your mother?" He sneered.

"As a matter of fact, yes," I said at the lowest volume I could muster and still be heard.

He stopped and his eyebrows arched. "Really?"

"Look, I don't have a lot of time. I pretended to be interested in renting this place because I didn't have a key to the front door, and the real estate agent is going to be walking in here any minute."

"There's a key hidden in a notch in the molding around the door, left side, about eye level," Ferry told me. "Even the super doesn't know it's there."

"Yeah, thanks for helping out, but it's a little late," I told him. "I need to ask you about Harry 'the Fish' Monroe."

It's not often that ghosts are absolutely still, but Ferry did not move at all on hearing that name. His face twisted, though, into the visual equivalent of a growl. "What about him?"

"He's dead." On Paul's instructions, I wanted to see if there was a reaction.

There was. Ferry's lower lip flattened out in an expression of indifference. "So am I. So what?"

"Exactly," I said.

"Exactly what?" he replied.

"It's an awfully big coincidence, don't you think?"

Ferry's brow wrinkled. "Wait. You think there's a connection between Monroe dying and what happened to me?"

Outside the bedroom, I heard Mom's voice getting closer, perhaps speaking a little too loudly so I'd be sure to hear through the closed door. "What does the bathroom look like?" she asked.

I wasn't worried about Alice finding me in Ferry's home office, which still had the desk and the daybed inside. She'd see only me, standing in an otherwise empty (of people) room. But I did need to talk to Ferry, and I couldn't do that with Alice watching; she might think it was just a bit unusual, especially when I got answers to my questions.

Ferry, of course, didn't care whether Alice saw or heard me and wasn't paying attention to her. He looked at me and asked, "Why is it so fascinating that Monroe and I died the same day?"

"Come on, Detective. If you were working the case and the mobster was killed the same day as the cop who was investigating him, wouldn't *you* wonder what was going on?"

Ferry shrugged and looked away. "Sometimes it really is a coincidence," he said in a tone so unconvincing I don't think Oliver would have bought it.

Was he still playing it coy? Was his reputation still an important issue at this late date? I decided to go right at it. "Weren't you on Monroe's payroll?" I hissed.

Martin Ferry looked the way I can only imagine he looked when his police-issued gun went off at him—astonished and angry. "What the hell are you talking about?"

Well, there was the thirty grand in his bank account. "Among other things—"

The door to the room flew open (or at least it seemed to fly open). I caught my breath and looked away from Ferry and toward Alice, who drearily led Mom into the room.

"This is the second bedroom," she droned. "It doesn't have to have the desk or anything in it. Obviously, we expect you to bring your own furniture. See, there's a closet." I had to wonder if this woman had ever closed a real estate deal in her life. She would've been so much better suited to a job at a mortuary; it's a very quiet job with very little interpersonal interaction. For most people.

"It's lovely," Mom said, although it really wasn't. There were cracks in the far wall, and the floor hadn't been sanded and refinished since Martin Van Buren was president. "But I'd really like to see the kitchen again."

Alice shook her head in wonder. "You seem really concerned about that kitchen," she said. But she gestured Mom toward the door. "I swear, everything in there works." They walked out, and I turned to face Ferry to confront him about his hefty savings deposit.

But he was no longer in the room.

Fourteen

"He left and didn't return the whole rest of the time we were there," I told Paul.

Instead of his usual routine of pacing and stroking his goatee, Paul had his hand up with the palm extended and was holding it near the ceiling fan in my new movie room. I had given up on the whole investigating thing for the rest of the day and was stripping the last of the paint off the paneling, so I wasn't paying much attention to what new energy games he was playing.

"That doesn't make sense," he answered after a moment. "There was no reason for him to be that upset. Unless . . ." Neither one of us wanted to finish the sentence.

Indeed, Mom had been thrown enough by our lack of success at Ferry's apartment that she'd just picked up Dad and left for home, saying she'd call the next day.

Paul seemed to be thinking something over as I got the remainder of the white paint off the last plank in the paneling and sat back, the bandana around my neck and the sweatband around my forehead more conceptual than helpful now. "There's no way of knowing where he went," he said.

I turned to look at him. He was squinting, his neck tense, the arm now pushed directly into the blades of the fan, which would have been very painful if he'd been capable of feeling pain. They were still going at the maximum speed. "What the heck are you doing?"

"I am attempting to transfer the energy from my being into the fan without sustained physical contact," he said, as if I surely should have realized that. "It's the next step."

"What is it with this 'energy' thing all of a sudden?" I asked. "What's the rush to move on to the next thing?"

"You really shouldn't take this personally," he answered, clamping his eyes shut with effort. "It's not that I'm abandoning you, it's that I'm trying to leave an existence that is fraught with some very daunting limitations for me." The light fixture underneath the spinning blades flickered a bit, and Paul opened his eyes, looking hopeful.

"Could you practice on something else? It's hot enough in here without you trying to turn off the fan." Rationally, I understood Paul's desire to get out of an eternity spent in one place doing basically the same thing every day until time eventually just ended. Emotionally, I was hot, tired, irritated and feeling rejected.

If Paul left, I'd be down to one ghost for the spook shows. Could I appeal to him not to leave to save my business? Or would he simply suggest I ask Dad to fill in for him?

Paul looked sheepish and lowered himself to the floor, deciding (apparently) to concentrate on the situation he'd actually asked me to relate. His mouth twitched.

"Did you get the impression that Detective Ferry was trying to evade the questions you were asking, or that he was offended by the suggestion that he'd been involved with Monroe?"

"Both," I said. "I don't know. Maybe neither. He did seem surprised, but I couldn't tell if it was because the idea was completely unexpected, or if he was shocked I knew about it. Could go either way. I'm confused, can you tell?"

Paul didn't answer, chewing the data over. But Melissa, coming into the room with Oliver (for Jeannie's benefit, please note that I'd closed the can of thinner and left the window open until any fumes could dissipate), was already talking anyway.

"I've been thinking about Detective Ferry's murder," she said, trying to perpetuate the myth that she *hadn't* been listening in on my conversation with Paul before she'd walked in. Oliver, who had no such pretense, was less than pleased with the slight smell of turpentine in the room, and while he didn't cry, he did wrinkle up his nose and look annoyed.

"I've told you a hundred times," I reminded my daughter. "We're not investigating Martin Ferry's murder, and *especially* not Harry Monroe's. We're just acting—"

"—as ghost liaisons for Lieutenant McElone," she parroted back. "And isn't that why you were over at the detective's apartment with Grandma today?" So she had a point.

"What have you found out about Maxie?" I asked in an attempt to change the subject. Paul was now pointing a finger at the floor lamp and getting no results. Oh, yeah, he was going to be a huge help on this investigation, I could just tell. If there was an investigation. Which, I'd just decided, there wasn't. I was done with this one.

"Not much," Liss admitted, putting Oliver down on the floor once she'd seen that I had removed all potentially dangerous substances and objects. Ollie tried to stand, thought better of it, sat down and picked up a clean, dry paintbrush I'd left on the floor for just such an occasion. He began to paint his face with it. "I didn't want to ask her straight out because she always seems to get mad when you do that."

"Yeah, but that's me," I pointed out. "She never gets mad at you."

Liss shrugged. "Even so. Instead, I asked her if she was

getting tired of doing the spook shows, because she always seems to want time off in order to go see her mom. I figured I could start the conversation like that."

Paul touched one of the bulbs on the floor lamp, which lit. He smiled, but then looked perplexed.

"Nice thinking," I told my daughter, ignoring the ghost pretending to be Benjamin Franklin out in the rain with a kite. "What did she say?"

"That she'd been tired of the spook shows from the very first day, but that she had a really great idea for them that she's going to try real soon." Oh boy.

"Did you find out what the 'really great idea' was?" I asked warily.

"No, but she was smiling really big when she said I'd find out."

There was no chance I was going to sleep tonight.

I checked my cell phone, after I wiped off my hands, for a message from McElone. Still nothing.

"I'm trying the best I can," Melissa said.

I looked over at her. "I wasn't suggesting that you did anything wrong, honey. I'm just worried about Kitty."

"Call her." Paul's attention was now directed at an electrical socket; he was staring at it like it was a luscious piece of red velvet cake. I chose not to think about why.

"But if Maxie's there now, she'll know I called."

Melissa thought about that. "Yeah, but she'd be a good distance away and would have to get all the way back here before she did anything about it." Melissa is always thinking and almost always has my best interests at heart.

"You're right. Enough," I said. I reached into my pocket for my phone again, and naturally that was the moment it decided to ring. I sighed just loudly enough to hear it myself and looked at the Caller ID.

I didn't recognize the number. Technically, I could have let it go straight to my voice mail and listened to the message later, but thinking the call might be coming from one of my absent guests, in which case I'd want to know immediately, I tapped Accept and put the phone to my ear.

"Hello?"

"Is this Alison Kerby?" The voice—male, deep—was not familiar. It sounded tentative, as one would when calling a complete stranger. But he sounded too old and authoritative to be calling about a political campaign, a credit card scam or a donation to one of the colleges I'd attended.

So I dodged. "Who is calling, please?"

"My name is Malcolm Kidder," he answered. I was about to try to cut off the pitch that was unquestionably on its way when he added, "I'm Anita McElone's husband."

My eyes must have grown to the size of hubcaps, because suddenly Melissa and Paul were staring at me with concerned expressions. "You're the lieutenant's husband?" I said, strictly for their benefit. Then *their* eyes grew to the size of hubcaps. I don't think any of us had ever considered the lieutenant having a husband before. Which was silly, in retrospect, considering that I knew she had three children; there wasn't any reason to think she *didn't* have a husband.

"Yes," Malcolm answered. "Has she ever mentioned me to you?"

What do you say to a guy who asks you that? *No, your wife has chosen to keep you out of every conversation we've ever had?* It seemed a little cold. "Of course," I lied. "She's talked about you quite a bit."

"She never brought my name up at all, did she?" he said, though not unkindly. Busted. I'm a remarkably bad liar. Paul had zoomed over to try to hear the conversation better, and Liss simply watched my face. "That's Anita. Business is business, and family is family."

"I'm sorry," I said, although I wasn't really clear why. It seemed like the thing to say at the time.

"Don't be; I don't mind," Malcolm said. "But I was calling to see if Anita is with you right now."

Well, *that* wasn't what I was expecting. "Did she tell

you she'd be with me?" I asked. Why would the lieutenant tell her husband to call me? Why didn't he just call her? She had a cell phone. Heck, I could give him the number if he didn't have it.

"No, but she said she had consulted with you on a case," Malcolm answered. "I know about all the ghost stuff. You know, your reputation is pretty well known around town." Of course, McElone lived in Harbor Haven. Harbor Haven can't stop talking about me and my haunted guesthouse. Put two and two together and . . . "The problem is that I can't find Anita, and I was hoping you might know where she is."

. . . sometimes you get five.

"What do you mean, you can't find her?" I said. Paul immediately put on his Sherlock Holmes face, but Melissa just looked worried. I waved a hand at her, trying to downplay her anxiety. McElone had probably just gone off investigating, and her cell phone needed a charge. It wasn't a big deal.

"I mean, I can't find her," Malcolm told me. "I know she's investigating the death of her ex-partner, but she hasn't called in. Anita *always* calls in, even more often than usual now that she's on a leave of absence working on this Marty thing. Do you know where she was planning on going today?" His voice, although still ostensibly calm and controlled, was showing edges of concern. If Malcolm was anything like his wife, his "concern" was the normal human equivalent of "total panic."

"No, she doesn't really tell me all that much about what she's up to," I said. "To be honest, the lieutenant never really briefs me entirely about the nuts and bolts of the investigation."

Malcolm's voice softened a little. "You don't have to call her 'the lieutenant,' you know. I understand you two are friends."

Friends? Was that what McElone told her husband we were? "Well, yeah," I stammered. "But I'm afraid I don't know where she is. I take it her cell phone isn't answering?"

Paul's eyes narrowed, which meant he thought something was wrong but hadn't figured out what it was yet.

"No, and I'm getting worried," McElone's husband said. "I haven't heard from her since yesterday afternoon, and I'm afraid something might have happened to her." Maybe he *wasn't* like his wife, so he wasn't saying that he was beyond panic now. That's what I told myself.

Suddenly, the look on Paul's face seemed to signal he'd figured out what he thought was wrong.

"She's been taken," he said to himself.

Fifteen

"You don't know that," I said to Paul. "You don't know
that Lieutenant McElone is even missing, let alone kid-
napped."

We'd been debating the issue for well over an hour now,
after I'd promised Malcolm Kidder that I'd call him back
at the number he'd used to contact me if I heard from his
wife. But I had a bad feeling in my stomach about whether
that was going to happen. During my argument with Paul,
Oliver had gotten bored, played with a ball, had a diaper
change, taken a short nap, gotten up, been given some
mashed potatoes and a piece of rye bread (Jeannie would
no doubt have a fit, but then, she wasn't ever going to find
out) and gotten bored again. He was now cranky, on the
floor of the den, sitting on an air-conditioning duct in the
floor and watching a DVD of *Dora the Explorer* that Liss
had found from her halcyon days. The fact that the flat
screen he was watching, left over from a television production's visit to the guesthouse, was ten feet above his head

probably didn't help. Every once in a while he grumped a bit, but he hadn't actually started crying. Yet.

"I don't like to make assumptions," Paul allowed, "but there are very few alternative theories that fit the facts as we know them."

Melissa, sitting on the floor with Ollie but not looking at Dora, stared up at Paul quizzically. "Are you sure?" she asked. "You don't think the lieutenant could have just turned her phone off or something?"

"If she had failed to respond only to your mom, that might be a very plausible theory," Paul said. "But from what we know about the lieutenant, the idea that she hasn't gotten in touch with her husband or children since yesterday is disturbing."

I didn't want to debate this idea any further. For one thing, Melissa looked upset, and I always try to avoid that. For another, I didn't want to deal with the fact that Paul's almost always right about these things. That wasn't a really encouraging prospect at the moment, either.

"Liss, can you do me a favor and get the take-out menus so we can decide on something to eat for dinner?"

Melissa looked a little suspicious—as well she might be, since dinner wouldn't be for at least two and a half hours—but she stood up and headed toward the kitchen door. "While you're up, please check the library and see if there are any guests there, okay?" I added.

Now she looked *really* suspicious, but she didn't say anything as she left the den.

"Okay," I said to Paul. "What do we need to do now?" If it was something I was going to object to—and I always object when Melissa is anywhere near danger—I prefer to keep the conversation between me and Paul.

Naturally, that was the very moment Maxie decided to drop down through the ceiling, looking unexpectedly happy. Although perhaps "unexpectedly happy" is redundant, as I never expect Maxie to look happy.

"Hello, housemates," she crooned as she floated gracefully down. "I'm back in time for the afternoon performance. Is there anything special you'd like me to do today?"

Was this really the same Maxie, the woman who will do anything she wants whenever she feels like it?

Paul and I, dumbfounded, watched her drift her way down until she was almost at my eye level, which put her a good foot lower than Paul. If you didn't look closely at the black T-shirt that read "Heck on Wheels," you could be forgiven for assuming you were in the presence of Glinda, the Good Witch of the North. (Notice we never meet the witch of the South in the movie? I'm thinking she was still smarting over the battle of Gettysburg.)

"Okay," I said when she finally came to a hovering stop, "who are you, and what have you done with Maxie Malone?"

There is one thing you can never say that Maxie lacks: nerve. Now she had the temerity to pretend she didn't understand. "What do you mean?" she asked.

"I take it your mom is doing well?" I said. It didn't seem likely that Maxie would fly into a rage over my mentioning her mother now, given the pleasant mood she was in.

And she didn't. "Oh yes," Maxie said. "As far as I know, she's doing just great."

"As far as you know?" Paul squinted at her.

Maxie seemed to come out of her trance; she shook herself and focused her attention on him. "I mean, she was fine when I left her." She looked at me. "Just now." I wasn't sure which was more dishonest, her tone or her face, but she was lying for sure. Which was good and bad, because while it probably meant that Kitty was okay, it also meant that Maxie was up to something, and that's *never* good.

I had a number of options. I could have tried to press Maxie for some indication of what was really going on. I could diplomatically try to coerce a more honest response out of her. I could use my mom or Melissa to find out, but that was going to take time.

So I chose Plan D, which was to completely ignore Maxie's strange behavior in favor of what was going on with Martin Ferry and Lieutenant McElone. "Something weird is happening," I told Maxie. She may sometimes come across as clueless, but Maxie's not stupid, and she can be helpful in analyzing a situation when she wants to.

"Nothing's weird," she said. "Everything with my mom is fine."

"This isn't about you," I told her, and got her up to date with McElone's radio silence.

Maxie absorbed the information and contemplated it for a moment. "Paul's right. Somebody's taken the cop."

Melissa, who was now walking back over to me with menus in her hand, looked at me with a little panic in her eyes. "Should we call the police?" she asked.

"And tell them what? That a colleague of theirs is conducting an unofficial rogue investigation into something she'd prefer they don't know about, and that she asked me to communicate with ghosts to help her out? The lieutenant was really clear about me not letting anyone in on that. Besides, reporting her missing, if that's the case, is her husband's call."

"Sounds about right to me," Maxie said.

But Paul and Melissa were looking more skeptical now. "Okay, it's a point," Paul said. "A number of points, in fact. Maybe you should call the lieutenant's husband back and suggest he make the call. A family member's concern would outweigh that of a colleague." It was so cute that Paul thought I was McElone's colleague.

"We have to do *something*," Melissa said. "I like the lieutenant."

"We will do something," I said. "But we're not going to do it until after dinner."

I looked down at Oliver, who was dozing, which was just as well: The *Dora* video had ended a few minutes ago. I let out a long breath. "Now there's a guy with the right idea," I said.

That afternoon's spook show was, I had to admit, a somewhat lackluster affair. The only guests in attendance were Joe Guglielmelli and Bonnie Claeson, who had gotten up in time to go out for (a late) lunch, spend a little time in town soaking up the atmosphere and then come back just in time to watch my household objects put on a show for her. Maxie's threatened new sensational effect had not manifested itself today, and my head hadn't really been in the hosting duties. Melissa had filled in when my interest had lagged. She's a trouper and allowed Maxie to do the "flying girl" bit down the main staircase, which always gives me heart palpitations despite my knowing it's perfectly safe.

Bonnie did seem to get a kick out of it, though. When she was awake, Bonnie was fully engaged, eyes bright, limbs tanned (a wonder, since she was never outside before one in the afternoon) and muscles often in motion. She also didn't say much but smiled a lot, which was another reason I wanted to order home for six more just like her.

Joe, looking interested but always seeming to expect something more spectacular, had additional reasons to look slightly disappointed after this less-than-enthusiastic display. But, like Bonnie, he did not complain, thanked me (and then the ceiling) for the lovely show and went back outside, saying he would head into town and try to find a good egg cream. I directed him to the Stud Muffin, where Jenny Webb can make anything you ask for in no time flat, as long as it's legal. (She can make it if it's illegal, too, but she tells me that takes longer.)

When the heat broke a little, I took myself and Oliver for a walk down to the beach.

For someone who lives on the Jersey Shore, I don't walk on the beach very much. I like the smell of the salt air and the sound of the surf, but to tell the truth, the feeling of sand between my toes has never much appealed. Still, I'll put up with the toe sand once in a while to clear my head.

Today, of course, I had Oliver with me, which slowed down the walking process to begin with, since I had to carry him.

A short while earlier, my phone had buzzed with a text message from Jeannie, which she'd managed to sneak through while Tony was allegedly not looking. Jeannie wanted to be sure her boy wasn't picking up bad habits from living in my house for a couple of days. I had texted back that aside from the smoking and drinking, he was exactly the same eleven-month-old she'd left. So far Jeannie had not responded.

"What do you think, Ollie?" I asked him. "Right now I'm trying to figure out if Lieutenant McElone has met with some foul play at the hands of the mob, which would be very upsetting to a number of people, including me. But that's not all—I know, you're shocked. In addition, I'm wondering what's been going on with Maxie and her strange absences, I'm worried about Paul figuring out a way to move on with his . . . eternity and I don't know whether the hat Rita saw was a ghost, and why it frightened her so much."

I looked around now for Rita's flying hat to determine if there was a ghost under it. The only ghosts I could see were an elderly lady, easily in her late eighties, in a swimsuit that left everything to the imagination right down to her ankles, which put her in the early twentieth century, and a young man, possibly a lifeguard, in a very small bathing suit that left very little to the imagination, making him more contemporary. The woman kept reaching down into the water as if to cool herself, and occasionally managed to splash some around. The guy was looking out into the water, possibly for swimmers or surfers in distress.

Neither of them wore a hat.

"Gah," Ollie answered.

"Okay, true enough, but we haven't even covered the Martin Ferry case yet," I went on. "The detective got himself shot by someone, he doesn't know who, four nights ago. His gun was locked in his desk, unloaded, but whoever it was still got to it and shot him with his own weapon."

Oliver gurgled a little.

"*And*, there are allegations, admittedly from some dead person I don't know, that Detective Ferry was a dirty cop, working with a guy named Fish when he shouldn't have been."

"Fiss," Oliver said.

"Excellent! You're brilliant!" I said to Oliver, who was getting a little heavy in my arms. I didn't want to sit him down on the beach because the sand might still be a little too hot for him to handle. Not that he seemed especially concerned about being carried around. You forget when you grow up what that must have felt like. Never having to walk, but still getting wherever you were going! It has its allure. Of course, you can only go where you're taken, but Oliver hadn't heard of France yet. Wait. Jeannie was his mother. Maybe he *had* heard of France.

"So I ask you, Ollie, how do I stay out of trouble and still find the lieutenant? She's the one who's been doing the real investigating, not me. Which is how it should be. I just want to run my guesthouse and not have to find out about gangsters. I don't want to know if Ferry was a dirty cop; that would be too upsetting. And if something has happened to Lieutenant McElone . . ."

"Why do you think something's happened to the lieutenant?" The voice was male and came from just behind my left ear.

I knew Jeannie had been anticipating Ollie's first sentence, but that was ridiculous.

Grinning, I turned around. "I didn't know you were

coming today," I said to Josh, who'd come up behind us. "I'll have to order more from the Greek place."

"I like to keep you on your toes. You know, there are times when you tell Oliver more than you tell me," he said. Ollie held out his arms, so Josh took him and said hello.

"That's only because Ollie doesn't worry the way you do," I told him. We started back toward the house, which was good because my feet were starting to burn.

"What's this about Lieutenant McElone?" Josh asked. "You sounded upset."

I filled him in on the conversation with Malcolm and what I had managed not to find out from Martin Ferry. "There are times I think I'm not really cut out for this whole PI thing," I ended up saying.

Josh pretended to ponder it. "Well, I'm not sure you'd be my first phone call . . ."

"Rat."

"How did you leave it with Malcolm?" Josh asked. He turned Oliver upside down, holding him by his ankles, facing out. Ollie couldn't possibly have been more delighted. Note to the babysitter (that's me, officially): Oliver enjoys being dangled upside down. Useful tip.

"He said that if he didn't hear from Anita—that's what we call her now, Anita—tonight, maybe we could get together tomorrow and brainstorm." Josh looked at me a little quizzically. "I know. He seems to think we are much closer friends and colleagues than McElone has ever let on."

"Maybe she's the kind of person who doesn't like to show her feelings," he answered. Climbing up a dune carrying an eleven-month-old by his ankles while dressed in a T-shirt, khakis and sneakers can't be easy, but Josh wasn't complaining, or even breathing hard. I guess lugging paint cans around all day keeps a guy in shape.

"I have to wonder if maybe Malcolm isn't playing it up a little more than it deserves," I answered. "I'll do whatever I can, but unless McElone answers her cell phone, how am I supposed to find her?"

We were about a hundred yards from my French doors, and Oliver still hadn't gotten tired of the inverted view of life; he was laughing and pointing at upside-down things. "Didn't the lieutenant give you some file she was working on for safekeeping?" Josh asked. "That might have—"

I was already running toward the house to find Paul. "You're a genius!" I yelled back at my boyfriend.

Oliver laughed. I look funny enough running when I'm right side up, so I can just imagine.

Sixteen

"I can't believe I didn't think of this earlier," Paul said.

"It was Josh's idea," I pointed out.

Josh, who was as usual standing by, fascinated by the invisible people moving things around the room, smiled indulgently at me. "I got lucky," he said.

"Save it to the hard drive," Paul said to Maxie. Intent on the task at hand, he was all attention and not listening to Josh and me banter. Paul was so absorbed, in fact, that he hadn't even tried to power the laptop all by himself.

Discovering this ability of his to transfer energy to electric devices would have really come in handy during Hurricane Sandy, but that was the way things went.

Maxie was punching keys with great intensity. "It's not a big file, but this thing is probably going to take some time to download it," she said. She shot me a look. Like the age of the laptop was my fault. Sue me for not taking money out of the college fund to buy a new laptop for a resident ghost.

"Do it anyway. The lieutenant wants me to keep this

drive safe, and I don't intend to lose it." Paul is always ethical, so I took him at his word. "When we're done looking at the download, we'll delete it." Mostly ethical.

Melissa was giving Oliver some puréed . . . something, sitting on the island and looking very responsible, while Oliver was attempting to feed himself and managing to still get some of his food in his mouth, although a higher percentage than just a month or two earlier—he was enough of a "big boy" now that he could sit in a high chair next to the center island in my kitchen and pick things up with his fingers, a task he appeared to find hilarious.

"How is the information organized?" Paul asked.

"Very carefully," Maxie told him. "The lady cop has a really disciplined mind. It's a little scary."

"Let me see." Paul maneuvered himself around Maxie, his body horizontal, his feet high in the air (in fact, partially sticking through the ceiling) to best see what was on the screen without getting in the way of Maxie's typing. The ghosts have some physical substance when in contact with each other. If I tried to touch them, my hand would go straight through.

There was a lot of technical gobbledygook that they shot back and forth at each other for a few minutes. If I could've funneled it to Josh, he probably would have understood it, but I wasn't picking up a word. Then Paul just floated there and looked for a while, and suddenly, he came out with an awed "Wow."

My head broke speed records snapping up. "What, wow?"

"The lieutenant is very thorough," he said.

"Yeah, newsflash."

"But there is one item that bears interest."

Maxie squinted at the screen as if it weren't right in front of her face. "You mean this?" she asked, pointing.

"Precisely."

"Okay, the two of you have to either come down here or

bring me up there, because I have no idea what you're talking about," I told them.

Josh walked over to Melissa, who slid down off the island, picked Ollie out of the high chair after toweling him off (which he did not find delightful) and lowered him to the floor. He (Ollie) immediately grabbed for the bar stool nearest to him and steadied himself, looking stupefied, amazed that he could accomplish such a tremendous feat. Once he was sure he wouldn't fall, Ollie grinned. "Gah," he said.

"Gah," Josh agreed.

"What do you see that's so interesting?" I asked again.

Maxie deigned to lower herself and the laptop just barely to eye level, meaning if Josh stood up, he'd see it plainly, while I had to stand on tiptoe a little. "This here," she said, pointing. Josh *didn't* stand up, because he lets me be in charge when we're talking investigations.

"I can't see it."

Maxie curled her lip a little. "Well, I'm conserving power by turning down the brightness," she huffed. "I mean, this thing can barely hold a charge as it is."

"Enough with the technological complaints; I'm sorry that I can't afford to buy a brand-new state-of-the-art laptop for a dead person," I said. She scowled, but now I was irritated. "What is it I'm looking at?"

Paul, always the peacemaker, rappelled down from the chandelier and brought the laptop—under a slight protest from Maxie—down to where I could see it. "There is one file that's encrypted," he said. "Out of all the files on the hard drive, it's the only one. It requires a password to get in. That sticks out as unusual and therefore worthy of examination."

"I can't see the name of the folder," I told him.

"H. Monroe," Paul read off to me.

"Harry 'the Fish' Monroe," Melissa said.

"Gah," Oliver answered.

I looked up at Maxie. "So . . . ?"

"So? So, what?" she said.

"So, how do you get into the folder? It might have some idea of where McElone was going in her investigation, and that might give us an idea of where she is now."

Oliver was cruising from one bar stool to the next, so Josh was busy keeping them from falling over if the baby (toddler?) yanked too strenuously. Oliver, apparently under the impression he was walking, looked quite pleased with his progress.

"It's password protected," Maxie reminded me. "I'm not saying I can't get in, but it'll take some time. You know the lady cop. Have any guesses what her password might be?"

That was a stumper. "Me? Until he called today, I had no idea what her husband's name was. I had no idea she even had a husband."

"Well, according to him, you two are besties," Maxie teased. "You must know *something*."

Ollie's foot slipped a little, and he fell on his diaper and started to cry. Liss was immediately on the floor next to him, but as the responsible adult in the room (after Josh), I walked over and picked him up. "It's okay, baby," I said. "It's okay."

He cried a little bit more, but his heart wasn't in it; what he really wanted was to be on the floor and try standing again. I held him close for a minute or two, and then he wriggled to be set back on his mission, gurgling with anticipation. Oliver pointed ahead like Columbus's navigator spotting land after weeks of desperate search. There were territories to conquer.

"I have no idea what McElone's password might be," I told Maxie. "Knowing her, it's a perfect blend of upper- and lowercase letters, numbers and symbols, all in a code that makes sense only to her. The woman is more efficient than is possible in normal humans."

"What's left for you to do?" Josh asked as he stabilized another bar stool for Ollie. "The lieutenant is missing, and you can't get into the encrypted file on her thumb drive yet.

Is there anything else on there that might point you in a direction?"

I turned to face up toward Maxie, and Josh, seeing that, instinctively did the same. "It's going to take a long time, and Paul's going to have to read most of this stuff," she said. "It's Lithuanian to me."

"Okay, get to work," I said, feeling very in charge and pleased that there was nothing that I personally had to do. "I'll continue to try contacting McElone, and if I hear from Malcolm again, I'll meet with him tomorrow."

Realizing that dinner would be arriving fairly soon, along with my parents, who had consented (well, Mom consented; Dad's not capable of doing much more than going along for the ride these days) to pick up from Zorba the Restaurant, which luckily makes better food than business names, I got some kitchen wipes and began sanitizing any areas—particularly the high chair's food tray—that Ollie might have come in contact with, or that he might later. If that kid had even a sniffle when Jeannie got back, I'd be hearing about it for the rest of my life.

"There is something else you can do," Paul said without looking up from the screen. "Given the latest developments, I think there is a witness you need to interview."

I didn't like the sound of that. "I said I'd talk to McElone's husband tomorrow," I reminded him. "I'm not sure if we can find Martin Ferry anymore. Who else is there to ask?"

"Harry 'the Fish' Monroe," Paul answered. "He just sent me another message. I know where he is now."

For a guy nicknamed "the Fish," it turned out that Harry Monroe was not terribly fond of the water. "All that ever happens in the ocean is you get wet and jellyfish bite you," he said. He said his buddies had saddled him with the "Fish" name because they thought a gangster working the Jersey Shore who didn't like the water was funny. Given that he was sitting just past the pier Josh and I were standing on, his body half submerged in the waves, his claim seemed incongruous. The fact that jellyfish couldn't even know he was there, and that there was nothing left of him to bite, didn't add to his credibility.

"Something else must have happened to you," I pointed out. "You're stuck out here in the ocean, yet you died in your car on land. How do you figure that?"

It was just before dusk, and Josh had driven me to the spot in Point Pleasant where Harry had apparently gone to sleep with his nickname (ghosts begin where they died), although his body had been found in his car. It hadn't been terribly difficult for me to spot Harry, who was unable to get himself to shore despite being within walking distance for most living people. In his dark suit, even transparent, Harry mostly looked ridiculous.

Josh had insisted on coming. He is fascinated by the investigation work I do, for one thing, and had been noodging me for a while to let him come along when the task was not being undertaken during his business hours. Also, he had made noises about "not letting you go see a mafioso— even a dead one—without someone along if you . . . want to make accusations." He had been standing within Melissa's earshot at the time and didn't want to emphasize the possible danger in visiting Harry.

Maxie, my first choice for a wing ghost on this mission, had begged off, saying she wanted to stay close to Liss and Oliver, but she had probably already found an excuse to go "visit her mom." *My* mom and dad agreed to help Liss watch Oliver and pass along any concerns from the guests. Given that Mom was the only visible adult in the equation, it had been impossible to ask her to come.

Right now, the only danger seemed to be that Harry was a little farther from the edge of the pier than I cared for, it was starting to get dark and slipping on the rocks was a very plausible threat. I had made sure to take off my shoes before we had ventured out this far. I wasn't bothering to record the exchange because ghost voices don't register on the recorder. I wasn't taking notes, because the sea spray would have pretty much obliterated them as I wrote. This was sort of like talking to a ghost on the *Will o' the Wisp* in Niagara Falls, which perhaps I should give a try someday.

"The memories are coming back in dribs and drabs," Harry the Fish said as his namesakes were no doubt swimming through his calves. "I don't have it all yet, but I don't remember anything after being in my car on the way to a meeting—and no, I'm not telling you with who. I sure as hell wasn't coming here."

"So tell me about Detective Ferry," I said. Best to get right to the point of the conversation.

"Listen, cutie, I am not going to tell you *anything* about my business, you understand? There's a code." A seagull flew through Harry's face, and he instinctively tried to brush it away.

"A code?" I repeated back, to give Josh some context. "I don't see where that code is really useful to you anymore."

"A code's a code. There are people I worked with—you know the phrase 'a fate worse than death'? They take it literally."

"Harry," I said, "Detective Martin Ferry was shot. You ended up out here somehow. Don't you want to know what happened to the two of you?"

"You bet your butt I do," Harry said. The guy was as charming as someone nicknamed "the Fish" should be (and keep in mind that I hate fish). "I don't care so much about the cop, but if I find out that somebody whacked me, there's gonna be some retribution from beyond the grave."

I edited the comment while passing it on to Josh. "Mr. Monroe," Josh said when I was done, "the detective's death and yours must be linked. Finding out what happened to him will help in finding out what happened to you."

"Who is this guy?" Harry asked me. "Why is he looking six feet over my head? There's nothing up there but sky."

"You're ducking the question, Harry," I said, without explaining to Josh. "If we can find out what happened to Martin Ferry, it could help figure out how you ended up here. What was your relationship with the detective like, anyway?"

"*Relationship?*" Harry parroted back. "You think we were dating?"

"I think that whatever it is, you don't want to talk about it," I answered. In "person," Harry the Fish wasn't quite as intimidating as you might think, especially since I knew he couldn't make it back to shore, so I was going for it. "And given that he was a cop and you were . . . in the business you were in, that leads to questions. You don't want to discuss how you knew Detective Ferry? What conclusions should I draw from that?"

Suddenly, I saw what must have scared the living hell out of the people who crossed Harry Monroe in life. His eyes narrowed, and his voice dropped to a menacing rasp. "Are you saying I'm a rat?" he said.

Josh must have seen my reaction, because his own expression became considerably more concerned. "Are you okay? What's he saying?"

I answered Harry, not Josh. Because I didn't know if I was okay. "I'm saying that you're not giving me a reason to think anything else."

"A reason," Harry said darkly. "Who are you that I should give you a reason?"

"One of the few living people left on the planet who can see and hear you," I answered, my voice considerably bolder than my digestive tract at the moment. "So if you want me to communicate your message, I need to know what that message is. How did you know Martin Ferry?"

Harry's lip curled a little, but just a little. The cute-grandpa act he'd been putting on had vanished. This was the killer, now quite literally stone cold.

"He was a cop, and I was someone in a business that didn't care much for cops," he said. "But we got along okay."

My eyes closed briefly. I was pretty sure I didn't want to hear what was coming next. "What do you mean, you got along okay?" I asked, dreading the answer.

"I mean we got along okay," the old mobster shot back. "Do I have to get in touch with some of my colleagues who are still alive?" His voice got deeper. "Or some who aren't but can get to where you live?"

Josh was not looking like his usual amiable self; he couldn't hear what Harry was saying, but he could see the effect it was having on my face and my posture. He stood closer to me and put an arm around my shoulder, which was damp from the spray and starting to feel cooler now that the sun was almost down. He looked in Harry's general direction.

"All this woman wants to do is help you, Mr. Monroe," he said. "Tell her the truth, and she can help. She has helped ghosts get through this transition before. If you ever want to get out of the ocean, she is one of the few people who can offer you assistance. So you threaten her, and you lose any hope you have of getting past this stage of your existence."

Harry 'the Fish' Monroe stared at Josh for what seemed like an hour and a half but was probably three seconds. "This guy your husband?" he asked me.

"He's someone who cares," I said. "Tell me about you and Martin Ferry."

"Martin Ferry was a cop," he answered. "Not all cops are Boy Scouts. Is that clear enough for you?"

It was clear enough.

Seventeen

"This is not good news," Paul said.

Josh and I had filled him, Dad and Mom in on our visit with the dead Fish. Oliver was fast asleep in his portable crib by now, and Melissa was upstairs, ostensibly getting ready for bed but more likely communicating with her friends online. In any event, she knew better than to come downstairs and participate in this powwow. I'd get her up to speed the next morning.

Meanwhile, Stephanie and Rita had come back from dinner more than an hour earlier, reporting no new hat sightings. Rita still looked a little nervous.

Don and Tammy Coburn had retired to their room, which I think of as the bridal suite, our most spacious guest room on the first floor. They said they'd had a lovely day at the boardwalk, where Don had won Tammy a giant stuffed tiger by spending enough tokens on Skee-Ball to pay off a car loan, from the sound of it.

Nobody had seen Joe Guglielmelli or Bonnie Claeson

for a few hours. If the Harbor Haven police didn't call, I could only assume that each was taking in the town in his or her own way. I don't require my guests to account for every moment of their time with me as long as they're getting what they want out of the visit.

Maxie was nowhere to be seen. She'd told my parents that she was out on another of her visits to her mom, so she could be anywhere. Literally. To his credit, Josh had reminded me to call Kitty in the car on the way home, but I'd been too busy texting Phyllis (oh yes, Phyllis texts) to see if she could explore the possibility that Harry had in fact drowned rather than having a heart attack in his car.

Phyllis's first reply text, "You think he drowned in his car?" had required more of a response than I'd planned, so Kitty had gone uncalled. But it was on my mental agenda.

"I'm aware it's not good news," I told Paul. "But what's really disturbing is that Harry Monroe seems to be saying Martin Ferry was a dirty cop."

Paul, his finger in the power slot of a large-screen TV I'd bought for the new movie room (even larger than the monitor the TV crew had left in my den) but not yet installed, looked downtrodden. "I don't understand," he muttered. "This television doesn't draw a large amount of energy. I should be able to power it."

"Maybe you need more fiber in your diet," I said, then waved a hand to get his attention. "Hey, remember? Martin Ferry? We're trying to help Lieutenant McElone? Harry the Fish is saying Ferry was on the take, and now even if we find McElone, I'm going to have to tell her that."

Dad, hovering near my mother as usual, turned his eyes into slits, which I knew meant he was thinking. He got the same look on his face when trying to decide what grit sandpaper to use on a decorative wooden banister. "I don't think that's what Mr. Fish was saying at all," he said. Dad was a terrific handyman and his clients loved him, but remembering names wasn't his best thing.

"Of course it is," I said, turning my head.

Josh noted the move. "Is that Jack?" he asked, and I acknowledged I was talking to my father. Josh had known my dad in life—Dad used to visit Josh's grandfather Sy's paint store (now Josh's paint store), which is also where Josh and I first met as kids. He waved at Dad, who smiled broadly and raised a compound knife I'd left on the floor by way of greeting. "Good to . . . well, I can't *see* you, but you know what I mean," Josh said in the knife's direction.

"He's a keeper, Alison," my father repeated. Mom, if she could have nudged him in good-natured embarrassment, would have done so. With all her years of interacting with ghosts, I was surprised Mom hadn't developed the ability to touch them.

I had to get the room back on topic. "What do you mean, Dad? You don't think Harry was saying Detective Ferry was on the take?" I asked.

"What you told me is that this Fish guy said some cops are not Boy Scouts. I think that's what he wants you to think," Dad explained.

That was a stretch at best. "We're going to exonerate Ferry based on a mobster's syntax?" I asked. "I don't want Ferry to have been a dirty cop, either, but like Paul always says, we can't make the facts fit what we want them to fit. They lead us where they go. Right, Paul?"

Paul, looking concerned, actually had his tongue stuck out, into the power port of the TV. "What?" he tried to say. It came out, "Blurrth?"

"Will you quit trying to be a backup generator and concentrate on the case?" I scolded him. I didn't have time to dwell on the irony that *I* was the one demanding that *Paul* pay attention to an investigation. It probably would have made my head hurt. "First of all, I don't know how to find McElone, and secondly, even if I do, I don't know what to tell her."

Looking properly chastised, Paul floated over from the

television. "The problem at hand is twofold," he said. "The most important matter in the short term is to locate the lieutenant and determine that she is all right. No member of the team can ever be left behind." He likes to say stuff like that, as if we were a real team and McElone was a member of it.

"So what can be done?" It was only the fifty-third time I was asking, but somehow it felt old already. (New Jersey's national language: Sarcasm.)

"We all should concentrate on our strengths. I will try to raise Detective Ferry again, since he was unwilling to speak to you on the subject of Monroe when you were there the last time. I'll also make a discreet check . . ." He seemed to catch himself midsentence, about to say something he shouldn't.

"A discreet check on what?" Mom asked.

"On Lieutenant McElone," I told her. "Paul wants to make sure she isn't on his side of the line now."

"You think . . . ?" Josh narrowed his eyes and seemed to be running his tongue over his front teeth. That's Josh being concerned. Then he shook his head to banish the thought.

Mom looked shaken. "Oh."

"All possibilities need to be explored," Paul said.

"What about me?" I asked.

"I think it might be time to start asking questions of the Seaside Heights police," Paul said. "And I think we have to assume that Lieutenant McElone's husband will be calling you in the morning. Meet with Malcolm Kidder as soon as you can and see if you can find out where the lieutenant was going. Be respectful, but we also need to know if there were personal problems between them. Circumstances don't always mean that the most obvious scenario is correct."

"Is there anything I can do?" Josh asked when he'd been told Paul's instructions for everyone else.

"Keep an eye on Alison," Paul said. "We don't know who we're dealing with yet, but there are certainly unsavory types involved here."

I turned to Josh. "He says there isn't much else that can be done, but he'll let you know if something appropriate comes to mind," I said. And off Mom's look, which was a little incredulous at my duplicity, I added, "You have a store to run. Run it."

"That's not what I said," Paul said. I gave him a look that indicated I was aware of that fact, and he stopped his protest right there. Josh's eyes flickered for a second, but he knew better than to go behind my back right in front of my face. He did not ask Mom for confirmation.

"I don't want you to do anything dangerous," he said.

"I won't," I promised, and meant both words. Then I kissed him, right there in front of both my parents and my ghost housemate.

"Okay, then," Josh said. He said his good-byes to my folks and Paul, then left.

Paul decided to get back to business. "All right. You have your assignments, and I have mine. If only Maxie were here, I could tell her what it is we need researched."

"And she could complain about the old laptop for the millionth time," I said absently. "Wait. Maxie." I reached into my pocket. "I'm not going to forget this time."

"Forget what?" Dad asked.

"She needs to call Maxie's mother," Mom informed him.

This time, I did indeed dial Kitty Malone and got her on the third ring. If Maxie was there, she'd be pissed that I was checking up on her, but I was long past caring.

"Kitty," I said as soon as the apologies for calling at night were made, "I've been concerned about you, and I just wanted to check in and make sure you were okay."

There was a long pause at the other end, then Kitty asked me, "Why would you be concerned about me, Alison? I'm fine."

Well, that was a relief, anyway. "It's just that Maxie's been spending so much time over there lately," I explained. "I know she loves to see you, but usually you come here. And she gets so upset whenever I ask about her trips there, so I was naturally a little . . . curious. I wanted to be sure you're all right."

"What do you mean, she's been spending so much time here lately?" Kitty asked, confusion in her voice. "I was going to call you to ask what the problem was, but, well, something keeps coming up when I reach for the phone."

"Problem?" I asked. "What problem?"

"I assumed there was a problem there," she answered. "I haven't seen Maxie in weeks."

Eighteen

I did not need another mystery to solve, and yet Kitty—or, more accurately, Maxie—was providing me with one.

I assured Kitty that I had no idea what was going on with her daughter. When we compared notes, Kitty said that as far as she knew, Maxie had last been by her house almost a month earlier—and that she'd told her mother (via written communication) that she wouldn't be coming by for a while, and that Kitty shouldn't come by the guesthouse either until Maxie told her it was all right to do so. When Kitty had questioned Maxie on the subject, Maxie had written "JUST DON'T COME OVER!!!" on a legal pad, so Kitty had dropped it, and she hadn't heard from her since.

"I'm sorry I didn't get in touch sooner," Kitty said. "I'm glad you called. I kept telling myself I really should call, but the fact is that I didn't want Maxie to get mad at me again, especially since I didn't know why she got so upset to begin with."

I'd started off informing Paul, Mom and Dad about everything Kitty was telling me, but as the conversation went on, I simply put the phone on speaker so we could have the discussion in real time. "I know what you mean," I said. "Maxie's been getting so bent out of shape whenever I asked a question, I didn't want to call you because I thought she would fly off the handle again."

Paul, who looked absolutely stumped by this turn of events, suggested I ask Kitty if Maxie had mentioned feeling any changes the last time they'd been together, a sense that perhaps she was moving on to some other plane of existence. I didn't want to ask—I knew that after their relatively recent reunion, Kitty would be very upset if she could never talk to her daughter again—but in this case, Paul's obsession with the next phase was relevant.

Kitty was silent for a long time. "She didn't say anything, but maybe she doesn't know how to tell me."

I wasn't so sure. "I could believe that she wouldn't want to upset you," I said, "but she'd take great glee in telling me that she would be moving out. She likes nothing better than getting my goat."

"Paul or Maxie moving on is not about you, Alison," my father said quietly. "It's involuntary." That seemed to shake him; he looked away.

I didn't know how to answer him. Instead, I asked Kitty what she suggested we do.

"Well, there is the direct approach, but I'm not sure that's the way to go with this," she answered. "She'll just hit the ceiling."

"Or go right through it," Mom said.

Kitty chuckled. "I really do wish I could see that."

"So what's the alternative?" I asked.

"Simple," came the answer, from Paul. I turned to look at him. He raised his eyebrows. "All you have to do is wait until the next time she says she's going to Kitty's house, and follow her."

"Do surveillance on Maxie?" I gasped.

Kitty, who had heard the suggestion for the first time, snorted a little. "That would be a trick."

I looked at Paul again. "Maxie can fly," I reminded him.

"I'm aware," he admitted. "You can't." No kidding, Captain Obvious.

"But I can," said my father.

"I haven't been sleeping much," Malcolm Kidder said to me the next morning. He was not the kind of man I'd have pictured as Lieutenant McElone's husband. Slim, almost slight, he had a goofy grin and a boyish manner that I would have bet money would draw an eye roll from the lieutenant as I knew her. Clearly, there were many sides of McElone I had not gotten to see before. Malcolm was one of them.

We were sitting on a bench outside the Stud Muffin, Harbor Haven's artisanal bakery and café. Oliver was entertaining himself climbing up the bench and back down again, just to see if he could. He could. It was only eight in the morning, so not yet stifling. Malcolm had suggested sitting outside while we could, to enjoy the early respite from humidity, and because the Stud Muffin was bustling (when better to enjoy a muffin or scone?) and a little noisy, with its high ceilings and bare walls.

Iced coffee seemed like a good idea. Mom, Dad, Paul and I had been up fairly late debating the merits of Dad's following Maxie around. It wasn't that we were worried about his safety—there wasn't much that could hurt Dad at this point—but it would be a really bad thing if Maxie were to realize she was being followed, mostly because Maxie is not a pleasant being when she's even a little bit irritated.

Maxie herself had wandered in about midnight in a strangely detached mood. When Paul had tried to engage her with new instructions on Internet research in the Martin Ferry murder, she had nodded a lot, but it was clear she wasn't listening. Paul had me write down the instructions and give them to Maxie, who grumbled about being treated like a secretary, not that we were doing that anyway.

Paul mostly wanted her working on decoding McElone's password to read the file on Harry Monroe, and after a while of staring blankly at everyone, Maxie said she would go out on the roof, where the Wi-Fi would still work but where she wouldn't disturb Melissa, and get cracking. I'm not sure anyone believed her.

Then we'd broken up the board meeting. Mom and Dad had headed home (leaving instructions for Paul to let Dad know if Maxie was about to "visit Kitty"); Paul had gone into the basement, where he does most of his Ghosternet communication; and I had straightened up the library, the den and the front room, keeping the baby monitor with me at all times, with not a peep from Oliver. It was too late to start in on more renovations in the movie room, so I'd once again promised myself to get an early start.

Then Malcolm had called at seven, saying he was sorry for the early hour but he couldn't wait any longer, and I'd packed Ollie up in his car seat and headed to the Stud Muffin. Having rousted Melissa out of bed, I asked her to greet the guests when they got up, and she grumbled a bit but agreed after I'd put out the coffee urn and the ice bucket. She probably made herself the first iced coffee of the day as soon as I was out the door.

"It must be nerve-racking," I said to Malcolm. Oliver steadied himself on the bench and took some chances, letting go with his hands to see if he could stand. Check. Walking was no doubt on its way. "When is the most recent time you heard from the lieutenant?"

Malcolm smiled. "I appreciate your avoiding the word 'last' in that sentence," he said. "Anita called me two nights ago and said she was on to something but she couldn't say what just yet. She was driving to Belmar, and she'd probably not be back until the morning. I haven't heard from her since."

"Okay, Belmar." I stole a glance at the voice recorder I

had on the bench next to Malcolm. "I hope you don't mind this; I like to use it to remember everything I need." The truth was that I used the recorder so that I could play my interviews for Paul when I got back to the guesthouse, so he could tell me what everything I heard actually meant.

"Not a problem," Malcolm answered.

"How have your children been holding up?"

He looked a little embarrassed. "They're fine. I, um, I told them that she was away at a convention in Atlantic City," he said. "I'm hoping this is over before they figure it out."

"Did she mention what she thought might be going on in Belmar?" One of the hardest-hit areas by Hurricane Sandy, Belmar was still recovering. There were homes in splinters that still had to be carted away, others that were being jacked up a few feet to better protect against any future disasters and some businesses that had simply never reopened.

Malcolm shook his head as Oliver reached out his hands to me and said, "Uh." I picked him up and sat him on my lap.

"All I knew was that she was trying to find out who killed Marty. She insisted it wasn't an accident like the Seaside Heights cops claimed, and she thought she could find out more after the two of you went to Marty's place. But where it led, I have no idea. Anita tends to tell me things after they happen. I don't know how much she ever tells the kids." He looked over at Oliver and chucked him under the chin. "Aren't you something?"

Oliver, believing that he was indeed something, laughed.

"Malcolm," I said, as gently as I could manage, "I think it's time to call the lieutenant's colleagues at the police department and let them know what's going on."

He nodded. "I already have. I spoke to the captain, and he assured me they'll do everything they can. But I don't want that to stop us from looking, okay?"

"Sure," I agreed, admitting to myself that I was thrilled

not to be the only living soul searching for McElone. I was going to be, as Paul had put it, "retracing the lieutenant's footsteps," which sounded like a bad idea to me. If she'd gotten herself missing doing this stuff, why should I expect something good to come of doing the same things? Wasn't there something about repeating an action and expecting a different outcome being the definition of insanity? Hadn't Einstein said that? Or John Lennon?

"Where had the lieutenant started? Had she talked to anyone?"

"You don't have to keep calling her 'lieutenant,' " Malcolm reminded me. "I meant it when I said you can call her Anita."

"That just doesn't feel right to me," I said. I gave Oliver a small toy duck I'd been carrying in my pocket. He looked at it, tried to stretch it and then threw it on the grass in front of us. I took this as a signal and put him on the grass as well. He sat up, grabbed the duck and threw it at me.

"That's not the way Anita tells it," her husband said, watching Ollie loll around on the grass, considering whether there was anything with which he could pull himself up. If he was standing, he wanted to sit. He saw a dog about twenty feet away, a beagle whose owner was naturally not using a leash, because why would you do that? He (Oliver, not the beagle) tried to muscle his way to his feet. He seemed to have it in his head that he could just walk over to the dog. The fact that he had never walked before didn't really appear to deter him at all.

"She seems to think the two of you make a very good team. She speaks of you with respect and affection."

I must have given him an incredulous look. "Lieutenant McElone?" I said, gesturing with my hand. "About yay high? Grumpy demeanor? General air of exasperation?"

He laughed. "That's the one."

"Well then, maybe I'm not who I think I am." It was a possibility, and it would actually explain quite a bit.

"Anita trusted you with this case," he reminded me.

"That should indicate a certain level of respect and affection. Maybe she just doesn't like to show it to you. She can be kind of embarrassed by such things."

I thought of McElone and the way she always fidgeted when I pointed out that she was afraid of my house. "But tell me what I can do to help find her."

"Well, any information you have on what she was doing in the investigation would help. It might point me in a direction."

Oliver rocked back and forth on the cushy disposable diaper under his blue shorts, trying to build up momentum that would take him to a standing position. This whole crawling thing had been fine for a while, but he was so over it now.

"I know what you know," I told Malcolm. "Martin Ferry was shot a few days ago. The police in his department believe it was an accident. The lieutenant didn't. She wanted me to . . . consult with some sources on possible information about the shooting, but so far we haven't come up with much to tell her. I knew she was going to conduct her own investigation, but she never told me how she was going to go about doing that. So I'm at a loss. You haven't heard from her in almost two whole days."

"But the cops, even the ones who work with her, will say we have an adult woman who has taken off and jump to the conclusion that she left because of trouble in our marriage," he said. "That's what they always assume in cases like this, because most of the time it's true."

"*Was* there trouble in your marriage?" Well, Paul had suggested I explore that possibility, and Malcolm had left the door wide open for me.

He looked at me with some intensity for a moment. "*No*," he said. "We're fine. That's why I'm worried sick about this. She never doesn't get in touch. She never doesn't come home at night. She never doesn't talk to her children before they go to sleep. My mind is not going in good directions right now."

"I'm sorry," I said. "I had to ask."

Malcolm nodded. "I know you did. Anita says you have to ask the questions even if you know the person you're talking to won't like hearing them. Maybe especially then. But we have no trouble in our marriage, certainly nothing that would make her slip away and not tell me where she was going. No, this is about Marty and what happened to him."

Oliver, meanwhile, had rolled himself onto his back like he was going to spring to his feet from a prone position the way Popeye the Sailor Man used to do. Alas, Ollie had not had his spinach that day (although I was sure Jeannie had sent some for him, assuming correctly that I would have none in the fridge), so he was not able to get himself vertical. He started to fuss. I stood up to let him see me, and that provided enough entertainment to quiet him down for a moment.

"So you knew Detective Ferry?" I asked Malcolm.

"Sure. He was Anita's partner in Seaside. He came over to the house a few times, even after she moved us here to Harbor Haven. Anita always said Marty was a good guy who was trying to act like he was a bad guy so people would respect him out on the street. I guess someone respected him enough to want him gone permanently."

Oliver was fussing again, so I lifted him just to the point that he was standing. He immediately looked for the irresistible beagle. My new role: boost bar.

"Any idea why?" I asked. Malcolm's perspective on Ferry wouldn't be colored by the same loyalty McElone might have had for her old partner. It might be interesting to get another take.

He cocked an eyebrow. "Well, Marty wasn't the easiest guy in the whole world to get along with. You could ask his ex-wife, Elise, or his daughter, Natasha; she's about to start college, I think. Elise, well, their divorce wasn't exactly smooth, you know?"

"You think his ex-wife might have wanted to kill him?" I asked.

Malcolm shook his head. "I think the shooting was business related," he said. "Anita said she gave you some files about things she'd been working on that might have had Marty's case files in it. Do you have that stuff?"

There was no sense in telling him that I'd given the flash drive to my deceased friend, or that he and the other ghost from my house were probably going over it right now. On the other hand, he might know what McElone's password for such things was, and that would be helpful information.

"I have it, but I haven't been able to open it," I said. "Do you have any idea how to open her encrypted files?"

Oliver actually tried to take a step and flopped down on his knee, which landed directly on the grass. He cried anyway, so I picked him up, kissed the knee (which had a little mud on it) and set him down again. By then, he'd forgotten the whole incident, but the dog was no longer in sight.

"You mean her personal passwords?" Malcolm asked. "No idea. She doesn't know mine, either. I guess it would have been a good idea to share. But be careful with whatever she gave you; if it's encrypted, it must be important."

"Who else can you think of that she might have talked to, besides the ex-wife and daughter?"

He made a show of thinking, stroking his chin the way Paul strokes his goatee, but without the goatee. "Obviously, the other cops he worked with. They seemed to give up on the case really fast. Someone might be covering. And he had a snitch, an informant, called himself Lay-Z. You might want to talk to him."

"There was a drug dealer Ferry was investigating. Buster somebody?" I wasn't going to see him if I could help it, but there was a possibility the mention would trigger something for Malcolm.

"Buster? I don't know a Buster. Maybe it's in the files Anita gave you."

I picked up the diaper bag and stood. "Well, I guess I'm off to talk to the cops in Seaside Heights," I said. I reached down, and Oliver held out his arms. "Come on, Ollie." I picked him up and put him in the stroller I'd parked next to the bench.

"Let me know what you find out," Malcolm said. "You have my number."

I shook his hand. "I will. And you do the same if you hear from the lieutenant—"

Malcolm raised his left hand and pointed a finger straight up. "Anita," he said.

"Right," I said. "Anita."

"Martin Ferry was a world-class pain in the ass," said Captain Charles Stella of the Seaside Heights Police Department. I had been anticipating such a response on the thirty-five-minute drive here, so I didn't blink. "But he wasn't bad at what he did, and he was an irritant, not a threat. Nobody wanted to kill him. It was an accident."

"How do you know that?" I asked. "What did the crime scene team report?"

"Crime scene team? What do you think this is, *CSI*? We sent over a detective because it was one of our own, but under most circumstances, the uniforms who answered the call would have been able to close the case." Stella was not an imposing physical specimen—I doubt he stood five feet seven—but he was solidly built and had a very authoritative voice.

I wanted to cower in intimidation and thank him for his time, but I had an agenda. "Were you here when Detective Ferry was working with Detective McElone?" I asked.

"No, she was gone before I got here," Stella answered, leaning forward on his desk and looking as attentive as he could. "But I met her two days ago, when she came by to ask me all the same questions you're asking now and suggest that somebody killed Ferry. Nobody killed Ferry. His gun went off when he was putting it away, and he got unlucky. There's no two ways around it."

"What's the evidence?" I said. "I've been to his apartment and seen the place, but I don't understand how the gun got out of his desk and shot him by accident."

Oliver, asleep in his stroller, wasn't helping me look terrifically tough, but I wasn't going to be all that scary even without him. Stella looked at Ollie a second because babies are interesting to look at, then regarded me with somewhat less indulgent eyes.

"What makes you think the gun was ever in Ferry's desk?" he asked. "Your Lieutenant McElone said the same thing. The gun was out, lying on the floor not far from his right hand. The desk drawer was open and the key was in the lock. So you tell me why you think someone came in and shot Ferry when he obviously was going through his routine, and maybe forgot there was a round in the chamber?"

"I'm not suggesting I know your job," I told Stella. "I'm not a police officer, and I'm only a part-time PI. So maybe you can explain to me—for the purpose of my own education—how the key dangling from the lock tells you he was putting the gun away. Doesn't it suggest that Ferry had put the gun away and then he . . . or someone . . . had unlocked the drawer to get it out again?"

Stella looked disgusted. "Because, as a 'PI' "—you could hear the quote marks in his voice—"no doubt you know that a key is used to open a drawer before you put something in it if it was locked before."

"It's also used to lock the drawer after you take something out," I said. "How can you tell by looking at it that the key was used for opening the drawer and not waiting for it to be closed again?"

Stella regarded me for a moment, and I wasn't crazy about his condescending expression. "You put the key in your pocket until you're going to lock it again."

"Maybe *you* do, but are you sure Martin Ferry did?"

Stella bit his lips, perhaps in an effort not to let what he was thinking pass between them. "Is there anything else?" he squeezed out.

"Yeah." I had no reason to try to butter him up now. "If I found a body on the floor with a gunshot wound and a gun right next to his hand, I might think it was a suicide. Why wasn't that considered?"

Now Stella regarded me with a sneer. "A cop eats his gun if he's going to off himself," he said. "Nobody shoots himself in the belly and waits to bleed out."

"He was shot in the stomach?" That fact was news to me, though I should have known it already. I wasn't sure why it made a difference, but it did. Even I knew that getting "gut shot" was a really bad thing. In the movies, it's always accompanied by ominous chords on the soundtrack and a wince from the otherwise stoic leading man.

Stella nodded. "I don't know how it was he didn't get to a phone and call for help," he said. "He couldn't have died instantly."

"Doesn't that merit further investigation?" I asked.

Stella looked me dead in the eye. "No," he said.

That did it; I'd have to go back to Ferry's apartment and try to persuade him to trust me again. Without McElone, it wouldn't be easy.

But that was the key.

Nineteen

After conferring with Paul via text in my car (and yes, Jeannie, I was parked while texting), I told my GPS to take me back to Martin Ferry's apartment. I don't know Seaside Heights that well; we tend to go to Point Pleasant when we want a taste of the boardwalk, usually in September when the crowds have thinned a little.

The whole way there I ruminated over the disappearance of Lieutenant McElone. According to her husband, she considered me more fondly than a mere annoyance, which was news to me. She was out of touch somewhere, possibly in danger, and I felt a sense of responsibility. But the only thing I could think to do—the only thing that no one else looking for McElone *could* do—was talk to ghosts for information. And the ghost with the best information to share was Martin Ferry. In McElone's absence, Martin Ferry was the best cop contact I had. And he had been shot dead. This is how my life works.

I pulled up to his apartment building with Ollie asleep

in his car seat, and felt bad about waking him to get him out of the car and into the stroller, and then out of the stroller in order to climb the stairs to Ferry's apartment.

At the door to Ferry's apartment, I set a grumpy Oliver back down in his stroller with the Superman action figure Melissa had found in the basement and cleaned up, then felt in the notch behind the molding for the key Ferry had said he'd left there. It took a moment, but reaching a little above my head, the fingers of my left hand found the key and extracted it.

An awful thought hit me as I put the key in the lock: What if Alice, the lackluster real estate agent, had managed to rent out Ferry's apartment already? Granted, it would have been swift for anyone, let alone Alice, to do so, but in that unlikely event, this could get awkward in a big hurry.

I opened the door cautiously, spotted no one—living or otherwise—and rolled Ollie inside. Then I made sure the door was locked behind me.

Ferry was not immediately visible in the living room, but both times I'd been here before, I'd found him in the spare bedroom where the computer was, apparently trying to will his fingers to work on the keyboard. I did the usual check of the other rooms and then opened the door to the spare bedroom.

I gasped when I first looked inside: The desk, the desk chair, the daybed and all the other furnishings that had been there before were gone. The room was completely empty, looking as sad and lonely as a room could.

Except for Martin Ferry, who was floating in its center, head in his hands. I knew he couldn't be asleep (ghosts don't sleep), but he could be resting. It wasn't that, though, I realized as I walked quietly inside. Ferry's shoulders were quaking, in spasm. His head shook. He kept gasping, as if he could take in air.

He technically wasn't crying, since it wasn't physically

possible. But in every other way, Martin Ferry was weeping silently.

"Detective Ferry," I whispered, afraid to startle him. Oliver, freed from the stroller, was crawling around the room looking for something with which he could pull himself up. There was nothing left.

Ferry turned suddenly at my voice; he hadn't known we were in the room. He blinked a couple of times and wiped invisible tears from his cheeks and eyes. "My daughter was here," he said. "She was right here—and she didn't even know I was in the room." The man was distraught, and I understood, even if I couldn't empathize. Every dead person I knew could see me, and I could see many of them, although not as many as Mom or Melissa, I'm told.

Accepting what's happened is a difficult task for any new ghost, and Paul tells me that the shock of death can be extra complicated when it's unexpected: Martin Ferry hadn't been ill, hadn't contemplated the idea that his life was about to end. He had been going through a routine day, and then he was . . . something else entirely.

"I know it's really hard to take," I said. "I'm sorry."

He didn't appear to have heard me speak. "She was crying, and there wasn't anything I could do about it," he rasped. "I couldn't let her know I was here with her the whole time." He descended toward the floor, at the same time contracting himself, bending into something past a sitting position, holding his ankles with his hands.

Maybe I could ease him away from the memory. "Where did your furniture go?" I asked.

Ferry didn't look up. "She took it with her. This was her room when she came to see me. She took the bed and the desk. Had some guy with her, and I didn't even know him." Then he did raise his eyes to mine. "I didn't even know she had a boyfriend."

"Did she take the computer, too?" I asked. Ferry had been trying to do something with the computer both times

I'd been here before now, and it was possible I could find out what, and why, through this avenue.

His eyes focused, and he started to become a cop again. "No. That was Lay-Z. Showed up here late last night, out of nowhere."

Lay-Z. "Your informant?" I said.

"Yeah. He must have picked the lock. He's good at that. He came right in, took the computer, walked out. Didn't look around, didn't take anything else, and he's the type who would." Ferry straightened up, slowly, and while he didn't pace the air, he was moving through it without conscious effort. "No, wait. He took a DVD, too. *Weekend at Bernie's.*"

"So what does that tell you?" I asked. "That he has ironic taste in movies?"

"That somebody sent him. Told him to get the computer and nothing else; don't make it look like the place was burglarized. Somebody wanted that laptop. The DVD was probably for him."

Oliver, having crawled to a spot under the window, was attempting to reach the sill and pull himself to a standing position. As this was occupying his time and didn't seem to be frustrating him to the point of crying, I saw it as a positive development and made note to tell Jeannie about it.

"The other times I was here you were all over your computer, and now someone took it. Why?" I asked Ferry. "What is there on your hard drive that would be valuable?"

"Notes. That's what I was trying to access, anyway. Notes about Buster." He finally seemed to notice Oliver by the window and swooped over for a look. "Hey, pal. You tryin' to climb up?" Ferry was about to reach down, then looked at his hands. "I can't help you much."

"Buster Hockney? The drug dealer you were investigating?" I knew that was who Ferry meant, but I wanted him to talk more.

He nodded. "Buster was one of Harry the Fish's competitors and was moving up in the area. He must have known I was getting close to him. When you showed up the first time, I didn't know what had happened to me, didn't know I was . . . like *this* yet. I was trying to get back up to speed, because I could tell my memory had holes in it and I thought it might have something to do with Buster."

"What made you think that?" This was the line of questioning I was most hoping wouldn't have had anything to do with Ferry's death, and here I was asking about it. Wait. There was still Harry the Fish. Second-most hoping.

He shrugged. "Instinct, I guess. Buster's a nut. I heard he put a guy in the hospital one time for pointing out some food stuck between Buster's teeth."

"Yikes. Why didn't you tell Lieutenant McElone about the laptop when she asked about your files?"

Ferry stared at me. "Didn't I?" Clearly, his mind hadn't been functioning at full strength that day. No sense in pushing it; he'd just start getting upset again.

"How is Lay-Z involved with Buster?"

"He ran some errands for Buster," Ferry said. "Nothing serious, but when I met Lay-Z, he thought he was going to be some big kingpin. I showed him how easy it was to bust him when he'd just been messing with some weed for the tourists, and he started to see that maybe he wasn't cut out to be Al Capone. He was just starting to get useful when I . . . *this*."

"I'm going to have to talk to him," I said, not the least bit pleased about what I was saying. "How do I find Lay-Z?"

Ferry shook himself fully alert. "You should leave it to Anita." He stopped, noticing her absence for the first time. "Where *is* Anita?"

I'd been waiting for the question. "She's missing," I said.

Ferry's eyebrows rose so high I thought they'd hit the ceiling. Literally. "Missing? You don't know where Anita is?"

Hey, it wasn't just *my* fault. I shook my head. "She hasn't answered her phone in two days. I spoke to her husband, and he doesn't know where she is, either. He's worried."

Ferry gave up on amusing Oliver and leaned back, almost through the wall. "That's not Anita. She'd never do that to her family."

"I agree. So you have to help me find her. You have to be a detective again, starting right now. What's the first thing I should do?"

Martin Ferry's eyes narrowed; he was becoming the man he used to be, just dead. "Find Lay-Z," he said.

Twenty

Josh Kaplan scoffed at the idea that I'd been acting like a baby when I'd called and asked him to come with me to meet a drug dealer because I was wary of . . . everything. "A baby would have just gone and met the drug dealer," he said. "They don't really have that much experience to fall back on."

Speaking of babies, I had not considered for one second bringing Oliver along on this trip. I might consider Jeannie a little overenthusiastic in her parenting and perhaps a hair overprotective, but taking a child along to meet a known drug dealer I suspected of involvement in at least one murder was a little extreme even from my laissez-faire point of view. I'd dropped Oliver off at my mother's house, and Mom had said she'd bring him back to the guesthouse in time for the afternoon spook show, then stay to make dinner. Dad, waiting to get a Ghosternet message from Paul about following Maxie, was hiding out at Madison Paint.

"Do me a favor and don't say anything like that when

Jeannie and Tony get back on Sunday, okay?" I said. "Tony will think it's hilarious, but . . ."

". . . but Jeannie will never let me exist in the same room as her child again, I know." Josh was wearing his work clothes with spots of paint on them and driving the Madison Paint van. I'd agreed to let him drive because the air-conditioning in his van actually works, which puts it one up on my Volvo. And his scruffy clothes might actually work to our advantage in this instance.

Martin Ferry had told me to look for Lay-Z, whom he described as "looking like a giraffe with a shaved head," working at a frozen custard stand on what is left of the Seaside Heights boardwalk.

They'd finally dismantled and removed the Jet Star, the roller coaster that had been blown completely into the ocean during Sandy. The absence of all that twisted metal in the surf was something of a relief after all these months, though weirdly, the damaged coaster had in fact become a sort of strange tourist attraction of its own in the area, as visitors came to take pictures of it to show how badly our shore had been battered and how people's lives and businesses were wiped away in a day and a half. I'm in the tourism business, and I think that's just beyond strange. Then, not long after the storm and just as people were recovering, came the fire in Seaside Park (started, ironically, at a different frozen custard stand), which had spread here to Seaside Heights, and most of the work that had been accomplished was wiped out. Re-rebuilding was once again on the agenda.

The one plus was that Snooki and her reality-TV gang had vacated Seaside Heights before the storm, so we didn't have to worry about them coming back and doing . . . whatever it was they were doing there.

Some of the boardwalk had been replaced with a modern-looking facsimile, made out of recycled material that had wood grain and probably no wood in it. It was a grayish white and, I knew from previous visits, did not threaten to impale your feet with splinters, which made me wonder how much fun it could really be.

"I feel bad about taking you away from the store," I said, determined to prove to Josh that I was in fact a bad girlfriend. "You have a business, and I should respect that more."

"You respect it fine. Sy is happy to stay for a couple of hours, and besides, the contractors all came and went by seven this morning. They're in even earlier when it's this hot, so they can quit at two in the afternoon."

Sy Kaplan, Josh's grandfather, is in his nineties and had recently given up his stake in Madison Paints, but continued to hang around in the store because it was where everyone he knew "who's still alive" congregated to talk and joke around. Actually, a bunch of guys who weren't still alive liked to gather there, too—in fact, my father was there today, always happy to join in with the gang until he was needed to tail Maxie.

Josh pulled the van into a parking space about a block from the boardwalk. The very fact that you could find parking a block from the boardwalk, at what was typically the height of the tourist season, was a testament to how not everything was quite the same at the Jersey Shore.

Josh and I walked up to the boardwalk and started strolling around, pretending it wasn't close to a hundred degrees out. There were some hearty sunbathers on the beach, and a good number in the water. It was the only sane thing to do in Seaside Heights on a day like today. Miniature golf here in August would take more out of you than a marathon in October.

We passed by the restored game booths but didn't even stop to make believe they weren't rigged or that I actually wanted Josh to "win" me a stuffed cloth monkey wearing a "Restore the Shore" T-shirt.

"There," I said, pointing. At the end of the boardwalk was a beaten-up frozen custard stand, an original, something that hadn't been replaced after bad luck had messed with the place. Homes came and went, roller coasters tried to swim to England, but Mickey's Frozen Custard had weathered the storm and showed every dent it had sustained from the wind, smoke and rain.

"Suddenly I'm in the mood for a custard," Josh said. He was wearing sunglasses, dark ones, so I wasn't really sure how his eyes looked, but his hand around my arm, which was already sweating, tightened a little.

We got closer to the place, which had not one customer in front of it (there were four Kohr's, the better-known custard place, locations operating on the boardwalk, and if you had a choice between those and Mickey's, well, that wasn't exactly a choice), and looked around for someone who might fit Ferry's description of Lay-Z.

He wasn't hard to spot, even from a distance: At least six feet three and weighing approximately seventy-eight pounds soaking wet, the kid—there was no other word for him—behind the counter at the custard stand had a shaved head and a neck that looked like it should have had handrails on either side. He was maybe nineteen years old and was still in need of a good acne medication, and gave the appearance of someone of normal proportions who had been grabbed by the head and feet and stretched by someone who didn't like him much.

"Put yellow and brown spots on him and he'd fit in at a safari theme park," Josh said.

There was no one else around, so we approached the stand and caught the eye of our prey. I had to look up pretty severely to do so.

"Welcome to Mickey's how may I help you," he said in what would have passed for a single breath if he'd seemed that animated. The script had been written, and he was reciting it; they weren't paying him enough to pretend he was interested.

"Are you Lay-Z?" Josh asked, forgoing the pretense of

ordering. Just as well; if I wanted a custard (and I did), I'd be better off at Kohr's anyway.

There was a glint of something in the kid's eyes that might have been wariness, anger or panic. "I'm just doing my job, man," he said.

"You know what I mean."

"I don't know what you're talking about." Variety was not his forte.

"Sure you do," I said. "I just want to ask you a couple of questions."

This really confused him; he looked us over carefully. Josh had enough paint splashed on his clothing to qualify as a Jackson Pollock canvas, and I looked like, well, me. You could put me in riot gear and I wouldn't seem threatening.

"I don't know anything," the kid said after a pause.

"We're not police," I assured him. "I'm a private investigator, and I'm looking into a matter that you might be able to help with."

I thought his eyes would leap out of his head. "You're a private eye?" he said.

After a thought, I shrugged. "Sort of."

"And who's he?" He pointed at Josh.

"I'm her enforcer," he answered. I gave him a look, and he said, "Okay. I'm her boyfriend. But frankly, we thought you'd be scarier than this."

Lay-Z drew himself to his full height (threatening to bump his head on the ceiling of the custard stand) and snarled. "You don't think I can take you, dude? I have a piece on me, and I'm not afraid to use it."

"Calm down, mad dog," I said, breaking the staring contest between Josh and our skeletal acquaintance. "Nobody wants to do you any harm, and we prefer that none be done to us. I just want to ask you about Martin Ferry."

Working on the boardwalk had given our host a very nice tan, but it lightened when he heard Ferry's name. "I didn't off him, man," he said to me, exhibiting a really poor assessment of my anatomy. "Anybody who says so is lying. Did that lady cop put you up to this?"

"What lady cop?" I asked. I described McElone to him and added, "*That* lady cop? She was here asking?"

"Yeah, but not here," the kid said. He was almost incensed at the mention. "She came to my *house* three days ago, on Monday. My mom heard everything, you understand? I don't care what she told you, I didn't kill Ferry, okay?"

"We don't think you did," I said. I questioned him a little more about McElone, but he seemed stuck on the idea that she'd questioned him within earshot of his mother. Josh, less concerned about a violent outbreak than he probably had been when we approached, dropped back a bit to let me do the talking. "But I think you might be able to help me."

Lay-Z, whose real name I had decided was probably Leroy or Larry, suddenly found the custard machine (which looked like it had last been serviced when people wore "bathing costumes" to the beach) fascinating. He picked up a wet rag from a sink behind him and started to wipe it down. "I can't help," he mumbled. "I don't know anything."

"Nobody's trying to get you in trouble, or at least we're not," I goaded him. "But I know that you took some things out of Detective Ferry's apartment after he died."

His back went stiff. He turned to me so fast he could have been auditioning for the Bolshoi Ballet. "You're lying," he said. That seemed to be his go-to explanation for things he wasn't crazy about discussing.

"I'm not. I know you took his laptop and a DVD of *Weekend at Bernie's*." I hadn't told Josh that part; it was obviously difficult for him to stifle a laugh, so he pretended he had to cough.

The Geoffrey Giraffe lookalike behind the counter, however, was not amused. "How can you know that? Nobody knows that."

"I have sources," I said. I considered for a nanosecond telling him that Ferry had seen the burglary and told me about it but immediately dismissed the plan. Having Lay-Z think I was Cray-Z wouldn't have been all that helpful.

"I'll give back the DVD," he said. "I have it at home." He'd probably have to sneak it by his mom on the way out.

"I don't want the DVD," I said. "But I would like to know who told you to go there and steal his laptop. Who'd you give it to?"

His face closed, a cold expression I hadn't seen before. I sensed Josh getting a little closer behind me. "Nobody," he said. The kid couldn't ad-lib to save his life, but if he kept on this path, at some point he'd be doing just that.

"Was it Buster Hockney?" I asked.

Suddenly Lay-Z looked like an old Little Orphan Annie cartoon: His eyes were wide, favoring the whites, and his mouth was a perfect O. If he'd put on a curly red wig, the effect would have been perfect.

"I don't know no Buster Hockney." His words couldn't have been more unconvincing if his nose actually grew while he was speaking. "Go away."

"I'm trying to help you," I said, although helping Lay-Z was actually about sixty-third on my list of priorities. "I know you were working for Buster. The real question is what he wanted with Martin Ferry's laptop computer."

"I don't know," the poor kid whined. "He didn't tell me that. He just said to go and get it." Suddenly his eyes widened as he realized what he'd said. "But I didn't."

"Yes, you did." Josh stepped forward, his voice sounding soothing and compassionate. Probably the opposite of the image I was projecting. "But nobody is interested in prosecuting you for that. What we need to know is how to find Buster and get Detective Ferry's laptop back."

I had no intention of looking for Buster Hockney, nor did Josh. He was trying to see what information we could get from Lay-Z that might be passed on to the cops in

Seaside Heights or Harbor Haven that could be useful in finding McElone.

"I don't know where Buster is," the kid said. "Honest. I don't find him. He finds me."

"Every time we asked you a question, you started by saying you didn't know," I reminded him, hoping to put a gentle tone in my voice. "And every time, it turned out you did."

"No, straight up," Lay-Z said. "Buster sends somebody to find me whenever he wants me."

Josh looked at him and folded his arms. "Who?" he asked.

"This guy Vinnie. And that's all I know, okay? Go away." Lay-Z was already looking around, as if he expected assassins to be stalking the place as we spoke.

"What's Vinnie's last name?" I said. "And don't start with 'I don't know,' just tell me and we'll leave you alone."

"Monroe. Vinnie Monroe. They call him Goldfish." *Aha!*

I nodded, then gave him five dollars. "For the frozen custard," I said.

"You didn't order any."

"I know." We turned to walk back to Josh's van, then I stopped and looked at Lay-Z. "What's your real name?" I asked.

"Lamont," he said.

I'd been so close!

Twenty-one

⚷

Paul Harrison stood in my kitchen sink and shook his head. "We have a great many things to deal with," he said.

Melissa, under Mom's supervision, had created macaroni and cheese burgers (which are exactly what they sound like—burgers with mac and cheese on them), something I'd never had before but which were now going to be my main source of cholesterol, I'd decided, and we'd gathered in the kitchen to try to make sense of everything that had happened in the past day.

Maxie, Paul and Dad had reported, had not left the house after the afternoon spook show and was in an unusually sullen mood (even for her), but everyone was too wary to ask her why. She was in the attic, allegedly looking into the lineage of Vinnie "the Goldfish" Monroe, whom everyone in the room had assumed was related to our somewhat damp pal Harry the Fish.

Mom and Liss—especially Liss—were basking in the glow of appreciation for the food, some of which had been broken up into very small pieces and given to Oliver, who also appeared to enjoy it heartily. With each bite I gave him, he would pound his fist on the high chair and make a happy noise. I was torn between wanting to tell Jeannie about this, because I wanted to show off how well Melissa could cook, and wanting to keep it a secret forever, so Jeannie wouldn't blame me when Ollie stopped wanting to eat mashed kale.

Malcolm Kidder had called while we were driving back from Madison Paint, where I'd gotten to see Sy and hear him tell us how only one customer, a woman looking for a pink that "wasn't too pink," had crossed the threshold while Josh was absent. Dad, chuckling over his old friend's story, hitched a ride back to the guesthouse with us.

There had been no progress by the Harbor Haven police, Malcolm reported, and "Anita" still hadn't called. Malcolm said he'd driven around, but the lieutenant wasn't in her usual stomping grounds, which didn't surprise him but had given Malcolm something to do.

I'd held off on telling him about Vinnie the Goldfish because I wasn't sure yet whether Lay-Z had been lying to get us to go away, or even if this Vinnie person actually existed. No sense getting Malcolm's hopes up if we'd simply been misled by a teenager with a wildly long neck.

"Perhaps we should talk to Lamont's mother," Paul suggested.

I gave him a look.

"Perhaps not. Let's see what Maxie finds out."

On cue, Maxie dropped down through the ceiling in her hide-a-larger-object trench coat, which no doubt meant she had the laptop with her. As she opened the coat, which vanished as soon as she was clear of the ceiling, I could see she was wearing her usual painted-on jeans and black T-shirt, this time bearing the words "Kiss My Grits." I had no idea what that meant, and was glad.

"I've been looking up Vinnie the Minnow," she said.

"Goldfish," the rest of us gave her back in unison.

Maxie nodded. "That explains things." She started tapping away at the keyboard, which she rested on the counter near the stove. Luckily, the stove was not in operation. Ghosts tend to overlook things like that.

Dad, picking up on a theme that I thought had been put to rest, was still looking grim. He pointed at me. "If you think you're going to start mixing it up with gangsters, young lady, you're not setting a foot outside that door without me, you understand?"

A sigh escaped my lips that was at least forty percent unintentional. "I already promised you, Dad, and I promised Mom, and I promised Liss, that there is no way I'm talking to any gangsters besides Harry the Fish, who really can't do me all that much harm from the second buoy to the left off the pier in Point Pleasant. So don't worry, all right?"

"So what are you going to do when you find this Vinnie the Guppy?" Maxie asked.

"Goldfish!"

She grinned. "I just wanted to see if you were listening that time."

I decided to forget that last part had happened. "I'm going to let the police know if I can make a connection between Vinnie and Detective Ferry," I said. "What I'm thinking right now is that I'll confront Harry the Fish with any evidence you can dig up and see how he reacts." I glanced at Paul, who beamed approvingly. It was like I had three parents in the room, and only one of them was still alive.

"I don't see how this gets us closer to finding Lieutenant McElone," Melissa said, wiping Oliver's mouth with a paper napkin, which he did not appreciate. "Aren't we supposed to be more worried about her than about what happened to Detective Ferry? I mean, it's bad that he's dead and all, but we can't make that unhappen."

As usual, Liss had managed to articulate what most of us in the room (I can never completely make any assumptions about Maxie) were already thinking: We needed to find McElone soon, or her situation might become just as unfixable as Martin Ferry's.

"Finding out more about what happened to the detective will only help us find Lieutenant McElone," Paul explained to Liss. "If we know who's behind it, we'll know their motivation for killing the detective, and that will help us figure out where the lieutenant might have gone for her investigation."

It was double-talk, but it was good double-talk. What Paul really could have said was, *We have no way to find McElone, so we're concentrating on the things we can do and hoping something will happen.* But that would have upset Liss. In fact, it would have upset me. Not thinking about what happened to the lieutenant was my new hobby. And now—*dammit!*—I was thinking of her as a friend.

"So what do you think we need to do?" I started to say. But I was about halfway through *think* when Maxie started bellowing from the stove area.

"Here we go!" she said. "Vincent Louis Francis Manfred Monroe is the grandson of Harry 'the Fish' Monroe."

"His grandson!" Mom exclaimed.

"Oh no," Josh said, grinning. "Bringing his grandson into the family business? The man is a monster."

Mom flattened out her lips. "It's not the same kind of business as you and Sy, Joshua," she reminded him, as if that were necessary. Josh nodded at her in apology for the imagined insult.

"Don't sass your mother-in-law," Dad chimed in, but luckily Josh couldn't hear him. I chose not to react, so I wouldn't have to repeat it to my boyfriend.

"*Anyway,*" Maxie went on, "Vinnie's only twenty-four, but he's been very busy the past few years. I found his juvie records—they're supposed to be sealed, but, you know,

I'm me. Got himself arrested the first time when he was sixteen for stealing someone's Hyundai in Asbury Park. Charges were dismissed after the aggrieved party appears to have dropped the complaint, saying she had just forgotten that she'd actually parked the car where it was found."

"Where was that?" Melissa asked.

"Spring Lake, only five miles away. Then when he was eighteen, Vincent found himself in some trouble with the law again, charges of possession of a controlled substance with the intent to distribute." She stole a glance at Melissa to see if she'd gone too far.

"What was he dealing?" my eleven-year-old asked as she helped Jeannie's eleven-month-old down from his high chair. "Weed? Coke?" I gave some thought to restricting her television hours, but that was a discussion for another day.

Maxie looked a little stunned. "Weed, mostly."

Liss nodded. "Figures." Oliver crawled over to me, and I advised him not to tell his mother that my eleven-year-old daughter thought she was a narc. But he was clearly not pleased about having nothing to stand and cruise on. The longer he stayed with us, it seemed, the more he wanted to be on his feet.

"In the past year," Maxie went on, "Vinnie has been doing much better. He hasn't been arrested once in close to sixteen months."

"What a guy," I said. "See? Rehabilitation works."

She shook her head. "Not so much. The unencrypted sections of Detective Ferry's files that Paul and I looked at have tons of references to 'Goldfish.' Personally, I thought the detective was partial to cheddar cheese crackers."

"For the record, I never thought that," Paul threw in.

"When you say they have references, what do you mean?" Mom asked.

Josh didn't say anything, and most men would. I always like to watch Josh during exchanges like this. He can't hear at least half the conversation, but a casual observer would have no idea anything special was going on around him. Now, he was sitting on one of the bar stools I use as kitchen chairs around my center island, smiling, watching me whenever no one he could hear was talking. He is a calm man, one who is content to be told what's going on when it's appropriate and not demanding to be the center of attention all the time.

Paul did not wait for Maxie to respond to Mom. "The lieutenant didn't have all of Martin Ferry's case files, but she did have some reports he'd filed in his investigation of Harry the Fish and Barnett 'Buster' Hockney, who appear to have been competitors," he said. "Vinnie's nickname comes up in connection with Hockney, but there are no direct links. I can't tell if Vinnie and Buster were working together against Harry, or if Harry was using Vinnie to spy on the competition. The detective did not name sources in his notes, perhaps to avoid them being found by the wrong person. That's why the data kept in the encrypted file is so vital to the investigation. I'm almost certain that's where his best information would be."

"But Lieutenant McElone encrypted the file," Melissa pointed out, holding Oliver by his right hand so he could cruise around the room searching for . . . something. They were making the rounds of the kitchen. "That would mean she's seen the stuff in there."

Paul stroked his goatee—always a sign that there was something new to think about—and considered. "You're right, Melissa. The lieutenant has information we don't, and it led her in a direction that doesn't seem to have gone well."

"Malcolm Kidder said he's been in touch with the Harbor Haven police and the Seaside Heights police," I said, mostly for Josh's benefit, who'd been so patient I felt he deserved to be rewarded. "So there's no point in duplicating that effort."

Josh, his eyes showing gratitude for being included,

asked, "Has Phyllis Coates gotten back to you? She was supposed to check on Harry the Fish's autopsy."

I put my arm around him. "That's actually a very good question." I pulled my phone out of my pocket with my free hand and speed-dialed Phyllis, who answered on the second ring.

"I hear from a couple of places that Harry the Fish drowned in his car," she said. Phyllis doesn't bother much with pleasantries, although she's always pleasant. Well, most of the time. There's also no point in asking who her sources are. She'd go to jail before revealing them—and actually did so once, for three days. "Now, how could you have known that?"

"I didn't call to talk about what I know," I said. "I called to talk about what *you* know. How does a guy drown and then show up in completely dry clothes in the front seat of his car?"

"It's unlikely he did it on his own," she answered. "I'm guessing a buddy or two helped him out. Maybe the Fish was the designated drowner that night." Phyllis sometimes thinks she's funnier than she really is. One indulges her.

"Why bother? Why not leave him in the ocean?"

Phyllis chuckled. No doubt she'd been steering the conversation into this area so she could drop a bomb. "Ah, but that's the thing, sweetie. Harry wasn't in the ocean when he died. His lungs were full of both fresh *and* salt water. Traces of seaweed, too."

Paul must have read my face. "What?" he demanded.

"He had both fresh water and salt water in his lungs?" I repeat things and make myself sound like an idiot just for the sake of some see-through people who populate my house. And yet have I ever been nominated for a Nobel Peace Prize? I have not.

Paul looked intrigued. Mom and Dad turned to face me. Melissa helped Oliver move around some more, but he wouldn't let go of her hand. Josh tightened his arm around my waist.

"That must mean there was salt water and then fresh, or the other way around," Paul suggested. "Otherwise, it would just be fresh water with some salt in it. I wish we could see the report."

Maxie lay back, the laptop on her outstretched legs. "If we're done here, I've got somewhere to go," she said, and then, without waiting for a reply, shot through the wall toward the beach.

"I'm on it," Dad said, and followed Maxie out at a discreet distance.

"This habit of hers is becoming inconvenient," Paul observed.

"Yep," Phyllis answered, unaware of the other conversation happening in the room with me. "My source in the ME's office in Ocean County isn't as good as the one in Monmouth, but that's what I'm hearing. There's also some evidence that Harry didn't drive the car to where it was found. Like there were no fingerprints on the steering wheel, and it was ninety-six degrees that day; he sure as hell wasn't wearing gloves."

The last time I'd seen Harry the Fish, he was thirty feet out in the ocean and couldn't move back far enough to reach land. And since ghosts usually start where they died, Harry *must* have been killed in the ocean. Probably. How could the water inside his lungs be from somewhere else?

"This is confusing," I said aloud, to no one in particular.

"It sure is," Phyllis agreed. "The cops are baffled. They say there's no evidence Harry had seriously annoyed anybody in his business recently. They think maybe this was personal."

"Personal? As opposed to what? Impersonal?"

"Personal," Phyllis repeated. "Like not business. They think maybe it was something like his wife, Teresa, was mad at him. In that family, you probably know a few people who would not have ethical concerns if you approached them the right way about filling a guy's lungs with fresh water. Tap water, probably."

Great. So we had the enlightening information that Harry the Fish wasn't drowned in Evian water. "Why would Teresa be mad at him?"

"Why is anyone's wife mad at them? I'm guessing Harry was fishing in uncharted waters."

Paul moved a little closer (as if he could be heard over the phone, or by Phyllis at all) and said, "Ask her about Vinnie."

"What about his grandson, Vinnie the Goldfish?" I asked. Sometimes it's fun to trip Phyllis up.

"Vinnie's a possibility," Phyllis answered. She's not so easy to trip. "Some of the cops say there was friction between the two of them, and Vinnie might have been looking for someone else to fund some of his . . . activities."

I only had one name left to use. "Buster Hockney?" I asked.

"Maybe. Buster wouldn't mind tweaking Harry the Fish a little. They were competing in some territories."

Phyllis has a good deal of experience reporting crime stories. "How do you approach a guy like Buster?" I asked, not commenting on how big a "tweak" drowning was.

"From very far away." And then she hung up; that's Phyllis. The last piece of advice wasn't a lot of help. I would have been glad Dad wasn't there to hear her say it, but my mother is a big snitch and would tell him at her earliest convenience anyway.

"There are two places to go next, assuming you are staying away from Buster," Paul said without being asked. Melissa looked up from tickling Oliver, who was lying on the kitchen floor specifically for that purpose. When she stopped, he looked annoyed. Who was interrupting his tickling? But Liss looked worried.

"I'm not going anywhere near Buster Hockney," I assured everyone. "What are the options?" I asked Paul.

"You can go see Vinnie the Goldfish, if you can find him."

"Option two, please." I wanted to see Vinnie about four percent more than I wanted to see Buster.

"Something Phyllis said struck a chord," Paul said, goatee a-stroking. "Something about thinking that Harry the Fish's wife might have had a personal motive, that it wasn't business."

"You want me to find Harry's wife?" We were increasing my willingness, but not that much.

"No. I think perhaps we should consider that approach when it comes to the murder of Detective Ferry. But start with his daughter."

Twenty-two

I'm not huge on interviewing grieving people. I feel like an intruder, an annoyance, someone who would be better off, say, hosting a spook show at her haunted guesthouse. But that's just me.

I had indeed been present for the Saturday morning ghost-a-thon. Rita and Stephanie had not attended (I think Rita was still rethinking the whole hanging-with-ghosts thing), but Joe had come and Bonnie, of all people, had risen early to watch as Paul had attempted the pull-out-the-tablecloth trick on my den's side table (he fails miserably whenever he tries, which is why I never put anything the least bit breakable on a table I bought at a yard sale for $10) and Maxie—who had shown up in the morning and I'll have more on that in a minute—had "walked" a pair of shoes up Joe's shirt with her hands. Her big special trick was still not in evidence, and I was starting to believe it did not really exist at all.

Don and Tammy attended their first ghost show that

morning, as they'd been far too busy touring the area and acting like newlyweds the whole time they'd been in the house to do so until now. They oohed and aahed at the proper moments, giggled with delight at the shoes going up Joe and then hit the road once again for Ocean Grove, where they'd heard there was good antiquing.

I'd gotten another non-update from Malcolm Kidder, who informed me that his children were starting to ask questions, and he didn't know how much longer he could hold them off. Personally, I think it's usually the best thing to tell kids the truth, but the last thing that man needed right now was to hear my parenting philosophy. He said there had been no further reports from either police department, and he was going to visit with an old friend of McElone's, who might have an idea of where she'd go if things got really hairy. He'd call back later, he said.

My father had returned from his Maxie-veillance the night before with little to report. "She rushed out to the beach, went up and down about a mile in either direction and then headed toward town. I followed to about Route 35, but she was too fast for me, and I lost her." He apologized a few hundred times. Paul, Mom, Liss and I got tired of forgiving him after a while and he stopped.

So my tasks for today were to talk to Martin Ferry's daughter, Natasha, and find out more about her mother, because ex-wives make really good suspects in murder cases, something I was certain to keep in mind in the event that my ex, The Swine, ever found himself more dead than he would prefer. I'd already established a really good alibi for myself by living three thousand miles from Steven and having as little to do with him as possible.

Natasha lived with her boyfriend, Rolfe, in an apartment in Highland Park over Ruthie's, a bagel shop and café. Although Natasha was to start college in Boston the next month, Rolfe was about to be a junior at Rutgers, which was just over the Raritan River in New Brunswick.

It was about to become a long-distance relationship, she said, and that would be difficult.

For an eighteen-year-old recent high school graduate, Natasha Ferry seemed very much like a twenty-four-year-old recent grad student about to begin her career in either astrophysics or public relations. She was a very self-possessed young woman, someone her father was no doubt quite proud of when he was alive, and even after.

Then I remembered she was barely seven years older than Melissa, living with her boyfriend and sporting a shoulder tattoo of a rose, and I decided on the spot to homeschool Liss for the rest of her life, possibly adding a moat to my front yard and assigning a ghost guardian to her for the rest of her life. Not Maxie.

I'd told Natasha that I was a friend of Lieutenant Mc-Elone's (which was true, if you believed Malcolm) and that I'd known her father (which was true, if having met him twice before he'd died and three times after counted as having "known" him) and that I was trying to piece together the circumstances of his death. That part was true no matter what.

"My dad and mom got divorced five years ago," Natasha was telling me. She'd offered me a cup of tea, but I figured I could go downstairs to Ruthie's if I got peckish and opted to pass. "I guess I knew things weren't good, but I was only thirteen, and I didn't want to understand. You know how it is." Unfortunately, I did. Melissa had cried a lot when Steven and I told her about the divorce, and it took about six months of talking with me and a therapist to convince her she had no blame in our marriage ending. I was still working on convincing her I didn't have any blame either, but that was more difficult, because even I didn't completely believe it.

"How harsh was it?" I asked, sounding like I was setting up a joke on an especially bad late-night TV show. Trying to smooth over my clumsy language, I quickly added, "I mean, did they ever learn to get along?" Better, but not much.

Natasha brushed at her eye for a moment but still looked very composed. "Not really," she said. "I lived with my mother most of the time through high school. That was part of their settlement; I don't think Dad liked it, but he knew that being a cop made it harder for him to be a single parent. Then in the last year or so, Mom started to complain about the child support checks. They were supposed to continue until I was out of college," she said. "That was part of the agreement, too. But Dad said his finances were tight, or at least that's what Mom told me he said. When I asked him, he told me he was sending the checks like he always had and didn't know what she was talking about."

Since I knew there was at least one pretty hefty deposit in Martin Ferry's bank account, his claims of poverty were a little suspect. I would ask him about that when I saw him again. Or if I had any luck at all, I'd get McElone to ask him. I'd decided now that she'd put me through so much by disappearing, I was no longer feeling so charitable as to spare her the suspicions about her ex-partner.

"Was your mother really angry?" I asked.

Natasha absorbed that for a beat, and then her eyes narrowed to slits—the way her father's had when I'd suggested something he found absurd. "Are you asking me whether I think my mother *killed* my father?"

That's exactly what I was doing. "No, of course not," I said. "I'm wondering about his level of stress, whether he felt pressure from her about the money." Nice recovery, huh?

Natasha didn't think so. "I see, so you're asking me whether I think she drove him to suicide." This interview wasn't going as well as I'd hoped, and I'd come in with pretty low expectations.

"No." This time, I really hadn't been suggesting that. "It's just not coming out right. I do think someone murdered your father, but given his line of work, the law of averages says it's probably more related to his job than his personal life. So I'm sorry if it sounded like I was making accusations; I wasn't."

Her face had changed into that of a little girl, and a sad one. "My father was murdered? The police said it was a gun accident."

"Did you believe that?"

She looked away from me. "I wanted to. But I didn't. He never was careless with his weapon, not ever. There's no way he'd ever leave it loaded or not secure it before he put it away. I knew. I just didn't want to know."

"So let's try to figure out who killed him," I suggested. "Did he tell you much about his work?"

Natasha stood up and started tidying up the room. Her avoidance tactics could mean that she was thinking, or that she was hiding something. I chose to believe the former. "He didn't really talk about his job that way to me, you know? He took me to Take Your Daughter to Work Day and things like that, but he wouldn't tell me the scary parts; he didn't . . . he didn't want me to be worried about him."

"So you don't know what he was working on when he died?"

She shook her head. "Not specifically. Every once in a while he'd get a phone call when I was spending the weekend at his apartment, but he never told me who it was, just business, he said."

"How did he act after those calls?" I asked. It was a Paul-type question, although we hadn't discussed this possibility precisely, because we didn't know the scenario would come up. It was the kind of thing he'd want me to ask.

"Like himself. He sounded, I don't know, almost mad when he was on the phone with whoever it was, but once he got off, he went back to being Dad. I really didn't think that much about it." There hadn't been that much untidy about the room to begin with, so Natasha had to stop straightening now. "You sure you don't want a tea? I could put it over ice." The apartment was not air-conditioned.

"Why don't we go downstairs and get something?" I countered. I felt like I should be buying Natasha a cold drink.

We went down to Ruthie's and ordered an iced tea for Natasha and an iced coffee for me. I got an everything bagel, too, because this was a new bagel place to me, and it's my sworn duty as a connoisseur to pass judgment on every unfamiliar establishment I encounter. (The bagel was very good, for the record.) We sat down at a table, and I asked her, because I was now officially out of ideas, if she knew much about Lieutenant McElone.

"Anita?" Everybody seemed to be on a first-name basis with the lieutenant but me, unless you asked her husband. "She was my dad's partner for a few years. Now she works in Harbor Haven, I think. She came by after Dad died, just to visit, you know. I think she asked some questions, but I wasn't really hearing anything just then." She stared down into her glass of iced tea.

"Did she say anything about investigating what happened to your dad?"

Natasha shrugged. "Maybe. If she did, it wasn't registering. I was in denial."

Elise Cranston Ferry lived in a single family house in Rumson. It was one of the smaller homes on the street, but considering that people like Billy Joel and Bruce Springsteen (the patron saint of New Jersey) have owned places in Rumson, being one of the less ornate places in the neighborhood was hardly a serious problem.

By Bruce's or Billy's standards, Elise's house was a shack. By mine, it was a very comfortable size for most normal people and maintained within an inch of its life. The paint job was fresh, the shutters sparkled, the windows were gorgeously clean, the roof probably wouldn't need replacement until Melissa was leaving medical school (a mother can dream) and the landscaping was downright impeccable.

I started to dislike and mistrust Elise immediately.

Still, after Natasha had called her to vouch for me, Elise had agreed to talk to me and ushered (*welcomed* would have been overstating it) me into her home once I identified myself at the front door. I'd walked up to the most adorable porch in history and been careful not to get the freshly painted floor planks dirty. We peasants have such unkempt feet.

"You have a lovely home," I began, which was code for *How the hell can you afford this, and why would you need child support from your ex-husband the cop?* Code is helpful, but it's not always completely pertinent to your intentions.

"Thank you," Elise said, indicating I should sit on the very tasteful sofa in her living room. I chose a side chair instead, as sofas are a little too "company" for someone asking questions about someone's murder. Or at least this one was.

She didn't say anything else and seemed to be awaiting my first question. She sat down on the sofa herself, as if to show off how much better it was than the chair. It did look very comfortable, but the chair wasn't bad, either. "Did you move here immediately after your divorce?" I asked, keeping up with the "lovely home" theme.

"Oh no!" Elise seemed to think that suggestion was hilarious. "I couldn't possibly have afforded a house in Rumson on Martin's salary, and he was one of those old-fashioned types who think it's a bad reflection on a man if his wife is working. No, I moved to an apartment in Belmar, third-floor walk-up, after we split up. It took me two and a half years to get here."

"How did you manage it?" That seemed like a fair question, and Elise, who wasn't the least bit condescending (to my disappointment), took no offense as far as I could tell.

"I started my own business with some of the money

from the divorce settlement," she answered. "We sold the house we were living in, and I took my half of the money to start up a soup delivery service."

"A soup delivery service?"

Elise smiled. "That was the reaction I got from banks when I tried to get a loan. Yes. I thought it was the kind of thing that could work. It's a cold winter night, you get home from work, you don't feel like cooking, but boy, wouldn't a nice hot bowl of soup be perfect? So you get on the phone or online, order it up, and it shows up piping hot at your door in the time it takes to change your clothes and set the table. Not bad, huh?"

In this air-conditioned room, it sounded great. Outside in the summer heat, I was betting the lure of steaming soup wouldn't be quite as strong. But mostly, I was shocked that there was a food delivery service—apparently a successful one—I'd never heard about. I was clearly slipping. It was a negative result of all this home cooking Melissa had been doing lately.

"Not bad," I echoed. "You've obviously done well."

She waved a hand; I had not yet truly grasped the enormity of her accomplishment. "I started working out of my own kitchen in Belmar, driving everywhere myself for six months, until I could hire a kid who had a car. Now I have five running kitchens in the area, and I employ thirty people." Clearly, there was more in her soup than lentils—she'd struck gold.

"That's great," I said. How to segue, how to segue . . . "So after your divorce, you made quite a bundle. Did that mean Detective Ferry wasn't paying alimony anymore?" As smooth a shift as in a '49 Studebaker in need of a ring job.

Elise's face darkened at the mention of her ex-husband. I have an ex-husband, and no doubt I don't look pleased when his name comes up, but this was actually a little bit scary. She went from the proud business owner to the Grim Reaper in under a second.

"*Detective Ferry* paid alimony until the day he died," she answered. "No matter how much money I made, I was owed restitution for the years I wasted on him. And then he stopped sending child support for Natasha, and I was about to serve him with papers when he got his brains blown out." I felt it best not to mention that Ferry had been shot in the midsection.

"I know what you mean," I lied. "My ex is often late with the child support. After what he did to me, that takes some nerve." To be completely honest, what The Swine did to me was sleep with another woman, which in the scheme of things was atrocious but not actually done to *me*. One rationalizes.

"Nerve!" Elise seemed to think I was excusing Martin of something, but I didn't know what. "Martin Ferry was a husband like King Kong was a headwaiter." That didn't make any sense, but there was no time. "He never spent any time with me. He was always out on a case, getting snitches to talk to him, spending time in the most hideous places. The man was a boarder in his own house. I'm not sure his daughter could've picked him out of a standing lineup."

That wasn't what Natasha had told me, for the record. She remembered Martin always taking time to play with her when she was little, and while he was "obsessed" with being a cop, he listened to her when she had a problem. It was clearly another Martin Ferry that Elise was describing.

Saying that to Elise would not help me, so I didn't. "Do you have any idea who might have been angry enough with your ex-husband to shoot him?" That was, after all, what I was really here to find out.

Elise sort of rolled her eyes and gave me her best long-suffering look. "I was angry enough," she said, "three years ago. Not now. I wasn't angry enough to shoot him now, if that's what you're asking."

"That's not what I'm asking," I said. That *was* what I

was asking. "Right now my first priority is actually trying to locate Lieutenant McElone, who was last known to be digging around in Detective Ferry's death—"

"What do you mean, locate Anita?" Elise said, suddenly concerned. "Anita's missing?"

It was interesting to me how everyone who'd known both McElone and Ferry seemed to have much stronger, and warmer, feelings for McElone. Except Lay-Z. I didn't know Martin Ferry terribly well, so I had an excuse, but even then, I'm fairly certain that McElone wasn't even on my holiday-card list.

I'd have to make a mental note to rectify that situation. If I ever saw her again.

"Her husband hasn't heard from her for a few days," I said. Maybe getting Elise upset would speed up the process of getting some information here. "And I was working with her on something, so it's odd that she hasn't been in touch. Do you have any idea where she might go if things were tough?"

There was no hesitation. "Have you checked her bungalow in Point Pleasant?" Elise said. "Martin told me that when a case was really bothering her, and she really couldn't crack it, Anita would go to a bungalow she had in Point Pleasant. It was like her place to think, I guess. So maybe she went there."

Suddenly I knew where my next stop was going to be.

Twenty-three

Except, I didn't go right to Point Pleasant. There just wasn't time before the afternoon spook show, and I did, after all, have to start watching the baby I was sitting, paying some attention to my own daughter, and running the guesthouse I'd spent pretty much every cent I had buying and renovating.

Also, I wanted someone to come with me when I went to McElone's bungalow. In case I found . . . anything.

Paul listened to the voice recordings I'd made at all my interviews for the day while I checked on the rest of my family and our youngest guest. Mom informed me that Dad had gone on another Maxie quest, although everybody's favorite poltergeist, once again using the "visiting my mom" dodge, had promised to be back in time for the afternoon performance.

Oliver was, as Mom had told me when I came home, obviously tired of this whole crawling business and was channeling his energy into the idea of standing and moving at the same time. He hadn't actually conceived of walking yet but clearly understood it had something to do with feet. He was staring at his own, no doubt wondering why they hadn't gotten the idea yet.

Wendy had come over to visit Melissa, and they were treating Oliver like any eleven-year-old girls would, as a remarkably interesting toy. Since he didn't really have to do anything to maintain this status, Ollie was being good-natured about it, which is another way of saying he hadn't noticed.

"He's trying to get the doll," Wendy said, pointing at Oliver's toy Big Bird. Mr. Bird inhabited the low table in the den and Ollie was propped up against the sofa, and his head positioning and eye movements showed he was trying to figure out how to navigate the distance, which was at least three feet. This was a conundrum for Oliver.

"It's not a doll," Liss corrected her. "He's a boy. It's an action figure." They had a good laugh over that.

Paul drifted in from the movie room with the voice recorder in his pocket. "The only lead we seem to have on Lieutenant McElone is this bungalow in Point Pleasant," he said. Paul needs a little help with his segue skills.

"Do you think she's there?" Mom asked him.

Wendy looked up, startled by the question, and saw Mom looking at what she would consider to be a spot just over the piano. She looked at Liss, who said simply, "Paul," and nodded. They went back to hovering over Oliver, ready to catch him if he stumbled. So far, the job was easy because Ollie hadn't tried to move yet.

"If she has gone to her hideaway, it answers one question and raises any number of others," Paul answered, not acknowledging the exchange between the two girls. "It's one thing for her to ignore your texts and calls, Alison, if she's stewing over the case. But it's something else entirely for her to uncharacteristically cut off contact with her family. That's very troubling."

"So I have to go to Point Pleasant. I'll call Malcolm and

see if he wants to meet me there. I wish you could come with me, Paul."

Paul, who was trying to light the chandelier with his pinkie, answered, "So do I."

"I'll go," Mom offered. I was a little reluctant, since Mom has a tendency to embarrass me on investigations, mostly by letting everyone know she's my mother. You never caught Philip Marlowe dragging his mom along on a case. On the other hand, he might have, if he'd had my mom.

"Meanwhile, we have made some progress in the files Lieutenant McElone kept on the flash drive," Paul said. "Maxie's not back yet?" He looked around to confirm her absence, then added, "I'll be right back," and vanished into the ceiling.

Before any of us could comment, Stephanie and Rita entered through the beach doors, having cleaned off their feet with a hose I keep on the deck. Wet feet I don't mind on my wood floors; sandy ones made scratches. A little sand coming into the house is inevitable—this is a shore town, after all—but I appreciate the effort of the guests to keep the place from becoming a beach all its own.

They seemed agitated. "Rita saw the hat on the beach again," Stephanie announced. "And I saw it, too!"

Mom agreed to stay back with Oliver because there wasn't time to pack him up, while the girls and I hustled out the beach doors and followed Stephanie and Rita onto the beach behind my house.

They led us to a spot near the public beach (which, frankly, overlaps my property a little, confusing lifeguards and tourists alike) and started looking around, shading their eyes with their hands.

"Do you see anything?" I asked, because at that moment, I didn't.

"Hang on." Stephanie seemed a little peeved, perhaps at herself for losing sight of what they'd concluded was a ghost. "I'm looking."

She kept looking for some time, and so did Rita. For that matter, Melissa, Wendy and I scouted the location for a while as well, no one saying a word. Finally Rita sighed loudly.

"We've lost it," she said.

I wasn't sure we'd ever had it, but I refrained from saying so.

"I'm not sure what to make of it," I said. "But I'll ask around, okay?" Stephanie nodded, and Rita looked a little less freaked out.

"Alison?" Wendy said.

"What's the matter, sweetie?" I asked. Wendy's voice had an edge to it. She was looking back toward my house, which was about two hundred yards away.

"Why is there a ladder up next to Melissa's room?"

I looked up toward the house and squinted, since the sun was starting to tilt in that direction. I didn't understand—or believe—what I was seeing.

There was indeed a ladder running up the right side of my house, all the way to the third floor, to Melissa's attic bedroom. I couldn't tell if the window was open, but I knew for a fact that I had not put that ladder there.

"That's my room," Melissa breathed. She sounded absolutely appalled, as well she might.

Someone had tried—and for all I knew, succeeded—to break into my house. I had no way of knowing if the ladder had been there two minutes or four hours. And my mother and Oliver were in the house.

I started running immediately, hearing vague sounds behind me. The crash of the surf, the wind, tourists on the beach, Rita and Stephanie asking why I wasn't looking for the hat any more. But Melissa and Wendy were right by my side the whole way.

Until we reached the property line, I wasn't even aware that I was winded. But once we got there, I saw Paul trying desperately to move his foot past the line he hadn't been able to cross since "moving in," and I started taking in long gulps of breath. I hadn't run that far in a number of years and wasn't pleased with the shape I was in.

"Your laptop is gone," Paul reported, watching Wendy pat me on the back like I needed burping.

"My laptop?" Melissa sounded panicked. She probably wasn't as concerned about the homework she hadn't deleted since June as the fact that she probably couldn't remember her Facebook password.

Paul shook his head. "Your mom's. The one Maxie uses. There is a ladder—"

"We know," Melissa told him, sighing with relief. "Wendy saw it from the beach."

Paul, who hadn't known we were going to the beach but had still managed to find us running back, didn't ask questions. "I should have been more vigilant."

I stood up straight again, having reoxygenated my blood. "Don't worry," I said. "If we find McElone, she'll only blame me, anyway. She doesn't think you exist."

"There is nothing she can blame you for," Paul said. "I removed the files from the desktop every time we logged off. It's all still on the flash drive, and we have that."

"You're a genius." I started to lead Wendy and Liss toward the house, quickly, with Paul backing up without walking. "Are Mom and Ollie okay? My guests?"

"No one saw anything, and nobody's hurt," Paul said. "If we'd known someone was in the house, I would have done something about it."

At least everybody in the house was okay. That slowed my pace a bit. "So you think whoever took the laptop was looking for McElone's files on Martin Ferry's murder?"

"They weren't going after it because of the high technology," Melissa said. Wendy giggled a little. I considered, and rejected, the idea of giving my daughter a day-old mackerel for her next birthday.

"It's true," Paul agreed. He would continue to have birthdays, but wouldn't get any older, which was a double annoyance for both of us. I suppose I could get him gifts for his birthday, but what do you buy for the man who doesn't have a pulse? "The only real value that computer has is the data they think is kept on it."

We walked inside after washing off our feet. Mom, with Oliver sitting on her shoulders, was approaching as we entered. Rita and Stephanie weren't far behind us.

"You heard what happened?" Mom asked. I acknowledged that we had. "It's terrible!"

Well, yeah, but that seemed a fairly oversized reaction. "It's bad, there's no denying that," I said. "I'm not sure it's terrible."

"Okay." Mom sounded skeptical. Ollie, on the other hand, was thoroughly enjoying his unaccustomed height and laughing with delight at how short the rest of us were.

"Am I missing something?" I asked. "Is he hurting your neck?"

"No, he's fine, but I guess you haven't considered the implications." Despite her protestations, Mom handed Oliver off to Melissa, who let him sit on *her* shoulders to avoid a grumpy mood.

"Of course I have," I said. "Someone broke into the house and stole my laptop. There are likely to be gangsters involved, and I'm probably going to have to go talk to them even though I'd rather do pretty much anything else. McElone is still missing, which can't be good, and someone not only knows where we live but where I keep the laptop, and was brazen enough to climb into Melissa's bedroom window—you're locking that thing and letting the air-conditioning do its work, young lady—to steal it. How much worse can that get?"

"Well, you're going to have to tell Maxie that her laptop is missing," Mom said.

Dad burst through the ceiling. "I followed Maxie. She'll be here in a couple of seconds."

"Okay," I said. "That's worse."

There wasn't time for Dad to give us a Maxie report

because she filtered in through the kitchen wall to the den immediately after. It was hard to read Maxie's mood, which was unusual: Lately, especially, she'd been either floating on a cloud of her own construction or breathing fire without a recognizable catalyst. Now, she was just sort of bland, barely paying attention.

That didn't last long.

"My *laptop*?" she screamed. "You can't be serious. Someone stole my *laptop*?" I refrained, nobly I thought, from pointing out that the article in question was actually *my* laptop, and let her go on. "How am I going to get by?"

I hadn't realized she was so taken with her role as Internet research arm for our investigative team. But as usual, I had misinterpreted Maxie.

"I need that thing!" she went on. "How am I going to see my Twitter feed? Check my Facebook page? Watch videos of people falling off things?" She turned toward me, the flames back in her eyes. "How did you let this happen?"

That figured. "Me? How is this my fault?"

"It's your house, isn't it?" This was progress, as she usually maintains that it's still *her* house. Maxie's tempo, swirling around the crown molding on the ceiling, picked up. She does laps when she gets agitated.

"This isn't solving anything," Dad said. If I'd said it, Maxie would have beaned me with the pasta pot.

"That's true," Paul said, "but finding Lieutenant McElone is the priority. Alison, when can you get to her bungalow in Point Pleasant?"

"Maybe tonight, after dinner," I said. I had to check for any other missing items and call the cops about the break-in. "I'll drive down after Oliver is asleep. But I need someone to come with me, and Josh is busy with an inventory tonight. Volunteers?" I turned toward the girls. "Over the age of twelve?" They looked crestfallen; a trip to a spooky bungalow! What could've been better?

"I'll go," Dad said. "When's the last time I was on a

stakeout?" I love the man, but his use of terminology is always just a little left of center.

"You've never been on a stakeout," I told him. "And you're not going to be on one tonight, either. This is more in the area of a going-to-see-what's-happening. But thank you. I don't know what we'll find."

Maxie, who had slowed down to a pace that made her at least visible to everyone in the room but Wendy, narrowed her eyes and dropped a foot or so toward the rest of us. "You think she might be dead?" she blurted. That ghost has tact like Jamaica has an Olympic bobsled team: It happened once, and shouldn't be expected again.

"Mom . . ." Liss began, sounding worried.

"I don't think we're going to find anything bad," I told her. "The fact is, I don't think we're going to find anything at all. But the first thing I need to do is call Malcolm so I can get the address, or we won't even find the bungalow."

"If I had my laptop, I could get her address," Maxie groused.

"I'll get mine," Melissa said, and was headed for the stairs, Wendy in tow, when Stephanie and Rita walked in.

I smiled at them. "Well, the good news is that everyone is all right and the only thing missing is mine," I said. "There's nothing to worry about."

Rita looked ashen, which isn't easy to do when you spend your day on a beach in New Jersey in August. "Was it a ghost?" she asked.

"Don't be silly," Stephanie told her. "A ghost doesn't need a ladder."

"No, it was not a ghost," I told them. "The police are being brought in." (I'd called, and they said they'd send someone "soon." This wasn't a priority crime in Harbor Haven, apparently.) "And we're taking precautions to make sure it can't happen again."

"This is a very exciting place to spend a week!" Stephanie said. She really seemed to be enjoying the intrigue.

"Yes," Rita agreed. I wasn't sure that she thought *exciting* was such a good thing.

I reassured them, and they went to their room to rest a little. I reached into my pocket for the cell phone to call Malcolm about the bungalow. And that was when Melissa and Wendy came down from the attic, carrying Liss's laptop, which she handed to Maxie. Wendy's mouth dropped at the flying computer; you'd think she'd be used to such things by now, but apparently the novelty had not worn off.

"I'm on it," Maxie shouted. "I'll find out who took my computer!"

"The bungalow, Maxie." I waved to get her attention. "Find McElone's bungalow."

"Yeah. Right." She stuck her feet out so she was horizontal and rested the computer on her legs. She dove into the keyboard with more vehemence than she usually exhibited.

I looked at Dad, who shrugged. Apparently his most recent Maxie excursion hadn't turned up any more than the last one. I decided to call Malcolm even as Maxie worked, since she would no doubt put her interests before everyone else's and see if she could track down the electronic signature of my pre–Civil War laptop, assuming it actually had such a thing.

Malcolm answered after a few rings; he sounded winded. "Alison?" he asked. He had clearly checked the incoming ID on his phone.

"Yes, Malcolm. I wanted to give you a progress report." I told him about Ferry's ex-wife, Elise, and about the burglary in my house, which seemed to worry him.

"Now the people behind this have Anita's files," he said. "That's not good."

"They don't," I pointed out. "The files are safe enough." Telling him where the flash drive resided was not an option.

"That's good, anyway. I've been searching for Anita in places where I knew she was asking about that Buster Hockney you mentioned. I've gotten a lot of grumpy looks, but not much in the way of information." I asked him about the bungalow, and he told me the address just as Maxie, who apparently *had* been listening earlier, swooped down with the laptop and showed me the screen. The website, listing real estate transactions, showed a small house, just a little larger than a cabana, listed in Point Pleasant. The transaction was three years old, meaning it had taken place just before the lieutenant left Seaside Heights and came to Harbor Haven. And the buyer's name was McElone.

I read back the address, and Malcolm confirmed it was the bungalow he and the lieutenant owned for "quick breaks." "We bought it a few years ago. But why would she go there and not tell me?" he asked. "I think it's a wild-goose chase, Alison."

"It probably is," I agreed. "But I'll let you know what I find there." I turned toward my daughter, who was tickling Oliver's feet as an amusement to at least one of them. "So. What's for dinner?" I asked.

She looked at her grandmother. "Um . . ."

There is nothing my mother likes better than to be needed, particularly for food. She would have rolled up her sleeves, if she'd been wearing sleeves. "I'm on it," she said. "Where's my backpack?" And off she went in search of whatever she keeps in that grade-schooler's book bag she carries around.

Oliver, having decided that tickled feet were fine but there were places to go, had maneuvered himself toward a dining chair and was, with Melissa offering counterbalance, pulling himself up to a standing position. "I think he's going to walk really soon," Liss said.

"Whatever." Maxie, back in whatever mood she was in before she heard of the theft, drifted off through the ceiling.

"He'd better not until his mom gets back," I told her. "If Jeannie misses his first steps, it's highly likely she'll never speak to us again." Jeannie had been waiting for her son's first steps—which would be a little early, but not much at this age—with the kind of anticipation generally reserved for Oscar nominations, the births of royal offspring or the culmination of a tense hostage situation, depending on her mood.

Melissa turned her energy to trying to persuade Ollie *not* to walk just yet. This was accomplished through pulling him onto her lap, which led to him standing up against the chair again, which led to the lap, then the standing, then the lap. Since babies love nothing more than repetition, Oliver seemed to be having a great time. Melissa, too, would no doubt sleep well tonight.

Paul, for once not trying to use himself as a human(ish) electrical socket, was pacing back and forth two feet off the floor. "There's something we're missing, and I can't figure out what it is," he said.

I'd had the same feeling, but for a different reason. "I know what we're not doing, if that's what you mean."

Paul stopped, which is not something you see him do often. The ghosts are always sort of in motion, voluntary or not. But now he was still. "What aren't we doing?" he asked.

"The obvious thing. The thing that has the highest probability of getting us the answers we need."

The ghost nodded, but he didn't look happy. "I didn't think you wanted to do that," he said.

"I don't. Have you got a better idea?"

"A better idea than what?" Melissa asked.

"We're going to have to talk to Buster Hockney," I said.

But Paul put his thumb and forefinger to his temple and grimaced a little. "Another message from Detective Ferry?" I asked. He looked so uncomfortable.

He shook his head. "No. Everett Sandheim. He wants to talk to you."

Twenty-four

"Maxie wandered around town for a while, and then stopped at the Dunkin' Donuts and sat on the sign outside for a while," Dad said.

We were driving to the Fuel Pit after a lovely dinner of baked ziti with ground beef that Mom had cobbled together from the meager ingredients I kept in my kitchen. ("Ziti Bolognese," she called it.) I wasn't driving fast because after seeing Everett, we were going to McElone's bungalow, and I really didn't want to get where we were going. But this was nothing compared to the idea of going to see a major drug kingpin and asking him if he'd killed one cop and made another one disappear. That I *really* didn't want to do, but at least it could wait until tomorrow.

The guests were back at the house, all of them, being entertained with karaoke night in the den (starring my daughter, the ham) and enjoying the air-conditioning. This was an event made possible by the karaoke machine my ex-husband had once given me in an attempt to reconcile.

The fact that he'd charged it on my Visa card was an indicator of how well that whole "reconciliation" thing went, if you couldn't have figured that out already from the fact that he was back in Southern California, I was driving down the Jersey Shore to look into what I hoped would be an empty bungalow and my guests were using it to sing renditions of "Tie a Yellow Ribbon."

"That's all she did?" I asked. "Maxie just sat on the Dunkin' Donuts sign?"

Dad snickered. "She had a little fun with the guy putting out the chocolate frosteds. Kept making one disappear then reappear on his tray for a while."

"That ghost is a menace to the Shore," I said. "They should call the next hurricane Maxie."

"I gotta say, she seemed sad up on that sign," Dad told me. "Like she was waiting for something that didn't happen."

"Maybe she wanted Boston cream and they didn't have any."

"Don't be mean, baby girl," my father said. "Maxie's not always the easiest person on the planet, but she's loyal and she's helped you out when the chips were down."

"Are chips ever up?" I asked. "How do I know the positioning of the chips?"

"You're being a wiseass to avoid saying that I'm right," he said. Dad could always see through me; it seemed logical that now I could literally do the same to him.

"How long did she sit there?" I asked, to show concern for a friend. A friendly acquaintance. A ghost who hangs around my house most of the time.

"About an hour. Always looking around to see if something was there, or at least that's how it looked. I can't really say that I understood what was going on."

Everett, in fatigues, was already waiting when we reached the Fuel Pit, which had closed for the evening. In fact, he was a little farther away from the gas pumps (and the restroom) than I'd ever seen him before. I commented on that when I got out of the car—and Dad just sort of floated out—to talk.

"A little bit more each day," Everett confirmed. "I've gotten quite far lately." He stood tall and straight, not at all like he had when he was homeless and mentally ill. "As I said, I am no longer confined just to this property. This afternoon, I got as far as the Stud Muffin, where, as you'll recall, we first met."

"You don't mind being there?" Dad asked. "It's not a painful memory?" Dad doesn't always know when he's picking at a scab, but he always wants to help.

"It is barely a memory at all," Everett told him. "Much of my time . . . in that state . . . is a blur to me now. I remember myself in this form, which might be why I appear this way now." He turned to me. "I wanted to let you know I've seen Buster Hockney. At the bakery this morning, I noted a man about six feet three inches tall, with a narrow build and a shaved head. The man was complaining because they would not take his credit card to pay for one cup of coffee. The card bore the name Barnett Hockney. I can only assume his nickname is Buster." In fact, that was true: Paul had noted it when reading McElone's files on Buster.

You'd think this all would be good news. I had asked Everett for information on Buster, and here he was with a description. That should have been a positive. But one of my best defenses against having to meet Buster was that I had no idea how to find him and didn't even know what he looked like. Apparently, that was about to change.

"That's . . . great, Everett," I said. "You've been a very big help."

"Thank you, ma'am. But let me finish my description: The man has a goatee, which he dyes blond, clearly not his original hair color. Is that helpful?"

"Very," I said, resignedly. "You're an excellent reconnaissance officer, Everett."

"One last thing: He did not seem like a gentleman, Ghost Lady. Be careful of him."

"She will," Dad said.

"It's that one," Dad said, pointing. It's possible his arm went directly through my head, because I didn't see his hand. I prefer not to think about it. "The blue one on the left." He pointed at the house, which he was saying bore the number of Lieutenant McElone's bungalow. I already had a knot in my stomach.

There was a space three houses down, so I parked. "Okay," I told Dad. "If you could go inside and unlock the front door, I'd appreciate it." He nodded and turned toward the car door to slip out. "Dad." He stopped and looked at me. The words tumbled out. "If it's really bad in there, don't let me in, okay?"

He gave me his best reassuring look and would have hugged me if he could, I'm sure. "I won't, baby girl." He was out of the car before I could think about it.

In fact, Dad moved so quickly—something he really couldn't do his last few years alive—he was almost inside the house before I'd even motivated myself out of the car and started down the street. All I could see of him were his feet entering through the side of the building. Of course, it was almost dark by this point, and Dad wasn't exactly easy to see under the best of circumstances.

I'll admit that I didn't rush to the door; I wanted to give my father plenty of time to peruse the situation inside and decide, as he did when I was little, if it was appropriate fare for me to view. It's funny how in times of stress you fall back on the things that you really resented when you were a child.

So when I got to the front door, I waited. A click in the lock would mean there was nothing to fear and I could walk in. No click would, in theory, mean that something had gone horribly wrong and Dad would be floating out shortly to alert me, and then we'd call the police.

There was no click.

In that second, I contemplated my relationship with Lieutenant McElone. I had great respect for her, believed her to be a very good detective and felt that no matter what, she would have my back if I needed her to do so. Were we friends? Despite what Malcolm seemed to think, I couldn't say I felt that we were; she always seemed annoyed whenever she saw me approaching. And yes, some of that was a game we played with each other—I took the role of the irritating amateur trying to keep up, and she was the crusty veteran who had better things to do with her time than school some pretender playing over her head. But the game was an exaggeration of the way we operated, not a substitute.

So why was I so devastated not to hear a click in the lock?

Dad startled me almost into convulsions when he stuck his head through the door and said, "What are you waiting for? I unlocked the door two minutes ago."

Heaving a sigh of relief (and struggling successfully to keep it from becoming a tearful sob), I turned the knob on the door. Sure enough, it opened. "So there's nothing gruesome awaiting me in there?"

"Nothing *gruesome*," Dad answered. "But it's worth a look."

I walked inside with a little trepidation, but no longer a sense of dread. "Thanks for coming, Dad," I said as soon as the door closed behind me. "You have no idea how much help that was just now."

"No charge, baby girl."

"You did a quick search," I said. I turned on the light in the main room, which was most of the bungalow. They're meant to be little more than cabanas, small structures to use when spending some time at the beach. This one had a main room with a large easy chair that had obviously come from someone's college apartment and a small galley kitchen (just a mini fridge and a microwave, along with a sink). Off to the right side was the door to a small bathroom. There was a futon to the left, against the wall. The back wall was dominated by glass doors that led to a tiny deck, and no doubt access to the beach beyond that. It was too dark to tell right now. "Is there somewhere in particular I should be looking?"

"I'm not sure," my father told me. "But there is something I think might be important."

"Where?"

"The kitchen. Look in the refrigerator."

That made as much sense as anything that had happened to me in the past few years, so I asked no questions and walked into the kitchen, which was only a couple of steps away. The fridge was tiny, mounted under the countertop, so I reached down and opened it.

"There's nothing in here but a quart of milk," I told Dad.

"Exactly. Take it out."

Hey, if he wanted to play a fun game, I could play a fun game. I removed the quart of milk—2%, in case you were wondering—and looked at it. "Yeah?"

"Smell it," Dad said.

Well, *that* didn't bode well. "Do I have to?" I asked my father.

"Go ahead."

I'd never had a reason not to trust Dad, so I did as he instructed, but I wasn't happy about it. I sniffed. "It doesn't smell like anything," I said.

"Exactly," he said again.

"Okay, Buddha, let's have it. What are you getting at?"

"Baby girl. The milk is in the fridge. It's cold and it's fresh. What does that tell you?"

It took a second, but I actually did catch up with the rest of humanity then. "She was here, and not very long ago," I said. "Wait. How did you know? Can you smell it?" Ghosts can't detect odors, as far as I know.

"No, but the sell-by date hasn't passed yet. I took a shot it wasn't from last year."

I decided to walk around the main room very slowly and examine everything. I started at the door and turned right immediately; the idea was to walk the perimeter. I had already seen the center of the room, and it wasn't much to look at. This wouldn't take very long; it was a fairly large room, but a sparsely furnished one.

"We're not far from where Harry the Fish is," I said to Dad. "Maybe you should go out and ask him if he's remembered anything else."

It wasn't that I didn't want my father around while I looked over the house. It was more that I wasn't afraid of being in the house anymore, because I hadn't found anything there that was upsetting and was unlikely to now. But Harry the Fish scared me even when he was dead. Dad could talk to anybody; he'd been a self-employed handyman.

"How will I know him?" Dad asked.

"He's the ghost in the business suit who's out at the end of the pier in the ocean with fish swimming through him," I said. "He's hard to miss."

Dad looked uncertain, but he almost never turns down a request I make (and *never* turns down a request Melissa makes; it's like he was born to be a grandfather and, thanks to the miracle of ghost technology, is finally getting the chance to fulfill his true destiny). He headed out through the back wall, saying that he'd be back shortly.

The walls in the room were wood-paneled veneer, like the ones in my movie room back at the guesthouse. But these were dark and uninteresting. The floor was the same, but real wood planks instead of veneer. There was a picture on the right wall, just before the kitchen entrance, of a marlin rising out of the ocean with a line running out of its mouth. The fisherman and the boat that must have been involved were not in the photo. I felt bad for the fish; he should have at least gotten the chance to face his attacker.

The kitchen, aside from the valuable information contained in the milk carton, was unrevealing. There was a box of Special K in the cabinet, for which the milk had no doubt been intended. It was open, and there was a clip on the bag inside the box. McElone might have had a problem with insects in the cabinets. That wasn't terribly revealing either, but it was sort of gross. There was also a large pot in a dish drainer inhabiting almost all the counter space next to the sink.

I inched my way around the main room, stopping to look into the very small bathroom, really a powder room with a shower. The basics in a house not meant to be a home. There was nothing in the medicine chest but sunblock and first-aid items.

The back wall was mostly made of the glass sliding doors that led out to the darkness. A light switch on the left side of the doors turned on the outside light, and I could see a small yard with a chain-link fence around it; beyond that, judging from the sound of the surf, was the beach. The house had sustained no damage from Sandy that I could see. It was probably on blocks, raised above the level of the beach, and there might have been man-made dunes protecting it, as my house had been protected.

On the left wall was a futon sofa that could clearly be converted into something on which a person could sleep. Above it was another framed picture, this one an "art print" of a dolphin wearing an academic mortar cap, "stroking its snout" with its right flipper. Quite the classy place, where the lieutenant came to think.

There was no sign of work being done in the room; the center featured a coffee table and the easy chair. No pens, no papers on the table. It was starting to look like this sweep of the place would turn up nothing.

Success, such as it was, came when I reached the front door again, this time from the left side of the room, the side into which the door swung when opened. There, behind the door and clearly having been overlooked, were two items: a length of rubber hose about two feet long and what, on close examination, turned out to be a guitar pick decorated like an American flag. They both screamed "CLUE!" at me, but I was damned if I could figure out what they meant. I texted Paul a photo and waited for a reply.

Dad floated in just about that time, shaking himself despite having no moisture clinging to him; I guess it's just force of habit. "Your pal Harry the Fish is a really tight-lipped guy," he said.

"No pal of mine," I answered. "He didn't tell you anything?"

Dad grinned; how little I knew. "He said he remembers seeing Lieutenant McElone on the day he died, but he still doesn't remember much else."

"Where did he see her?"

"Here. In this house."

"Did he talk to her?"

Dad shrugged. "He thinks so, but he's not sure. His memory's not great, he says."

Okay, that was unexpected. "Why was *he* here?" I asked Dad.

"He said they used it for meeting sometimes, just to be funny. It was a cop's house, but she was rarely there and Lay-Z was good with locks."

I took a moment to digest that information. It was completely outside my realm of comprehension, but it was interesting. "What I could use right now," I told Dad, "is a detective."

He regarded me, floating a foot off the floor, holding his right hand to his chin. "Really. And here I thought you were the detective on this case."

"I'm a placeholder," I said. "What I need is a professional, but the only actual cop alive who will talk to me is missing at the moment."

"That's a problem," he agreed. "So what do we do?"

"We go see a cop who'll talk to me but isn't alive."

Twenty-five

Martin Ferry was actually "sitting" on the front stoop of his apartment building when we got there about twenty minutes later.

"I see you've learned to get past the door of your apartment," I said. Nobody on the street looked up as they passed, mostly because there wasn't anyone on the street. But I also wear a Bluetooth headset when I'm walking around with ghosts so that it looks like I'm on the phone. Technology is a grand cover when you communicate with the dead.

Ferry looked at me and scowled. Scowling was apparently his default expression. "I willed myself to do it," he said. "They're getting ready to rent out my place. All my stuff—what's left of it, anyway—will be gone in a couple of days and then there'll be people living there. A young couple with a baby." He rolled his eyes and then looked at me. "You'd be right at home."

I got him up to date with what Dad and I had found out

from Harry the Fish and from his old pal Lay-Z. Ferry shook his head when the young man's name came up.

"That kid's gonna get himself killed by being stupid," he said. "Watch it happen."

"What about what Harry Monroe told my father?" I asked. Dad, bobbing up and down with his feet about an inch into the pavement, watched without commenting as I dealt with Ferry. "How he said he'd seen Lieutenant Mc-Elone at her bungalow just before he died. How do you figure that?"

"There are two reasons a guy like Harry the Fish goes to see a cop of his own volition," Ferry said, chewing over a mouthful of nothing by way of pondering. "Either he was an informant for her, or he was going to kill her."

I liked one of those options a lot better than the other, but I hadn't considered either one before. "An informant? You think Harry 'the Fish' Monroe was giving Lieutenant McElone information? Wasn't he pretty high up for that?"

Ferry shrugged. "There were few higher in his end of the business. But hey, Whitey Bulger ran the mob in Boston while talking to the FBI for decades. Go figure."

I didn't want to ask, but my father, who is the captain of the Olympic just-dive-in team, had no such qualms: "Do *you* think he went there to kill Lieutenant McElone?" he asked from his perch next to me.

Ferry got a grin that only cops, EMTs and other first responders can get, a gallows-humor sort of face. "Harry ended up dead," he pointed out. "If he went to kill Anita— and I doubt he did, because that's the kind of thing he'd send someone to do—he clearly didn't come out of it so well." Ferry turned and looked at me. "Besides, you said he died the same day as me. We both saw Anita alive after that." He had a point.

I reached into my tote bag and pulled out the length of rubber hose I'd found at McElone's place. The guitar pick took a little more digging, but I managed to extract it, too.

"I found these things at the bungalow," I told Ferry. "You think they mean anything?"

"Somebody likes to play guitar and irrigate crops?" he said. Cops are not funny. They just think they are.

"Detective," I said. "Your friend is still missing. If these objects can help us find her—"

He put on a "you're not a cop so you don't get it" expression, but answered, "You're right. Let me see the hose." I held it out for him just as a young couple, hand in hand, turned the corner and walked toward me. I got two very odd stares, but they kept walking.

Ferry looked over the hose, and I turned it so he could see the object from various angles. "You said Harry drowned, right?"

"Yeah, part fresh water and part salt water," I reminded him. "Why?"

"Was there a bathtub in the bungalow?"

"No, actually. There was a shower stall, but that was it. I'll ask again: Why?"

Dad gave me a look that said he thought I was being disrespectful to the officer trying to do his job. I believe you have to give cops a little attitude or they don't respect you, but I didn't have a look for that, so I turned my attention back to Ferry.

"Because you can drown someone in a bathtub, but you can't in a shower," Ferry said. "If they started to drown him at the bungalow and then took him out to the ocean to finish the job, they might use the hose to keep feeding in water while they carried him. But they couldn't do that because there was no bathtub in the bungalow."

"Wait," Dad said. "Think about the kitchen."

Think about the kitchen? "The great bird flies over the mountaintop," I answered nonsensically. "What do you mean, 'Think about the kitchen'?"

Ferry turned his attention to Dad with the trained concentration of an investigator.

"The kitchen in the lieutenant's bungalow," Dad explained. "All she had there was a mini fridge and a microwave oven."

I felt like I was getting the idea, but I didn't know what it was. "So?"

"So what else was there?"

I knew better than to be a smartass now; give me credit. I closed my eyes. "A couple of cabinets, a box of cereal, a few dishes. A sink. A small countertop with a dish drainer."

I opened my eyes and saw Dad grinning. I was getting close. "And in the dish drainer?" he asked.

"A big pasta pot."

Dad pointed at me. "Right. So what does that tell you?"

Ferry, predictably, got there before I did. "No stove? No cooktop?" he asked. Dad shook his head. "So why a pasta pot when there was no place to cook pasta? It's not like you could use it in the microwave."

"What am I missing?" I asked. "What does the pot tell us?"

"That maybe there was another way to drown a guy." Ferry was already "up on his feet," pacing back and forth over the front steps to the building. "Maybe they did start drowning him at Anita's place and then dragged him out to the ocean."

"They?" I asked.

Ferry glanced sideways. "Seems like it would take more than one person."

"Why do that?" Dad asked. "If you're going to drown him, drown him. Why do it in two places?"

Ferry scratched his head. He looked like he should have been wearing a hat. "Maybe just because they *wanted* it to be confusing. A mixture of salt and fresh water in his lungs? Maybe they wanted it to last longer, really make Harry suffer. I don't know."

"They found Harry the Fish in his car, in a dry suit," I reminded both men. "But he's still out in the ocean, and he hates it. He hated the water when he was alive."

Ferry wandered a bit too far, and I saw his foot freeze in midair. That's what happens when a ghost who's tethered to a spot tries to go too far. They simply can't move beyond whatever barrier is fencing them in. "Damn," he said absently. He shook it off. "Okay, so let's say Harry the Fish was snitching for Anita. Some of his friends find out about it and they decide they disapprove. They lure him to Anita's bungalow, maybe find out how she contacted him. And once he's there, they show their disapproval by filling a pot with water and sticking his head in it. Then, just to be mean, they finish the job in the ocean. Once he's dead, they bring him back to shore, dry him off, put him in dry clothes and stick him behind the wheel of his car to be discovered."

"It fits the facts," I said. "There's one problem."

"What's that?" Dad and Ferry chorused at once.

"Who does that? How crazy do you have to be to go to all that trouble?"

"Pretty crazy," Ferry said. "There's only one guy I know batty enough to make it plausible, and that's Buster Hockney. What we just described would be one of Buster's more subdued days."

A shiver went up my shoulders into my neck.

"Did you find anything that indicated Buster and Harry's grandson Vinnie the Goldfish were working together?" I asked Ferry. "I couldn't tell whether they were friends or enemies."

"I could never find out," the detective admitted. "They spent a lot of time together toward the end—my end, and Harry's—but I couldn't get close enough to figure whether Vinnie was trying to undercut his grandfather or get enough inside dope, if you'll pardon the expression, to help Harry put Buster out of business."

"What kind of guy is Vinnie?" That question was from Dad.

"Like Buster, but without the creativity," Ferry said. "He's mean and violent, but not what you'd call the sharpest tool in the shed."

"So what do I do now?" I asked Ferry.

"If it was me, I'd squeeze Lay-Z a little more," Ferry said. "The kid knows more about Buster than he's saying, and he might be able to put Buster in the bungalow the night Harry died."

I didn't relish the idea of going back to the custard stand, especially if it was going to get me closer to Buster Hockney. "What about you?" I said. "We seem to be concentrating on what happened to Harry Monroe, but we're not getting any closer to finding out who shot you, Detective. What can I do that I haven't done yet?"

He avoided my eyes. "You've done what you can do," he said. "Let it go."

That was not the Martin Ferry I . . . honestly didn't know very well. "You're being evasive. Have you remembered something? Is this about the thirty thousand dollars?"

This time Ferry did turn toward me, his eyes flashing with anger for a second. He forced himself to relax. "No," he said. "I haven't remembered anything about that night. And no, the thirty thousand has nothing to do with it. That money . . . well, that money came to me legally, is all I'm going to say."

Dad looked at him skeptically. "Detective, if we're going to help you—"

Ferry didn't get a chance to temper himself this time; he just turned and shouted. "You're NOT going to help me!" he yelled. "You can't help me! I'm dead! There's nothing left that can be done for me, okay?" And then he wasn't there anymore.

Like I said before, it takes some ghosts more time to adjust than others, and the ones who died violently are especially likely to be angry. Even Paul, who otherwise had a very mild demeanor, bristled when his killer was mentioned in his presence. Luckily, the subject rarely came up.

"That went well," I said. ˙

It turned out I got back to the house at a reasonable hour, mostly because there wasn't a chance in hell I was going to look for Buster Hockney at night, even if I'd known where to look (oddly, Ferry had vanished without leaving an address lying around on a cocktail napkin for me to use). Besides, Jeannie and Tony would be back late the next afternoon, and I wanted to at least be able to say I'd checked in on Oliver the last night he stayed at my house.

He was, unexpectedly, still awake when Dad and I returned with a few quarts of Jersey Freeze ice cream in tow (I'd have brought Kohr's frozen custard, but you can't really transport Kohr's when it's hot out—the stuff is partially melted when you get it, and besides, you absolutely need the cone). I handed the quarts off to Mom for quick storage in the freezer. The ice cream would stabilize from the trip, and maybe I could get Oliver to fall asleep in the meantime. But first, I needed to know why he was awake at this hour.

"He was asleep for a while, but then he needed a diaper change," Melissa reported. "So he cried and I went in to help him, and then he was awake. We figured he could burn off a little energy with the folks."

Indeed, all six guests were in the den, and the karaoke machine was still warm, indicating they'd been having quite the time. Even Rita, who had been wearing anxiety on her face in place of sunscreen, finally seemed relaxed and happy. Maybe I should stay away from the guesthouse more often.

"You should have heard Joe singing 'Piano Man'!" Bonnie Claeson told me as soon as I walked in the door. "He sounded just like Billy Joel!"

Joe smiled but looked away. "I didn't."

Bonnie hooked her arm through Joe's, which was a surprise to me but apparently not to anyone else in the room. It was dawning on me that I hadn't been around much for the past few days.

Stephanie gave me a look that indicated Bonnie might be exaggerating things a tad, but she grinned nonetheless. "I did 'You've Got a Friend,'" she announced proudly.

"I wish I had heard it," I said. I almost believed me, I was so convincing.

The two ghosts in the room (besides Dad, whom I don't always count as a ghost) were not concerned with ice cream, babies or karaoke: Maxie was complaining that Melissa wouldn't simply surrender her laptop permanently, and Paul was asking for an update beyond what I'd texted him after Martin Ferry had evaporated.

"I'll be right there," I said, ostensibly to Mom but really to Paul. "I have to see about my pal Ollie." I dropped down on my knees. "Hello, Ollie. Hello, Ollie. What's the boy doing up so late? Huh? What?"

"He's not a puppy," Maxie said. "He's sort of a human."

Oliver wisely ignored Maxie, perhaps taking his cue from me. Tammy and Don were sitting on the floor next to Ollie, rolling a toy train back and forth in front of him, giving him no incentive at all to go back to bed. You had to admire their enthusiasm, if not their grasp of the larger situation.

"Detective Ferry said he'd gotten the thirty thousand dollars legally," Paul said. I guess he figured that just because I couldn't talk to him right now didn't mean he couldn't dive in. That's Paul. Though I was grateful that he was contributing to the investigation instead of competing with the local power company. "There are only a few ways that is a plausible scenario."

"Maybe we shouldn't stimulate Oliver quite so much right now," I suggested to Tammy Coburn. "I think he needs to get some sleep."

"Oh, of course!" Tammy said. She looked horrified that she'd done something "wrong," and leaned back. I'd have to explain later that I wasn't trying to criticize her behavior. This is the life of an innkeeper.

"He could have inherited the money," Paul went on. I'm not sure if he was talking to anyone but himself. "He could have won it, in the lottery, perhaps. He could have had a side business, a legitimate one. Or . . ."

"What?" I said, pretending to talk to Oliver, who was annoyed that the train was no longer going back and forth on the floor next to him. He pulled himself up on the armchair near the spot where we were sitting and reached a hand out toward the train, trying to figure how to grab it.

"It's possible there's another way Ferry got thirty thousand dollars, especially if he was in need of it, if he'd fallen into debt, perhaps." Paul's goatee-stroking was reaching a fever pitch.

"Is it something I need to research?" Maxie asked. "I could borrow Melissa's laptop . . ."

"Forget it," Liss pretended to tell Oliver. It wasn't that we didn't want to let the guests know there were ghosts in the room—we are billed as a haunted guesthouse, after all—but I didn't want to bring all my guests into my sideline as an investigator. Besides, it was more that repeating each line of a conversation can be tedious, time consuming and, in this instance, a little too close to smearing a man's reputation in public.

Oliver moved a foot toward the train and caught himself on the chair. Too scary.

"It wouldn't be a matter of public record," Paul said. "There would be no paper trail without access to all sorts of accounts we don't have."

"What is it?" Again, me cooing at Ollie. You get good at it after a while.

"I'm not prepared to say yet," Paul said. "It's possible the information would be embarrassing to the detective,

and I would not want to be the cause of that." Unexpectedly, he turned toward Mom. "Loretta, I think we need
more information out of Detective Ferry, and he appears to
become agitated when it's Alison doing the asking. Would
you mind going over there tomorrow morning?"

I thought that was a touch insulting, but I didn't want to
say anything. I just humphed, but nobody seemed to notice.

"I'll go along with her," Dad told Paul. "For backup."

Mom was watching the conversation but not reacting.
Clearly, she didn't think she'd need backup but was just as
happy to have Dad along for the ride. She nodded imper-
ceptibly, drawing on a lifetime of interacting with ghosts
and making sure no one (for a long time, including me)
could tell.

"Good," Paul said. "I'll send you a message with the
questions I need answered." He pointed to his head to indicate this would be a Ghostergram (a Ghosternet message
aimed at one spirit) to Dad.

"I think he wants to walk," Tammy said, pointing at
Oliver.

"Stop him, Liss," I warned. Melissa pulled Oliver, who
looked surprised and irritated, onto her lap. Tammy seemed
shocked, so I turned to her. "His mom's coming back tomorrow," I said. "Don't want her to miss his first steps."

"How would she know?" Stephanie asked.

That stopped me. It was a good question. "Okay, let him
walk if he wants to," I said to Liss. She did nothing, but
Oliver pulled himself back up to a standing position and
eyed the train again. His left foot was definitely in on the
plan, but his right hadn't necessarily gotten the memo yet.
He pivoted.

The guests gathered around. They weren't all parents,
but they all had some family; it was a decent bet each of
them had probably, at some time or another, seen a child
take his or her first step. So you'd think they wouldn't find
this moment quite so magical.

But even Maxie was paying rapt attention. Paul ceased going on about clues or stratagems for the moment. He was watching, too.

But once Oliver, until now focused on the amazing train toy that he just *had* to have, noticed the volume level in the room drop to a whisper, he looked up to investigate. There were so many eyes focused on him that he must have found it completely overwhelming. He leaned forward, then back, fell on his diaper and started to cry.

"Aw . . ." Melissa said, and she reached over to give Ollie a hug. "I think he's more tired than he knows." He sobbed on her shoulder for a moment, then regressed to sniffling, which indicated he probably was on his way to sleep. Liss has an unerring instinct for kids; someday she'll probably be a great teacher or a great mom, or both. Assuming she decides not to take over the world. While being a mom and a teacher.

Paul watched Melissa carry Oliver in the direction of his crib, hitched his shoulders and looked back down at me. "So Lieutenant McElone had been in the bungalow recently. What does that tell us?"

"Time for ice cream," I said to the guests. That was also intended to inform Paul that I was tired and didn't want to talk about this anymore tonight. "Who's interested?"

Nobody, as it turned out. Stephanie and Rita headed up to their room, thanking me for a lovely evening I had not attended. Joe and Bonnie begged off, saying they wanted to go for a walk on the beach now that the temperature had moderated somewhat. Tammy and Don had plans to drive all the way to Vineland, about a two-hour trip, to go to the last drive-in theater in New Jersey. There was, they said, a midnight show. I began to think they did not sleep.

Mom, however, did sleep. "I think I'm going to hit the road," she said once the Coburns had left. "It seems I have somewhere to go in the morning, and I'm not as young as I used to be."

"But you're still younger now than you'll be tomorrow,"

Dad reminded her. He thought, for reasons that defy logic, that he was being encouraging.

My mother shot him a look, saw he was innocent and smiled. They have the kind of marriage that has truly prevailed over every possible obstacle, even the biggest one. They left together, talking about their plans to come back to welcome Jeannie and Tony back tomorrow.

When Melissa returned from putting Ollie to bed, we were alone in the room with our two resident ghosts. And I was fading fast.

"Alison," Paul began.

I held up a hand. "Not tonight, Paul. I don't have anything left. Tomorrow morning, I promise. Early." And I started toward the staircase to go to bed without even putting the karaoke machine away. It could wait.

Out of the corner of my eye, I noticed Maxie's body tense as if she'd heard a noise outside. "Boo-yah!" she shouted, and blasted her way across the room to the outside wall. She was gone in no time.

"Boo-yah?" Paul repeated. He shook his head in confusion.

But it confirmed a suspicion I'd been having for some time now. "So that's what she's been doing," I said.

Melissa looked at me, grinning; at worst she's on my level and usually ahead of me. "You think so?"

"I'd bet on it."

Paul scrutinized us carefully, his eyes showing a total lack of understanding. "You've discovered where Maxie has been rushing out to every day and night?" he asked.

"I think so," I said. "But I'll have to confirm it, of course. I'll do that tomorrow, too." And I turned back toward the staircase.

"Alison!" Paul called after me. "Aren't you going to tell me?"

I turned back and gave him an eyebrow raise. "Are you going to tell me where Detective Ferry got the money?"

Paul thought but shook his head. "I don't think that would be appropriate without asking the detective first," he said.

"Then you'll have to wait," I said, and didn't stop on my way to bed.

I did in fact sleep like a rock that night, then woke early, in time to straighten up and get the coffee and tea going before the guests started straggling in. Even in the early morning, the air-conditioning was necessary, but it was more for the humidity than the temperature at this time of the day.

Rita came in first, sans Stephanie for the first time since I'd met her. She said her wife was still sleeping, so she'd come down for coffee and to sit quietly in the den for a while. I provided her with the coffee, and she availed herself of the ice I'd put out and sat with a cool drink. But it was soon obvious that she had come down to talk to me without Stephanie present, so I made myself an iced coffee and asked her if she'd been enjoying her vacation so far. This was an appropriate question because one, I'm an innkeeper, and two, Rita and Stephanie were leaving the next day, but I asked knowing it was an avenue toward whatever she *really* wanted to discuss, so I was ready for her response.

"The house is lovely, and I really adore the town," she said. "But I have to admit, even with all the talk in the brochure, the ghost stuff really sort of . . ."

"Scares you?" I said. "That's not unusual. But I can assure you, the ghosts in this house are incredibly friendly and no threat to anyone." As long as you didn't catch Maxie when she was grouchy.

Rita sipped her drink and scanned the ceiling. "It's not here. I feel perfectly safe inside the house, believe me, Alison. But what I saw out on the beach—"

I had prepared for this, especially since I now had an

idea of what she'd seen. "What you saw was a hat," I told Rita. "There might have been a ghost under it, but it was a hat. I'm thinking if there was a spirit, he was holding it up as a signal to someone else, and that's why you saw it. Otherwise, you'd never have had the chance to notice it."

"So I'm not going to see ghosts all the time now?" Rita's eyes were wide.

"Definitely not. It was a random incident. It's no different from the ghost shows you see every day here in the guesthouse. You're not developing a supernatural ability. You saw a hat. All that says is you're more observant than most of the people on the beach that day."

Rita sank back in the easy chair, smiling. "Really?" she asked.

Paul rose up through the floor and watched me for a moment. "Really," I told Rita, without turning my head toward him.

Rita looked happier than I'd seen her since she arrived. "Thank you, Alison. You're a really good hostess."

I never know how to react to that sort of thing, so I thanked Rita, picked up my iced coffee and headed out to the deck, knowing Paul would follow. I leaned on the railing, looking out at the ocean, and without looking at him, said, "What?"

"I'm trying to think of a way to solve Lieutenant Mc-Elone's disappearance and Detective Ferry's murder without you having to meet Buster Hockney," he said.

"That would be the goal. And?"

"And so far, I haven't come up with one."

"That's a huge help, Paul. Good morning to you, too."

He floated out to a spot in the air directly in front of me so I'd be forced to look at him. "I believe the lieutenant is in a good deal of danger," he said. "The amount of time she's been missing is troublesome. We need to act quickly."

"Nobody understands that better than I do, Paul. But whenever you say, 'we need to act,' what you mean is that

I need to act, and that's dangerous and scary." Out of the corner of my eye I saw that Melissa was awake and getting herself a cup of coffee. She sometimes prefers it hot, even in weather like this. Of course, she was indoors, where there was air-conditioning.

"If I could think of another way—" Paul began.

My phone rang, so I dug it out of my pocket. Seeing that the caller was Malcolm Kidder, I answered. "I'm hoping there's good news, Malcolm," I said.

His voice did not reward me; he sounded weary and tense. "I've been up all night, Alison. I still haven't heard anything. Someone broke into the house when I was out yesterday and tossed the place, but they didn't find what they wanted. I'm worried."

I closed my eyes; the problem was closing in around me. "I am, too," I said. "I'm thinking I might have to do something stupid."

"What's that?"

"I might have to go see Buster Hockney." I opened my eyes. Paul, not looking happy, nodded his head.

Malcolm absorbed that information. "I don't think that's a great idea," he said.

"Neither do I. Do you have a better one? I'm open to suggestion."

"Maybe," Malcolm said. "Can I come over? I think we can figure something out."

I looked at Paul. "Of course you can come over here, Malcolm," I said for the ghost's benefit. Paul looked impressed. "You know where I am?"

"I have GPS. I'll be there in twenty minutes." We hung up.

I told Paul what Malcolm had said. "I hope his idea can get us closer," Paul told me. "Anything that keeps us— you—away from Buster Hockney—"

My phone rang again. This time, I recognized only the local exchange. There was no name on the Caller ID, so it was someone who hadn't called me before or whom I hadn't stored on the phone. Maybe Martin Ferry had learned to use a cell phone. Weirder things have happened. Believe me.

I pushed the talk button. "Hello?"

The voice was male and a little tentative. "Is this Alison Kerby?" Good phone calls never start that way.

"Who is calling, please?"

"My name is Thomas McElone," he said. "I'm calling because I haven't heard from Anita since yesterday, and I'm concerned."

Those sentences had way too much information in them for me. "You heard from the lieutenant *yesterday*?" I said. Paul immediately stiffened up and stopped floating freely.

"Yes, but not since," he said. "Have you heard from her?"

"No, I haven't heard from her for days. Are you a relative of hers?"

"I'm sorry, Alison, I forgot we haven't met. I'm Anita's husband."

Twenty-six

Thomas McElone—if that's who he really was—clearly did not respond well to stunned silence. "Hello?" he said.

I looked at Paul, who was definitely wondering exactly who had punched me in the stomach. "You're Lieutenant McElone's husband?" I said, just so Paul could hear it. His brow wrinkled, and his mouth opened a little.

"Yes, I am," Thomas said. "Is that a problem?" I didn't blame him for being confused; I was as baffled as I've ever been.

"No, it's not a problem, but if you're her husband, who is Malcolm Kidder?"

I dealt with stunned silence better than he did, but I've had more practice. "I don't have the faintest idea," he said after a moment. "Why did you ask?"

"A man named Malcolm Kidder has been in touch with me for the past few days, and he says *he* is the lieutenant's husband," I told him. Why not reveal all? If Thomas could explain it, he was way ahead of everyone else in this game.

It hadn't occurred to me that it was unusual for the lieutenant to have a different name than her husband's, and I told Thomas so. I'd never changed my last name, not when I was married and certainly not since my divorce. In fact, Melissa has my last name because The Swine and I had agreed on it when I was pregnant with her (and yet I *still* didn't see our divorce coming!).

"That's reasonable," he said, which marked the first time anything had been reasonable for about a week.

"Put the phone on speaker," Paul said. So I did. I hadn't counted on Melissa, coffee cup in hand, wandering out onto the deck as we spoke, but I would have told her all about this later anyway.

"Who do you suppose Malcolm Kidder is?" I asked Thomas, but I was looking at Paul and Melissa.

"Like I said, I have no idea," Thomas said. "But if you need proof, I can send you a copy of our wedding picture."

"Yes, please do," I said. I wanted to give the impression that I was professional, but also I really wanted to see McElone in a wedding dress. I put the phone on mute and told Melissa to find Maxie and get her laptop, pronto. She was off like a shot. That coffee works wonders.

Punching the mute button off, I asked, "So you heard from the lieutenant yesterday?"

"Yes. She'd been calling in every day and coming home every night, but last night she didn't come home, and now she's not answering her personal cell phone."

Maxie appeared at the attic window in her trench coat and descended quickly to the spot where I was standing and Paul was hovering. I texted Thomas my e-mail address, and he said he would send the photograph immediately. Maxie heard that and nodded; she'd check for it.

"Just now? I've been calling her cell phone number, and she hasn't been answering me for a few days," I told Thomas.

"Did you leave voice messages?" he asked.

"My daughter tells me no one listens to those," I said. "She says you just look and see someone called, then you call them back."

Thomas was silent for a moment. "Maybe not when they're missing," he suggested.

"Maybe, but she still didn't call me back. Not even before you said she stopped getting in touch with you."

"She . . . I'm not sure how to put this . . ."

I could tell what was coming, so I decided to put Thomas out of his misery. "She thinks that I'm a pest, and she decided somewhere along the way that contacting me in the first place had been a bad idea, so she stopped taking my calls, is that it?"

I heard Thomas exhale. "Not *exactly*," he said, "but pretty close."

"Really? Which part am I wrong about?"

"She doesn't think you're a pest. She thinks you're a nut."

Maxie turned the laptop around to show me a somewhat younger Lieutenant (probably Officer) McElone, her face very near that of a rather dapper young man with very broad shoulders. She wore a flattering white dress with not too much lace, and he was in a business suit, not a tuxedo. They looked like they had a nice future together.

"Okay, you're either a wizard with Photoshop or you're Lieutenant McElone's husband," I told Thomas. "Assuming this is you."

Maxie nodded again and punched a few keys. A page of images on a search for "Thomas McElone" showed at least twelve pictures of the man in the wedding photo. It seemed to me he couldn't possibly be devious enough to get his picture plastered all over the Internet just to fool me.

"I can come over there to prove it," he said.

Great. So both of McElone's husbands would be here soon. *Hey, wait!* "Malcolm Kidder is on his way over!" I shouted to the heavens. Everyone, including Melissa, who had just come back from her trip upstairs, froze. Maxie recovered first and started typing again.

"The guy who said he was me is on his way to your house?" Thomas asked.

"Sort of." Malcolm hadn't actually said he was Thomas McElone, he'd said he was Anita McElone's husband. But that was splitting hairs.

"Hold on," Maxie said. "Uh-oh."

Uh-oh? That meant things were getting worse. How could things possibly get worse?

"What?" Melissa said.

"I've been running a search on the computer for the name Malcolm Kidder," Maxie said. "It never occurred to me before to do that, because we thought he was the cop's husband."

Paul's face looked worried. "What did you find?" Maxie showed him the screen, and I believe that if it were possible, Paul would have blanched. "Oh, my."

"Oh your what?" I said, forgetting that the man on the phone could hear me.

"Is someone there?" Thomas asked. Then he paused. "Is this one of those ghosty things Anita tells me about?"

"There's something in one of Lieutenant McElone's files from the flash drive," Paul said. "'Malcolm Kidder' is a known alias for Vinnie 'the Goldfish' Monroe."

Twenty-seven

I had, at this point, about fifteen minutes before my doorbell was going to ring, and the finger on the button was going to be that of a criminal/drug dealer/generally feared guy who was now moving up quickly on the list of possible murder suspects. He also might have something to do with Lieutenant McElone's disappearance.

"I'm on my way," Thomas McElone said, and hung up his phone.

What was needed, quickly, were two plans of action. First, I had to get Melissa and Oliver out of the house. That required an adult with a car and a driver's license. Or a skateboard. There wasn't enough time to summon Mom (who was probably going to see Ferry per Haul's request) or Josh, Wendy was visiting her grandmother in Bergen County (too far away) and Jeannie was probably steaming frantically toward Port Elizabeth as we spoke.

I could have simply asked Maxie to protect the kids and

sent them out to the beach (Paul couldn't get past the property line), but I needed Maxie for my plan to stop Vinnie Monroe once he got to my door from, you know, killing me at all. (I didn't know if that was actually his plan, but in these cases it's best to err on the side of caution, I believe.) It's not that I wouldn't put Melissa's life and Oliver's before my own, but given the option, I preferred to keep all of us alive at the same time. Call me greedy.

Another option would be to ask one of the guests to supervise the kids for a while. That would be reckless, since I really didn't know any of the visitors well; a little insulting to my eleven-year-old, who can take care of herself under most circumstances; and bad business, as the vacation brochure I circulate does not mention the guests being required to perform babysitting services in order to prevent the odd homicide.

Fourteen minutes. Luckily, I think fast.

My cell phone was out in seconds, and I had Phyllis Coates on speed dial. I didn't even give her a chance to say hello. "I have the story of the year for you, but you have to be here in five minutes," I said.

The great thing about Phyllis is you don't have to say more. "On my way." And that was it.

I looked over at Melissa. "Please get Oliver ready to go," I said.

"Go where?"

"I don't know yet. Phyllis will tell you."

Liss didn't look pleased, but I hadn't actually told her she was leaving, too, and she'd seen the look in my eyes. So she rushed off toward Ollie's room. I turned toward Paul. "I have a really bad plan," I said. "But if you don't have a better one, that's what we're going to do."

He didn't have a better one.

We moved into the movie room, the least populated spot of the guesthouse at the moment. Bonnie and Joe wandered in to ask about museums in the area, and I directed them to

Allaire Village in Wall Township. It's very historical, and if you come stay at the guesthouse sometime, I'll tell you about it.

True to her reputation, Phyllis showed up in four minutes in a 1973 Dodge Dart that she had probably driven through a few brick walls and kept going. I hesitated for a moment, weighing whether staying in the house with Vinnie Monroe was less dangerous than riding in Phyllis's car, but decided that if Phyllis was still alive having owned the Dart since the Nixon administration, she was probably the best bet.

I outlined her assigned duties. Phyllis, while not especially motherly, is fond of Melissa and really wanted the story I'd pitched her, though I refused to divulge it completely unless she cooperated. Knowing the kids' safety was on the line, she did not argue.

"I'll take them over to the *Chronicle* office," she suggested.

I'm guessing my face looked a little nonplussed. "Yeah, because there's nothing there an almost-one-year-old could possibly find to hurt himself with, right?"

Phyllis gave that some thought as Liss wheeled in Ollie's stroller, complete with Ollie. "Where are we going?" Melissa asked. She'd been told now that she was on the passenger list. A short *discussion* had ensued, but she had accepted her fate when I'd promised to text the second they could come back.

"There's an IHOP in Neptune," Phyllis said, glaring at me just a little. "Your mom's buying the pancakes."

I agreed, giving Phyllis some cash and Ollie's car seat, and the three of them were out the door with about six minutes to spare before my personal idea of Beelzebub showed up at the door. I looked at Paul, who was about knee-deep in the floor but still pacing, goatee-stroking and thinking. Maxie had stashed Melissa's laptop on top of the bookcase on the assumption that Vinnie might be the person who had taken "hers" and would want the other if he saw it. She was in a corner of the movie room working herself into the proper state of irritation to perform properly, something that is not difficult for her to do.

"How serious is this going to get?" Paul asked.

"That depends on how serious Vinnie turns out to be."

The doorbell rang at that moment, a few minutes early. That figured. My heart took a quick leap, then I reminded myself that we had a plan and walked what would appear to be calmly to the door. Paul trailed behind me, while Maxie went out through the front wall to see our visitor and warn us if he was behaving badly before I opened the door.

But she appeared amused when she came through the front door—or, more accurately, when she stuck her head through it and looked at me. "All clear," she said.

"What does that mean?" I asked, but she was gone again.

Even Maxie wouldn't purposely lead me to danger, so I opened the door. And found Josh standing there. He gave me a peck on the cheek and walked through, carrying two one-gallon cans of wood stain.

"Oh, for Pete's sake," Paul said. I did not respond.

"I was making deliveries in Harbor Haven, so I figured I'd bring over the stain for the movie room," Josh said.

I smiled at him. "I haven't decided on a color yet," I reminded him.

"Yeah, but this is the one you were going to pick, and I was in the neighborhood."

If he'd been here ten minutes earlier, I wouldn't have had to call Phyllis. "Listen, we've got a situation here." I got him up to date on the confluence of McElone husbands about to descend on my house, and Josh's face hardened.

"I think I'd better stick around." I knew that tone. I wasn't going to be able to persuade him otherwise.

"Okay, but stay out of sight. Come on." I picked up one can of stain, Josh got the other and we headed for the movie room.

Once we got there I opened the storage closet and put the stain inside. Best to keep all this stuff behind a closed door, especially with a houseful of guests and a very small child who could learn to walk and who knows what else at any minute. But I considered the situation and looked at Josh.

"Get in the closet," I said.

He actually blushed. "We don't have that kind of time, Alison."

"I like the way you think, but what I meant was, I don't want you visible when Malcolm-slash-Vinnie gets here. The element of surprise can't hurt."

Paul nodded his approval of my plan. "Is there something in there he can use as a weapon?" he asked.

I looked at Josh. "There might be a piece of two-by-four in there, too. If you need it."

Josh stared at me. "You're serious?" he said.

But there was no time to argue; the doorbell rang at that moment, and Maxie appeared through the wall at the same time. "This one has got to be the bad guy," she said. She hadn't seen "Malcolm" before, but I was willing to bet she was right.

"Okay," I said, "time to let the raging maniac inside." I gestured toward the open closet door, and Josh sheepishly walked in. I closed it behind him. "Can you hear in there?"

"I can hear fine; the question is whether I can see, and the answer is no." There is no light fixture in the closet.

"You're not in there to read," I said, and walked out of the room toward the front door. "Just absolutely don't come out unless I say your name. We have a plan. Okay?" I didn't wait for an answer.

I composed myself at the door. I'd met this man before, but he'd been playing a part, and doing so very convincingly. Now I had to do the same, pretending I wasn't aware of his true identity and wasn't starkly terrified of him. I took a cleansing breath and tried to think of people I really liked who reminded me of Vinnie "the Goldfish" Monroe. No one came to mind.

"What are you waiting for?" Maxie asked behind me. "Christmas?"

I declined comment on Maxie's helpful attitude, put a concerned look on my face that I hoped would be at least a little believable and pulled the door open. The man I knew as Malcolm Kidder stood there, his best tormented-husband expression on. I wondered now why I'd ever bought it; that face looked so phony.

"Malcolm," I breathed, as if grateful he'd finally arrived. "I'm so glad you're here. Come on in."

"Thanks," he said. "It's hot out there." He walked in wearing cargo shorts whose right-hand side pocket seemed to be carrying something just a little too heavy. It bounced a bit. I wasn't interested in finding out what that might be.

"Yeah. You want a cold drink or something?" I didn't want Malcolm Kidder anywhere but in my movie room, but if I really did think he was Malcolm Kidder, that's what I would have said.

"No, that's okay." Good. "I've been thinking about your meeting with Buster Hockney."

I looked around as if concerned that a guest would hear. "Let's go in there," I said, pointing toward the movie room. "I'd just as soon keep the investigation separate from my guests, okay?"

Let's-just-call-him-Vinnie-and-be-done-with-it looked down the hallway and seemed to be sizing it up. "That doesn't seem very private," he said. "There aren't even doors. How about if we talk somewhere else, like your room. The guests don't go there, do they?"

My bedroom was the last place I was going with this guy. "Don't worry," I said. "The movie room is far away from the guest areas, and they know I'm renovating in there, so they don't go near it." And before he could come up with a reason that wasn't a good idea, I started down the hallway.

"Nicely played," Paul said, walking just ahead and above me, but backward so he could watch Vinnie.

"I don't see why I can't just hit him with something and tie him up," Maxie suggested. She was behind me, no doubt sizing up Vinnie and finding him wanting from the tone in her voice.

"Because we need him to tell us where Lieutenant McElone is," Paul reminded her. "Stick to the plan."

After one of the longest twenty-foot walks of my life, Vinnie and I were "alone" in the movie room. He pretended to look it over as a courtesy but was probably trying to figure out the best place to hide my body. If it was in the utility closet, he'd be in for a surprise, but the actual possibility of that scenario took some of the fun out of the thought.

I noticed, though, that Maxie had already morphed into wearing her trench coat and Paul was wearing a long pea jacket (in this weather?) so they could "import" any objects they might want while Vinnie was here. That emboldened me. A little.

"So what do you think I should do when I meet Buster?" I asked Vinnie. It was an ironic situation, and there was no reason not to roll with it.

"Malcolm" looked startled. "When you meet Buster?" he asked. "Do you even know how to *find* Buster?"

"Oh, that's right. I forgot to tell you." I thought it was going well, but Paul frowned, indicating I was playing the scene a little too frivolously. "I managed to get past the encryption on the lieutenant's folder and found some files she had on Buster. I assume she got them from Detective Ferry's computer or somewhere, but she had a list of Buster's usual haunts, and where she believed his whole operation had its headquarters."

I could tell that he was trying to keep his emotions from

showing on his face. But he definitely had a number of questions running through his mind, not the least of which was whether I was lying. "But you said your laptop was stolen," he said. "How could you have gotten that information?"

I waved a hand. "You forget," I said. "Your wife"—and it was a real effort not to punch the word *wife*, but I managed—"left me all her data on a thumb drive. I plugged it into another computer, and after a while I realized how to get through her encryption software." I will admit for the record that Maxie was feeding me the line about the firewall; I honestly don't know encryption software from a Rottweiler.

"You figured out her password?" Vinnie, who no doubt had my laptop in his possession—a major reason it was becoming difficult to keep Maxie from smacking him around with something—would surely want that information (if I'd really had it) so he could get into the same files I was making up.

"Yeah, it was easy. Funny, I never thought 'Anita' and I were that close, but once I met you I realized I knew her pretty well. It didn't take long to get her password. I'm surprised you haven't been able to do it."

I walked over to the last section of wall that had needed prepping for stain and blew a little sawdust off the paneling. It was just a question of time . . .

"So what was her password?" Vinnie asked.

Bingo! "Well, what do you think it is? I mean, you're married to the woman. It should be a pretty simple equation. Think: what are your children's names?"

Now, that was going to present a dilemma to my guest. I was willing to bet he didn't know the names of McElone's children (after all, I didn't); he'd been very careful not to mention them by name in any of our conversations and had not introduced himself as Thomas McElone, so he might not even have known her husband's. But I'd just suggested I could break her password using the names of "his" children, and if he made some up, I would know they weren't right. You could almost smell him thinking furiously.

"Well, the important thing is that you got the information," he said. "Where does Buster have his headquarters?"

"He turned the tables on you," Paul said. "Shall we go to Plan B?"

I shook my head a tiny bit; not yet. "Come on," I said. "Guess the password. Start with your children's names."

Understand: The goal here was not to get Vinnie to out himself, although that was coming. The key here was to show him that *I* was aware of the deception, to gain me some respect. Because what was coming next would be especially effective if he thought I was the person controlling it.

The problem was, Vinnie wasn't playing along according to plan. Instead of responding, he reached into his cargo shorts pocket and pulled out a small handgun with the alacrity of Billy the Kid drawing on a rival in a saloon. And I was willing to bet his grin was even nastier than Billy's.

"Okay, Alison, you've had your fun," Vinnie said. "Now give me that thumb drive. It'll go much easier on you if you do."

"How much easier, Vinnie?" Might as well define the terms.

Vinnie whispered for effect. "I won't make it hurt as much."

Twenty-eight

Paul had not anticipated Vinnie's aggression coming so quickly, but Maxie is pretty much always ready to smack someone, so she had picked up a metal roller tray from the floor and was wielding it more or less like a baseball bat.

"Hold it!" Paul warned her. "He has a gun on Alison."

"I know—why do you think I'm trying to hit him?"

"If you don't knock him out—or even if you do—the gun could fire."

"Oh."

I saw the doorknob on the utility closet slowly begin to turn. I had to make sure something happened quickly to keep Josh safe; he'd rush out if he saw the gun trained on me, and he might get hurt.

"See," I said to Vinnie, "there's not that much upside in threatening me."

He took a step closer, the grin still on his face. "I disagree. I'll get the information I need, and you'll stop asking everybody a lot of questions that are becoming a problem.

I get what I want, and you get dead. Win-lose. That's the way it usually works with me."

"You're forgetting something. Didn't you see the sign at my front door when you came in today?" That was the signal; Paul went into the library for a chair and Maxie went into the closet—and possibly through Josh—to get a rope.

"The one that says the place is haunted? That's how you're going to intimidate me?" Vinnie chuckled. "I'm in the intimidation business, lady. You're going to have to do better than that."

The ghosts were in place, so all I said was, "Okay."

But Paul held up a hand and stopped Maxie from moving. "First we need to get the gun off Alison," he said.

Maxie shrugged. *Thanks, Maxie.*

But she zipped herself over to the window—the room is rife with windows, which is going to make watching movies in here something of a challenge during the day—and flapped the curtain. Hard.

Sure enough, Vinnie turned for just a moment, in reaction to the movement. But that moment was plenty of time.

Before he could turn back, a chair had been thrust into the backs of his knees, forcing him to sit down. Then a rope seemed to appear out of nowhere and tied him securely to the chair at the chest and the ankles. The gun was removed from Vinnie's hand while another rope coiled around his chest. His hands, though pinned down pretty well by the chest ropes, were nonetheless in the process of being duct-taped behind him when he realized what had happened to him.

"How the hell did you do that?" he demanded, staring at me.

"I didn't." I gestured toward the ghosts, whom he could not see, just to annoy him. "These are my friends Paul and Maxie. They don't like it when someone threatens me."

Vinnie sputtered and sneered at me. "I'm not some rube tourist," he said. "You can't sell me on this ghost crap. How did you get me tied to this chair?"

I saw the doorknob on the closet shake just a touch. Josh was conflicted, but he did what I'd asked him to do—he waited to hear his name before coming out.

"If you're not going to believe me when I tell the truth, would you prefer I lie to you?" I walked closer to the center of the room, where Vinnie was attempting to walk the chair out of the room. Maybe he thought he could walk all the way back to wherever his headquarters *really* was (I had no idea where that might be). Maybe he thought he could bang the chair against the wall and it would fall to pieces, like the balsa-wood ones do in the movies.

It didn't matter what Vinnie thought; he wasn't going anywhere. A canvas bag I'd discovered in my basement appeared out of Maxie's trench coat and found its way over his head. Disoriented, he stopped moving and yelled a little.

"Believe in ghosts *now*, Vinnie?" I asked.

Paul brought the gun to me. "Just in case," he said.

I'm not much for guns. They tend to go off and kill people. They're heavier than you think they are and, to me, have a very volatile feel to them. I was afraid to breathe heavily.

Men like guns, right? I called out, "Hey, Josh!" Before I could blink, he'd opened the closet door and was heading toward me. He assessed Vinnie's predicament and let out a quick laugh. "You want to hold this?" I asked him, and then didn't wait for an answer before handing it to him.

"He doesn't believe?" Josh asked, awkwardly gesturing toward Vinnie with the gun. Then he realized what he was doing and held it with both hands. Maybe not *all* men like guns that much.

"No," I answered. Maybe we could use that to our advantage. "Hey, Vinnie!" I shouted. I don't know why; the bag over his head probably didn't affect his hearing all that much. "Let's start with an easy one: Where's the laptop you stole from my daughter's bedroom?"

Vinnie's voice was muffled, but no less annoying. "Suck eggs," he said.

"Laptop, Vinnie, or I let Paul and Maxie at you. You don't want that."

"I don't know anything about somebody putting a ladder up to your house and stealing stuff, lady."

My lord, he was stupid. "Who said anything about a ladder?" I said.

"Alison, the lieutenant is the priority," Paul reminded me.

I turned toward Vinnie. "You told me the lieutenant was missing *before* she was missing. What was the point of telling me that?"

Vinnie looked, of all things, annoyed. "I knew she was *gonna* be missing. Why wait? If I could get you to look for the info she gave you, I could get it back. I could be 'Malcolm,' and you'd give it to me because it was, like, an emergency."

I hated that he was right. If I'd thought it would have gotten McElone back, I would have happily handed over the thumb drive to the man I'd thought was her husband. "Okay, Vinnie. Where is Lieutenant McElone now?"

"I don't know!" Vinnie's voice was a little less confident. "Let me out of this thing!"

"You knew she was going to be abducted and you don't know where she was taken? Come on, Vinnie. Do I have to get dead people to work you over?"

"Take this thing off my face!"

I considered. He couldn't see ghost stuff if his head was in a bag. "We have your gun, Vinnie," I said. "If I take the mask off, you can't be trying to walk your way out with that chair. I need it for guests, and it won't fit in your car." I took the bag off his head. Vinnie's face was red—I'd be embarrassed, too, if all that stuff had happened to me—and his hair was mussed. More than anything, he looked mad.

"You don't know who you're dealing with, lady!"

I tossed my hair a little. I've always wanted to do that. "Well, neither do you," I said. "Where's the lieutenant?"

"I. DON'T. KNOW!"

"I could hit him with the can of stain," Maxie offered. I shook my head.

"What?" Vinnie demanded.

"I wasn't talking to you," I said.

Vinnie looked at Josh. "Who's *he*, a ghost?"

"Do I look like a ghost?" Josh asked.

"How would I know?"

"You pretended to be Lieutenant McElone's husband," I said, trying to regain some control of the proceedings. "You knew she was missing, even a couple of days before she actually was missing."

"I hear things." Can you swagger while tied to a chair? "I'm a player."

"Okay, player. I'm going to ask you again: Where can I find her?"

"Which part of 'I don't know' don't you understand?" the criminal in the room asked.

"Okay, Maxie," I said. "Hit him with the gallon of stain. Maybe a knee first."

Maxie gleefully picked up the can and started moving toward Vinnie, even as Paul was telling her, "It's a bluff; you're not really going to hit him."

And sure enough, when Vinnie saw the stain can float past his face and seem to draw a bead on his knee, rising in the air and starting to swing, his eyes got wide and his mouth made a gargling sound. "Hold it," he managed to croak out. "Hold it."

I held up a hand dramatically in Maxie's direction. She giggled as she stopped the gallon can's swinging. "What do I get for stopping her?" I asked.

Vinnie opened and closed his mouth three times without making a coherent noise, and then managed, "It's a *her*?"

Maxie started to swing the can again.

"No!" he shouted. I held up the hand again, and again Maxie stopped.

"What do I get?" I repeated. "Because the next time I'm not going to stop her."

"I really don't know where McElone is," Vinnie said. "But I can tell you what happened to my grandfather."

Frankly, at this point I didn't care what happened to Harry Monroe, but it was something. "What did you do to him?" I asked Vinnie.

"I didn't do anything. I just gave someone a name, that's all. I didn't have any interest in getting rid of the Fish. He wasn't a threat to me."

"Whose name did you give to whom?" I said. I would like it pointed out that I used proper grammar even under some duress.

Vinnie looked away. Josh gave me a look, eyebrows high, asking. I returned one that said, "Hey, if you have an idea . . ."

"Your grandfather drowned, then was put in his car in dry clothes," Josh recounted. "That would indicate pretty strongly that he didn't just have an accident while swimming. Somebody killed him. Alison has friends in the police, Vinnie. You want the killer to be you? Go right ahead and protect the guy."

Vinnie, perhaps realizing what he'd just admitted to, stopped talking.

"Enough," Paul said. He floated down to Vinnie with a great air of purpose, pointed his finger and straightened his arm. If he'd been holding a stick and yelling something in fake Latin, he could have been one of Melissa's friends playing Harry Potter.

But the effect was very much the same. I didn't see anything come out of Paul's outstretched finger, but Vinnie certainly reacted as if he'd stuck his toe into an electrical outlet after taking a dip in the ocean: His body stiffened, his eyes widened and veins in his neck stood out.

"Paul . . ." I said.

Paul nodded and dropped his arm. Vinnie's body relaxed; he slumped in the chair and let out a series of coughs.

"What the hell was that?" he finally managed.

"That was my friend," I said. "You *really* don't want my other friend to give you a massage." Maxie, a gleeful look on her face, stretched her fingers out in anticipation. "So I'll ask you one last time. Who asked you about doing in Harry Monroe, and who did you recommend to do it?"

"I got a call from Teresa, my grandfather's third wife," Vinnie said, after testing his bonds once again and making no progress with them. "She thought the old man was straying a little bit outside the paddock, if you know what I mean."

"I know what you mean," I said, thinking that Vinnie had employed all the subtlety of a Three Stooges short. "So Teresa wanted you to do something about Harry?"

He nodded. "I told her I don't do that when I don't have to, and especially not to family." He looked around the room, trying to find his tormentors. "And I *don't!*"

"But you weren't above giving Teresa the name of someone who would," I said, trying to get him back on topic.

"Yeah. I figured it wouldn't hurt my business dealings to take over for the Fish, and maybe then I wouldn't need Buster to supply some . . . side enterprises I have going. So I slipped Teresa a phone number."

"*Whose* phone number?" This wasn't getting me closer to McElone, and Vinnie was just annoying me now.

"Lay-Z," he said.

We grilled Vinnie for another ten minutes before Thomas McElone showed up. Thomas, as the husband of a very thorough but by-the-book police lieutenant, was probably a little shocked by the scene of Vinnie tied to a chair with his hands duct-taped behind him going on about undead spirits in the house. It took a little while to convince Thomas that Vinnie Monroe *really* didn't know where the lieutenant might be, but he was a good match for his wife—he wouldn't consider breaking protocol to question the Goldfish, and insisted we at least cut the duct tape on his hands and then call the Harbor Haven police.

It took about six minutes for them to show up, assess the situation and cart the Goldfish off to a tank where he wouldn't be bothering anyone for a while.

I had texted Melissa with the all clear, and she informed me via return text that they were having far too much fun at the IHOP to come back now, but that they would be returning as soon as they could convince Phyllis that peek-a-boo was not necessarily the most original idea since the invention of the wheel. I figured that wouldn't take terribly long.

Thomas was baffled by the mention of Lay-Z as a hit man, but he was familiar with the name. "Anita said he shows up in Martin's records," he said over an iced tea in my kitchen. "But he didn't have a violent history at all."

Maxie had taken Melissa's laptop upstairs again to start looking into the idea of Lay-Z as a killer, which seemed awfully unlikely to anyone who had actually met him. But Paul, eager to see what Thomas might make of the latest revelations, was sitting in the refrigerator, mostly, his head and hands sticking out but the rest of him hidden from view. He rested his head on his hand, listening. If I weren't already very much into takeout, this might have turned me off to eating anything that came out of my fridge again.

Paul was looking intently at Thomas, a tall, standard-built, unassuming man, with a soft voice and eyes that didn't seem to miss much. Thomas McElone's tension was evident in his face but not in his manner. There was nothing Paul enjoyed better than hearing what he called "information" from a "subject." When Paul was a little boy, he'd probably thought *Green Eggs and Ham* was "information" and his mother was a "subject" who channeled Dr. Seuss.

"I know you're not supposed to go on impressions, but Lay-Z just doesn't seem the hit-man type," I told Thomas. "I met the kid. I'm surprised he can tie his shoes in the morning. Was more upset that he'd been interrogated in front of his mother than the fact that the cops were asking him questions about a murder."

"Anita didn't seem to think he was a legit suspect, either," Thomas said. "She'd known him as a minor dealer in pot and a snitch to Marty Ferry. I guess he had everybody fooled. The question is, what now? We can't tell the police that Vinnie said Lay-Z killed Harry Monroe. It won't hold up in court, and I guarantee you he's lawyered up by now."

But something else was eating at me, and inappropriate as it was, I had to ask: "Thomas, what would the lieutenant be talking about when she mentions the wet handcuffs?" It would give me ammunition the next time I saw Martin Ferry, but there was no point mentioning that to Thomas.

He looked confused for a moment, and then he let out a bark of a laugh. "The wet handcuffs!" he said. "Where did you hear about that?"

It was a good question; Paul was looking at me like I must be insane. "The lieutenant mentioned it the last time I saw her but wouldn't tell me what it meant. Is it something that can help us?" I was sure it wasn't, but I'm not above making myself look like an idiot for the sake of some good gossip.

"No, no," Thomas said, shaking his head and smiling that special "in" smile you can get when thinking of a private thing. "It goes back to when Anita was a rookie cop and partnered with Marty, who didn't take kindly to her."

"He didn't want to work with a woman?" I tried.

"He didn't care that his partner was a woman. He didn't want a partner at all, but they got along well enough. It was just—there was this one time, early on, when Marty was waiting for Anita to start their shift, and she's in the ladies' room. He says he's waiting and waiting and she won't come out. The sergeant's giving him a look, and Marty is getting antsy. So he busts into the women's restroom looking for Anita, and finds her rinsing off her handcuffs in the sink."

I knew McElone to be a fastidious person, but that seemed a little extreme even for her. "Why?" I asked.

Thomas laughed a little harder. "Turned out she had dropped her handcuffs in the toilet, so she was washing them off." He laughed even more, almost to the point of hysteria. I let out a little burst myself, I'll admit.

"And he still wanted to work with her after that?" I asked.

Thomas grinned. "He said it was the turning point in their partnership."

Paul, who had been choking back a laugh himself, now looked at me with excess sternness. "Amusing. But that didn't help our investigation," he said.

"No wonder she was so upset when the detective died," I said to Thomas, trying to bring things back around. "And now to hear Lay-Z might have shot him, this skinny teenager he was trying to help . . ."

"Lay-Z didn't kill Harry the Fish," came a voice from above. Alas, not divine inspiration: it was Maxie, coming through the ceiling. "I looked it up. He has an alibi. He was being held by the Seaside Heights police for possession when Harry was being drowned."

I had to make a show of "finding" the laptop in my oven, of all places (thanks a heap, Maxie!), to show that information to Thomas. He rubbed his chin the way Paul rubs his goatee when perplexed.

"Well, we're back to square one," he said.

But as it turned out, we were even further back than that. After Mom called to tell me Ferry had not told her and Dad anything useful, Phyllis Coates called my cell from her car as she drove the kids home (Phyllis has Bluetooth) with the opener, "I hear you scared Vinnie the Goldfish so bad he lied about somebody killing his grandfather."

How could Phyllis have known about Lay-Z's alibi? "Lied?"

"That's how the cops see it," Phyllis answered. "They say Vinnie's going on about ghosts torturing him with invisible lightning bolts. They think he's the craziest person in the Monroe family, and that's a real competition."

"What are you saying?" I said. But I knew what she was saying.

"I'm saying they let Vinnie go ten minutes ago," Phyllis answered.

Twenty-nine

"So let's sum up," Paul said after I got off the phone and started to freak out.

"No. Let's not." I wasn't in the mood for more pontificating.

Thomas had presented me with a thread of hope: "There's a possibility," he said, when we were done marveling over the wet handcuffs, Lay-Z's alibi in the death of Harry the Fish Monroe and Vinnie's quick exit from the holding cell, "that the Monroe case doesn't have a connection to Marty's murder. And Anita was only investigating Marty's murder. So there's a possibility."

"You said that already," I told him.

"Right. Anita had already gone to see Lay-Z, who she thought was working with Buster Hockney. But from what you told me, Vinnie, who works with Buster, is trying to implicate Lay-Z. The last time I talked to Anita—that is, the most recent time I talked to Anita—she was looking into a lead. One that she said had come from Marty's case file. Did Vinnie have the computer that was stolen from your house?"

Paul and I exchanged a look, and it wasn't a happy one. "We never got an answer to that, did we?" he said.

Maxie took that moment to finally notice Thomas, annoyed that her breakthrough hadn't gotten her effusive-enough praise. "Who's this one?" she asked.

"So," I said by way of an answer, but aimed at Thomas, "the lieutenant, that is, *your wife*, had a lead, and you think the case file could show it to us. Why does it matter if Vinnie has the computer? The files are not on the laptop."

"No, but he could be trying to find Anita for his own reasons," Thomas said. "And since he now knows for sure that you can't locate her, he'll start asking around to people we don't know and can't find. He's our best lead to where Anita might have been going."

"So what you're saying is that we should have followed Vinnie when he left here," I said. "That's not a tremendous amount of help right now."

"You might not think so," Thomas said. "But I noticed a car in your driveway as I was arriving that just had to be Vinnie's, so I dropped a prepaid cell phone into the backseat."

"How did you get the phone into Vinnie's car?" Josh asked. "Didn't he have it locked?"

Thomas's grin widened a bit. "Vinnie drives a convertible," he said. "With the right GPS software, which I happen to have on my own phone, we should be able to track him and stop in on all the places he might want to visit after he leaves." Thomas had a smile on his face that mirrored one I had occasionally seen on his wife; it signaled that he had done something he considered brilliant.

We followed the bouncing GPS signal on Thomas's smartphone for about an hour without leaving my kitchen. For one thing, the guests' last morning spook show—for which Maxie swore she would produce her "special surprise"—was scheduled to take place soon. For another,

Jeannie and Tony were coming to pick up their son and hear how I'd completely botched the job of watching him (I imagined Jeannie would think) the whole time they were away.

My mom and dad showed up around eight thirty, by which time Phyllis, warning me that the story "just keeps getting better" but noting that IHOP makes "a hell of a chocolate chip pancake," had dropped off the children and gone to what she was now referring to as her "day job" running the *Chronicle*. After spending more than six minutes in a row with Phyllis, Melissa was sure to start lobbying for a job delivering the paper, but I was holding out until she was thirteen because that was how old I'd been before I could bike around town throwing newspapers at doorsteps.

Ollie was joyously cruising around the kitchen while I brought Melissa, Mom and Dad up to speed on the morning's revelations. Mom looked particularly concerned about the moments spent with Vinnie, but got over it when Paul told her there had never been any real danger because he was there. Or words to that effect.

Thomas, who had been introduced around, was making a careful list on a legal pad of places the GPS noted Vinnie having visited after his departure from the police impound lot. At least I hoped that was what he thought, because I certainly didn't want him coming back again. Thomas checked his list against some of his wife's files, which he'd printed out from whatever computer trail she'd left him, and what I'd gotten from my printer via Maxie, claiming I'd done the work myself. Maxie snorted in amusement but understood why I wasn't giving her credit.

"He started at the Crunchy Crisp Donuts on Route 35," he reported. "I'm guessing it wasn't for caffeine, because I doubt he needed an adrenaline rush after the time you gave him."

"If not for refreshment, then what?" I asked.

"He probably has someone there who launders some money for him, or at least keeps a stash in the store safe," Thomas guessed. "He's going to need some ready cash to pay informants for the information he needs. He might not know where Anita is, but now he'll keep going until he finds somebody who'll tell him, so he can tell Buster Hockney."

I marveled at the man. "You're not a cop?" I asked.

Thomas grinned. "Never made it through the academy," he said. "I work for the PBA, the police union, in the accounting department. That's how I met Anita." I wasn't sure how crunching numbers led to meeting a uniformed cop, but that was a story best left for another day. "The kids are more like her, you know. I had to take them to their uncle's house in Totowa, drove almost an hour and a half, because they were threatening to work the streets trying to find their mom."

"Where'd Vinnie go after the donut place?" Melissa asked. Melissa is the chairgirl of the getting-things-back-on-track committee. Her grandmother beamed at her.

"You're so smart," she said. Oliver was right next to my bar stool, paying no attention to me but plenty to the turkey baster Liss had taken out for him to play with, which had inevitably gotten left on a low shelf under the microwave cart. He reached for the next stool, grabbed hold and continued on his way.

Thomas put up his hands to acknowledge that he'd strayed from the task at hand. "From there it was an address in Asbury Park, which is listed in Anita's notes as the home of Lamont Mancini, someone who had some connection to Harry the Fish but wasn't considered terribly important."

"Mom," Melissa said.

But I was on a thought. "Lamont," I said to Thomas. "That's Lay-Z."

"Yeah, but the owner of the building is listed as Lenore Mancini," Maxie reported.

"Probably his mom," I muttered. Thomas was poring over the list and didn't react.

"Mom," Melissa said a trifle more urgently. I looked at her. Nothing seemed urgently wrong, so I held up a finger to indicate I'd be with her in a minute.

"Possibly," Thomas said, reacting to my comment about Lay-Z. "It would make sense for Vinnie to go looking for Lay-Z after you questioned him; he made a show of not caring, but clearly there's a connection. Marty thought he was a good source of information."

"*Mom.*" Okay, I looked. Melissa pointed toward the floor. Oliver was walking toward the turkey baster, so engrossed in his task he probably didn't even realize what he was doing. Mom gave a delighted squeal, and Maxie actually applauded.

"Go, Ollie!" she shouted.

Melissa rushed to Oliver, who looked up at her, got the message he was standing and immediately sat down. Everyone had a chuckle over that until I said, "Just make sure he's not doing that when Jeannie gets here."

The gathered assemblage agreed, and Liss propped Ollie back up to see if he would walk again. He got down and crawled over to the baster, which he picked up and showed to us. What the hell; we applauded again.

"It's always amazing when they do that," Thomas said softly. He got a faraway look in his eye. We had to focus on getting his wife back.

"The list," Paul said. Paul has no use for babies because they can't help him solve cases. It's a good thing we had Paul.

I looked over at Thomas. "Okay, so after visiting Lay-Z, assuming that's who Lamont becomes when he walks out his mother's door, where did Vinnie go?"

Thomas propped his forehead on his right hand and looked over his spreadsheet data. "Long Branch," he said. "An address that doesn't appear on Anita's records at all."

"That seems like the place to look," Mom said. "You've looked everywhere the lieutenant had listed and you haven't found her. Maybe Vinnie found her."

"Maybe," Thomas said. "But anything that gives us new information is helpful; we should look there first."

Paul nodded his approval; I think he was considering

offering Thomas a job at his detective agency. The fact that there is no detective agency means very little to Paul.

"I can't actually leave right now," I told Thomas. "I have obligations here at the guesthouse, and Oliver's mom and dad are coming to pick him up soon."

Ollie looked up. "Ma?" he said.

"Soon, baby, very, very soon," Melissa told him. "And you can walk for her. She'll love that!" Ollie squeezed the rubber ball on the turkey baster, and air shot out the other end. He laughed.

"It's okay," Thomas told me. "I'll go check it out. I'll keep in touch. If Anita's there, I'll let you know. If not, we'll decide where to go from there."

I agreed to that, feeling just a little guilty that I wasn't dropping everything to look for the lieutenant just when she might actually have needed help for the first time since I'd met her. But I told myself the woman would most likely prefer to see her husband when she was under duress.

Thomas left almost immediately after, as did Maxie, mysteriously saying she had to go get ready for the morning performance. Maxie gave the laptop to Melissa, because it was Melissa's computer, which led me to wonder why she hadn't simply done that before. I didn't ask. With Maxie it's always better not to ask.

"Did you check on that thirty grand that Detective Ferry has in his bank account?" I asked Paul.

Paul looked quite smug, like the smartest boy in the class being asked what two plus two equals. I could have asked Oliver, but he was busy squeezing the ball on the baster. "As a matter of fact, I did contact the detective, and he confirmed what I'd already deduced," Paul said.

Maxie stopped just before the ceiling. She loves to see me get shown up, and besides, this was good gossip.

"So?" I asked.

Paul glanced surreptitiously (he thought) toward Maxie. "So?" he repeated.

"You first."

"The lieutenant got the money from his ex-wife," Paul said. "You'll recall that Elise is doing quite well for herself. He was behind in some bills—things were difficult after the divorce—so she sent him some of the money she got from selling the house they'd owned, especially after she'd parlayed the profit from the sale into her soup business."

"Wait. She gave him thirty thousand dollars from their home sale, and then got mad when he didn't send child support payments on time?" Mom was confused, and I couldn't say as I blamed her.

"He says she thinks it's the principle of the thing." Paul turned toward me and folded his arms like he was a genie about to grant my wishes for great wealth, a handsome prince and a team of elephants. "She knew he needed the money, and it wasn't for gambling debts or frivolous spending, so she gave it to him because she could. Every marriage is different." He raised an eyebrow. "So now you tell me what *you* know."

"What?" Maxie asked. "What does she know?"

"Why you're acting weird," I said.

"I'm not acting weird. *You're* acting weird!" She flew up into the ceiling in a typical dramatic Maxie exit, and we all turned our heads up to watch. Except Josh, of course.

"What's up there?" he asked.

"What was up there isn't up there anymore," Mom told him. "But she'll be back."

Josh nodded. Sure.

"So what's the big secret?" Paul said.

I looked at Melissa. Maxie and I have a complicated relationship, but we don't really want to hurt each other. This looked like it was important to Maxie, for reasons I couldn't understand yet. Liss smiled a tiny bit and shook her head an even tinier one.

"I've got nothing," I told Paul. "I thought I could get her to talk if I pretended I knew what she was up to."

"I knew it," Paul said, but he's not the type to gloat. He caught himself and put up his hands to indicate it was all right. "You tried."

Sure, dead boy.

Ollie suddenly looked up, opened up his arms and took three steps toward the back door. "Ma!" he shouted. I saw Liss reach into her pocket.

Sure enough, a beaming Jeannie was standing in the doorway in shorts and a T-shirt that read, "I Survived the Bermuda Triangle." Tony, eyes fixed on his son, stood behind her, naturally, carrying two large shopping bags.

"Oliver!" his mother shouted. "You're walking!" Her gaze shot up from her tiny son toward me, and her eyes narrowed a little. "When did that start?"

I felt my mouth open and close, but the voice that I heard after that awkward moment was Melissa's. "Just now!" she exclaimed. "He's so excited to see you!" She held up her cell phone. "And I got it all on video for you!"

Jeannie chuckled and swooped down to pick up her son. "Oliver Woliver," she singsonged. "What a big boy! You're walking!"

Ollie made a gurgling sound and then said, "Da." He held out his arms toward Tony.

Jeannie did her best not to look hurt and handed their son over to her husband. She got herself all the way into the kitchen, and hugs were given and received all around. Paul and Dad, the only ghosts left in the room, went unhugged but didn't seem all that put out by their exclusion.

"Bermuda was *fabulous*," Jeannie said. She took a furtive glance at her husband and added, "What we saw of it."

Tony, seemingly engrossed in watching his son, blushed.

"This was *just* what we needed," Jeannie went on, despite no one having asked; I think we were all trying not to acknowledge what she'd just said. "A little time alone as a *couple*." She looked over at Josh. "You know what I mean."

"Easy, tiger," I told her.

Oliver, disturbed that only one parent was paying him undivided attention, held out his arms again. "Ma," he said.

My phone vibrated as Jeannie took her son away from Tony, who disappeared into the movie room to note my lack of progress. Then Jeannie took Oliver into the den to change his diaper, which probably didn't need it—Jeannie just wanted to assert that she was the mom.

The call was from Thomas, who reported that the Long Branch house, while clearly used for selling drugs, was abandoned, and his wife was not there. "But Vinnie's doubled back," he said. "He went to Harbor Haven from here." He gave me an address just off our main drag. I read it out to Josh, who looked it up on his iPhone.

"It's a pizzeria," he reported. "Luigi's III."

"Luigi's has been closed since the storm," I said. "Why would Vinnie go there?"

"That's a good question," Thomas responded. "I think I'd better go check."

"I'm closer," I said. "Is Vinnie still there?"

"No. He took off and is still driving in the direction of Asbury Park."

"Okay, so it's not dangerous to go to Luigi's. I'll just look inside for the lieutenant and come right back." I looked around the room; volunteers to join me were already trying to angle for a seat in my trillion-year-old Volvo wagon. I looked up at Dad. "You want to come along?" I asked.

But I'd miscalculated the angle; Josh thought I was looking at him. "Of course," he said. "Just let me check in with Sy."

"No," I answered. "You've been away from the store long enough. This isn't going to be a big thing, I promise. If it looks sketchy, I won't even go inside." Josh seemed confused. First I'd asked; now I was sending him away? "Your grandfather is over ninety years old. You can't leave him in the store this long by himself," I continued.

"I'll go," Melissa began. I think she was a little relieved to be relieved; that is, that Jeannie and Tony had taken custody of Oliver again and she didn't have to worry about him quite so much.

"You won't," Mom told her. "I'll go."

"No, you won't, either." This was getting silly. Now I was turning down assistants by the armful. "I'll go"—I gestured toward Dad—"by myself. I'll be fine."

Mom and Liss saw and nodded. Josh, probably realizing now that I hadn't been asking him in the first place, smiled a private smile, kissed me lightly to remind me that I liked that and left, making me promise to keep him posted every step of the way.

I made my apologies to Jeannie and Tony (who had come back from the den and the movie room, respectively) and told them I wouldn't be long. Then Dad and I headed for the front door. I asked Melissa to tell the guests that the morning spook show would be pushed back to eleven (then asked her to make sure it started then in case I was late) and braced myself for a stifling ride in my old rattletrap of a car.

Outside in the swelter, we had just about reached the car—in fact, Dad's left leg was already inside, and I hadn't unlocked any of the doors yet—when Paul appeared at my side wearing his long leather jacket.

"Isn't it a little hot for that thing today?" I teased him.

He reached into the jacket pocket and took out Vinnie's gun. "Take this," he said, forcing it into my hand. "Just in case." And before I could argue, he was gone.

I sighed a little at Paul's burdening me with the thing, for which I naturally had no license if I got stopped. "I've never shot a gun in my life," I said as I got into the car.

"Let's go for the no-hitter," Dad said, and put the gun in the glove compartment.

The drive to Luigi's, which took every bit of seven minutes, was mostly hot. New Jersey in the dog days is enough to give dogs a bad name. I was surprised my Volvo could actually make it all the way to the abandoned pizzeria. Just getting through all that hot, heavy air in the noonday sun was a tough job for my poor Swedish car. The thing had never really acclimated to its adopted country.

I parked across the street from Luigi's. The place had suffered serious damage during Sandy, and the owners had decided that it wasn't worth the effort to repair the building. Parts of the roof were still gone, and "FEMA" was spray-painted on the sidewall, for all the good it had done. Luigi's was never my favorite pizza place—too oily—but it hadn't deserved a fate like this.

"Looks like they made one too well done," Dad said. "That's going to take a good deal of wallboard compound." He can't help sizing up construction projects.

"I think it's beyond compound," I told him as I got out of the car. Dad simply stood up where he'd been "sitting" and floated his way out to the sidewalk. Then I sighed, remembered Paul's advice and took the gun out of the glove compartment. I slipped it into my cargo shorts in the right-side pocket.

It wasn't, at least, demonstrably hotter outside than it had been in the car. There was almost no one on the street, which wasn't terribly surprising, given the heat. A lot of businesses had been hit hard by the storm, but most had rebuilt. The restaurants would probably see more business at night, and the small shore souvenir stores that were too far off the beach itself for tourists to drop in now would make their rent when the sun went down and people started coming out to eat.

A small, somewhat disheveled woman was walking in front of Luigi's. If she had been pushing a shopping cart or wearing more clothing, I might have thought she was homeless. When Everett was the official Harbor Haven homeless man, he used to look like he was dressing for the Yukon even in the middle of a heat wave; he couldn't afford to lose a valuable piece of clothing and have to replace it when the first cold winds of winter started to blow.

I walked across the street quickly to intercept her,

although she wasn't exactly tooling down the street at warp speed. "Excuse me," I said. "May I ask you a question?"

"That *is* a question," the woman answered. New Jerseyans. You have to love us.

"A different question."

"Fire away, honey," she said.

She wasn't homeless, and she wasn't dirty. She was simply middle aged and not especially concerned with her outward appearance. The woman was thin and wearing a loose cotton dress that had probably fit her better back when Ronald Reagan was in office.

"Has anyone been hanging around here lately?" I asked. Boy, did that sound like a stupid question. "Anyone, just like, just spending a lot of time near this building?"

The woman looked at me, then at what had once been Luigi's. Then back at me. "Yeah, because this place just naturally draws the tourists, right?"

"I'm serious," I said. "Are you around here a lot?"

"No! I'm from Pennsylvania." It figured.

"Tell her you're sorry to have bothered her," Dad said. "I see someone down the street who's a lot more suspicious." He pointed.

Sure enough, about a hundred yards up the street near a surf shop (where the prices were inflated by a degree of about two hundred percent) was a young man with a sunken chest watching us. Through a pair of binoculars.

"Don't move," Dad said. "He'll run if you look like you've spotted him."

I turned toward the woman and did as Dad had said. "I'm sorry to have bothered you," I told her.

"Seek help," she said, and walked back up the street. Pennsylvanians.

I reached into my pocket for the Bluetooth device I use when I talk to ghosts on the street so people won't think I'm psychotic. Of course, I do live with the delusion that people actually pay attention to what I'm doing.

Except this guy *was* watching me with binoculars. So there's that.

"What should I do?" I asked Dad.

"Let me go down and check him out," he answered. "You don't want to spook him if he's a lead." Note the irony of the ghost using the word *spook*.

I agreed and watched Dad float down the street, hands in his pockets, trying to look nonchalant. Dead for six years and the man still forgets most people can't see him.

To make myself less conspicuous while trying to appear unconcerned, I walked to where the entrance to Luigi's had once been and leaned back on the large plate-glass window in the front. If I smoked, I would have definitely lit one up just then. You can't look less concerned than when you smoke. It tells people, "Yeah, I know I'm making myself gravely ill, but I look good, don't I?"

Not having a nicotine habit or a desire to start one, I tried to keep an eye on Dad without actually looking in that direction. He was still ambling through the air. Granted, he can't exactly move like Usain Bolt, but he seemed to be taking an especially long time to get where he was going and then come back. And because I was trying not to be seen, I averted my eyes most of the way.

Since I didn't smoke, I decided to indulge the other great addictive habit of the twenty-first century—I texted Josh to let him know things were still all right. That took about fifteen seconds, and then here I was again, left without a thing to do but wait.

When I looked up, both my father and the Peeping Tom were gone.

That didn't seem promising. But presumably I was no longer under surveillance, and Dad would report back when he had something to report, so I decided to do what I'd come here to do: look inside Luigi's.

The windows, as you might imagine, were not immaculate. They were so filthy it was difficult to make much out inside the place. Of course, there were no lights on inside Luigi's, either, although the missing patches of roof let some sunlight shine in. I could make out shapes. Not much else.

I tried the door. Open. Go figure. Well, why bother to lock a building that's been decimated by an enormous storm? The owners had abandoned it; the insurance company had probably dropped the policy. Most likely the building was waiting for some government functionary to stamp the DEMOLISH order on its Form 1564-D. In triplicate.

I thought that Dad might be concerned if he got back and didn't find me where he'd left me, but glancing inside the pizzeria and then coming back out wouldn't take long. Also, I decided to leave the door open, leaving a metaphorical trail of bread crumbs for him to follow.

The building was essentially divided into two spaces. The larger was the former pizzeria's business space, where there were still a few tables and most of a counter, but no longer a refrigerated case for sodas and certainly not the flat-screen TV that had once hung near the ceiling. What hadn't been damaged in the storm had no doubt been taken not long after, when it became clear that the owners weren't coming back.

There was no sign of McElone, but I hadn't really expected any. Vinnie had come here, perhaps to talk to a "business associate" who might be in the area—for all I knew, Lay-Z—or to see if someone else had an idea of what had clearly been going on behind his back.

There was some fire damage; it was possible that the storm had exposed some faulty wiring and triggered damage, but it wasn't related to the fire that had taken the Seaside Park and Seaside Heights boardwalks—those were miles from here. The place was certainly dusty and dirty; I noticed myself taking care not to touch anything. I walked inside and looked around, seeing nothing but dirt and abandoned tables.

The back part of the building had been devoted to the kitchen. The wall separating it from the dining area was

still intact. That meant I'd have to walk to the back through
the room as it was, and the lack of living things was certainly a good thing for me right now.

Even better, from my perspective, was that there was a
*non*living thing there. There was a woman's ghost sticking
out of the pizza oven (no longer working, not that it would
have bothered this woman if it had been set at five hundred
degrees—she was dressed in the style of the eighteen hun-
dreds, wearing an oppressive amount of clothing even if this
weren't the second-hottest day of the decade). But her expression was more concerned than uncomfortable; she didn't feel
anything, but she seemed engaged. A lot of ghosts I see more
or less ignore the living. We are not part of the world they
inhabit; it's like the relationship we have with bacteria. We
know they're there, but we rarely think about them other than
when we're using a disinfectant wipe on the kitchen counter.

This woman, though, was watching me intently.

I looked up at her. "You haven't seen a police detective
around here, have you?" I asked. My mother always says
we should engage with people because most of them are
quite nice. This, despite having lived in New Jersey almost
all her life.

The ghost looked flabbergasted. Her mouth moved, but
no sound reached me. That happens sometimes, and it's
incredibly annoying. But I could more or less lip-read her
question: "You can see me?"

"I can, but I can't hear you," I said. "I'm looking for a
friend, and I'm afraid that she might be here. Do you know
of a woman being held here?"

She nodded.

Jackpot. Sort of. "Please," I said. "Show me." My heart
was already starting to beat faster. This was no longer the
danger-free environment I had thought it was. Should I go
back and find Dad? No. He was keeping the bad guy away.

The colonial ghost headed for the back room, the kitchen.
I followed. She went through the wall; I favored the door,

which was of the swinging variety, with one of those port-hole windows, impossibly grimy, right at eye level.

Once inside, it was harder to see. There weren't as many holes in the roof back here, which meant not as much light. It took my eyes about ten seconds to adjust. The ghost was hovering to my left and up toward the ceiling, talking and pointing. But it was too dim for me to read her lips in this light, especially now that she seemed to be speaking faster and in more complex sentences. "What?" I asked.

I couldn't see McElone anywhere in this room. There were tables and sinks, but absolutely no female police lieutenant being held against her will. I'm not that great a detective, but I know when there's no one in the room.

My stomach tightened a bit, though, when I saw where the ghost was hovering. It was next to a door that could only lead to one place: the pizzeria's basement.

Now, I wanted to find McElone and help her come home to her husband and children. I wanted to find out who had killed Martin Ferry, and I wanted, more than anything else, to be done with this case so that I could go back to just being a Jersey Shore innkeeper again. But going down into a basement that was most definitely without light, in a hurricane-ravaged former pizza joint, was definitely not at the top of my to-do list. I looked up at the ghost. "She's down there?" Maybe I should wait until Dad came back.

The ghost nodded and pointed more urgently. *Dammit!* She was serious about moving *now*.

I took my cell phone out of my pocket and hit the flash-light app. Blowing out some air, I opened the basement door and looked inside. The door went right through the ghost, but she moved downward immediately afterward, and the darkness in the stairwell made seeing her that much harder.

I concentrated on the stairs themselves, making sure I didn't fall down into the basement. My phone wasn't fully charged. If the battery died, I would have no source of light down here at all.

Except I found that wasn't entirely true. There were dirty windows up near the ceiling, in the foundation of the building, but only two. They shed some light inside, but not what you'd call reading intensity. It was enough that I could see shapes and, with the phone/flashlight in my hand, a little bit more. The beam didn't travel all that far. I had to get close to things to see them.

What I could see was that there was a furnace in the far corner, with the usual plumbing pipes and heating pipes and electrical tubing running up around the studs in the ceiling, up to the higher floors. There were decrepit stacks of pizza boxes down here, and large gallon cans, some of which still bore the labels of tomato sauce companies.

There was also a closet, to my left and at the far end of the space. Perhaps *closet* is a little too grand a term for what it was. The small area had been separated from the rest of the basement, just framed out and then finished with plywood. No wallboard or plaster. Just wood. It looked like what it was: a really big box. Next to a pegboard on the wall on which some tools were hung, the box looked both imposing and sort of comical, like it had been slapped together by children. But the front panel was hinged on the left side and had a large padlock run through a rung on the right side. What could a pizzeria possibly have in its basement that needed to be locked up? Imported mozzarella?

Well, it was the most logical place to look if you thought someone was being held against her will down here. Besides, the ghost was moving toward the large box and pointing wildly at it, her hand going inside and disappearing when she'd point. You don't have to hit me over the head. More than once.

"Hello?" I called. Maybe if I had some confirmation that someone—presumably McElone—was inside, I'd have the added incentive I needed to find a way past that lock. Maybe I should go back upstairs and find Dad. Except—and I know this is crazy—I didn't want to disappoint the Revolutionary War–era ghost, who was clearly frantic.

So I asked the version of Dad I'd had in my head for the five years he wasn't around (it's a long story). And what he told me was logical: *Get inside and see what's there. Then you'll know what to do.* How to get inside? The tools on the pegboard (a back saw, a hammer, a couple of screwdrivers and a pair of pliers) were all a little rusted out and not going to stand up to much. I doubted I could break the lock with them; it was a pretty thick one and, I noted, not nearly as rusty.

But Dad had taught me about doors and locks before. If this had been a keyed lock, I might have been able to pick it (I don't like to brag, but I'm not bad with locks). Unfortunately, this was a combination lock, and not being a professional safecracker, I had no idea how to deal with such a thing.

So I decided not to worry about the lock—it was easier to deal with the hinges.

I knew that with the screwdriver and the hammer, I could push the pins of the hinges up and take them off the outside of the workroom door. This was designed to keep someone in, not out. It was less than a minute before I had gotten the hinges open on the left side of the box and pushed the plywood away so I could see inside.

Inside the box was a metal locker, like the ones high schools have in their hallways. And there was some banging coming through the metal walls.

Someone was in there.

This lock was harder to deal with. The hinges on the door were inside, so I couldn't pull the same trick. And there was another padlock through the handle of the locker door. The screwdriver and the hammer weren't going to do me much good now. I hung them back up. You always put your tools away because you want to know where they are the next time you need them.

Reluctantly, I took the saw down from the pegboard. Ideally, you'd want a hacksaw for cutting through metal, but I didn't have a selection handy. I attacked what I saw as the thinnest part of the lock with the saw and persisted, back and forth, for quite some time. The banging inside the locker stopped. Had the air run out in there? No. The locker had air vents in it; high schools know about bullies. The person inside—assuming it was a person and not some scary animal I would certainly regret awakening— understood I was working on a way out. I kept sawing, telling whoever—or whatever—was inside that it was okay, I'd have them out in a minute.

Truthfully, I knew there was no chance I'd be able to saw all the way through that lock with a back saw. But eventually I had made enough of a wound to the lock that it was vulnerable to attack. I got the hammer again and swung it, hard, at the lock. Once. Twice. Eighteen times.

Success: The lock gave way, and I could unhook it from the handle. Then I pushed the handle up and opened the locker door.

Inside stood Lieutenant Anita McElone, her hands bound behind her, a little bent at the knee because she is a tall woman. I helped her out of the locker—her legs had not been bound—and out of the wooden closet. There was duct tape across her mouth, which I removed, trying to be very gentle about it. It came off, but probably stung pretty badly.

"Oh for crying out loud," she said as soon as the tape was off. "All the people who could have gotten me out, and it's you?"

"Try not to be too gushy," I answered. "I don't respond well to hero worship."

"Untie my hands." McElone had no time for appreciation. "Use the saw if you have to."

I quickly cut through her bonds, made of a relatively thin rope, with the help of my Swiss Army knife. "What the heck is this all about?" I asked, knowing not to wait for effusive thanks. "Who killed Detective Ferry?"

"I still don't know," McElone answered, rubbing her

wrists to get the feeling back. "Let's get out of here before she gets back."

"Who?"

"Lenore Mancini," she said, starting toward the stairs, behind the flickering beam from my cell phone. I followed her, holding the phone higher over her shoulder so the light wouldn't simply bounce off her back.

"Lay-Z's mother?" How did that add up?

"Yeah. She seems to think I'm trying to destroy her boy, and the only way to save him is to take care of me."

Just as her foot hit the first step, the battery on my phone gave out and we were plunged into almost total darkness. McElone turned around and looked at me.

I couldn't see the look on her face, but I could picture it. "Remember I busted you out," I said.

McElone started slowly up the stairs. "Buster Hockney told her I was going to get him put away or killed, and he sent her to my bungalow. She caught me flatfooted, okay?"

I didn't know why, but she was keeping her voice very low. It occurred to me that she preferred to keep Lenore, if she were to come back, from knowing where we were, but the creaking of the stairs under our feet would certainly give our position away.

"Why didn't Buster come himself?" I asked.

"I've only seen him once, at my bungalow when they knocked me out and took me. Didn't get a chance to ask him."

Despite going up really slowly because we couldn't see, it wasn't a really long staircase, so we were almost already at the landing. "What's Buster got against you?"

"Lenore says he wants some information from me." She pushed hard on the door to the upper floor, and it opened. "Lenore says Buster tried to send Lay-Z, but she intercepted the call. Won't let her son get caught, and she knows he can't handle himself. The kid has all the survival skills of a deer in the headlights."

As we made it into the light of the pizzeria's kitchen,

McElone testing her weight very tentatively on the floor to see if the creak was too loud, she froze in her steps and held her right hand up at a ninety-degree angle, ordering me to stop. I halted without another step.

"Lenore?" I whispered.

McElone turned toward me with a look of great irritation. I held up my hands and mimed zipping my lips closed, which is something you actually shouldn't do outside a Bugs Bunny cartoon. McElone rolled her eyes and turned her attention back toward the dining room door.

The footsteps were coming closer. McElone, stuck in the middle of the kitchen, looked for a weapon to use, but the knives, pots and pans were long gone. Flinging an empty pizza box wasn't going to be terrifically effective.

The door swung open, and in walked the disheveled older woman I had met in front of Luigi's, still in the ill-fitting cotton dress and still looking like she was maybe one bad day away from being homeless. I exhaled in relief that it wasn't McElone's imprisoner.

But McElone stopped me with her right hand, pushing on my shoulder.

It was just about then I realized the woman I'd met only a few minutes ago was grinning at us. And leveling a gun right at McElone.

"Lenore," the lieutenant said.

Thirty

Alas, this was not the first time I'd been held at bay by someone with a gun. It wasn't even the first time today, thanks to Vinnie. But it was the first time I'd ever seen Anita McElone look unnerved.

"I thought she would go away," Lenore Mancini said to McElone, gesturing at me with the gun-free hand. "Then since you wouldn't talk to *me*, I thought if she got the impression that something was up, she'd find you and then you'd spill your guts to your pal."

McElone glared at Lenore with something resembling fury. "My *pal*?" she sneered. "The crazy ghost lady? You thought I'd bare my soul to *her*?"

"Hey," I said. "I'm right here in the room."

"This is very distressing," Lenore answered. "I'm really starting to get the impression that I'm not going to get an answer to Buster's question from you."

"You're not. I'm not giving you Martin Ferry's files."

"That's not helping," I murmured.

McElone didn't respond. But she did seem to be trying to turn her back to me. "Don't stand in front of her," Lenore ordered, circling around to keep McElone and me stymied and without a clear path to the exit. "Stand right by her side." She held the gun closely on McElone. McElone moved to my right side but did her best to create distance between us. Personally, I was not only terrified of dying but starting to feel a little insulted.

And that's when I remembered that I had Vinnie's gun in my pocket. Funny how something you put out of sight vanishes from your mind as well.

I've never shot a gun at anyone, and I don't imagine I ever will. But I was standing next to a trained police officer who, I'd been told, was among the best in marksmanship in her department. I had no qualms about letting *her* shoot somebody if doing so would remove the danger to my own life.

Morals are stretchy things.

The cargo shorts I was wearing had side pockets, and the gun was on the right side. But there simply wasn't a casual, nondescript way of reaching down for the pistol; I had to bend my knee to meet my arm or lean over to reach into the pocket.

"See, now I have a problem," Lenore told the lieutenant. "Buster says I have to keep you alive until I find out how to get into those files. But you tell me there's absolutely nothing I can do that will convince you to tell me what I need to know. Personally, I think you're wrong: There are a lot of things I could do, including threatening your children, but I don't have time for that sort of thing; it takes planning. So I'm stuck with the question of whether it might not be easier for me to just shoot you."

I wanted to vote for "keep trying," but my focus right now was on not being noticed, so I took the rare opportunity to stay silent.

Meanwhile, I developed an imaginary itch on my right

calf. Yeah, it was corny, but hey; there was a gun pointed at me and I needed to get to my right pocket. But as soon as I reached down, Lenore caught the movement from the corner of her eye and turned a bit toward me. I saw McElone tighten up a bit, but she couldn't lunge forward.

"What are you doing?" Lenore demanded.

"I'm scratching my leg; I have a mosquito bite. What's your problem?" I could definitely take the offensive when necessary. Besides, I was starting to convince myself that my leg really *did* itch.

"Straighten up," she said. Then her face brightened, as if she'd gotten an idea. She looked at McElone. "Suppose I was going to shoot this one first," she said. "You'd want to prevent that, right?"

McElone looked me up and down as if deciding whether she wanted to purchase me. She was rapidly dropping on my list of favorite police officers, and until now, she'd been the only one on the list. Ferry, after all, was dead and therefore officially retired.

"I'm not going to tell you anything about those files," McElone said slowly. "So shooting her or anyone else won't do you any good."

It wasn't what I considered a ringing endorsement.

"Whether it does me any good is my business," Lenore answered. "Whether you can live with yourself after I kill her is yours." That was *definitely* not what I wanted to hear.

"The way you talk, I won't have to live with myself very long," McElone told her. Immediately, Ferry leapfrogged her on that favorite-cop list.

"Have it your way," Lenore said, and she turned to face me directly. Anticipating her move, I decided I was having a massive itching fit and bent over to get the gun. I'd barely put my fingers on it before I yelled, "Here!" Then I grabbed the gun by the handle and flicked it toward McElone.

The lieutenant looked absolutely baffled as the gun flew

through the air. I saw her flinch at the movement, heard her say, "What the—" and decided that my downward movement should continue, so I rolled onto the floor. I heard something fly over my head; I was guessing it was a bullet.

My head was turned in just the right direction to see the gun I'd tossed hit the floor; it fired but was pointed at one of the old pizza ovens, which didn't do much good to anybody. I rolled, sure the next bullet was on its way.

"Alison, stay down!" McElone called. Since my plans had not included getting up, I was happy to comply. The center island offered plenty of protection. I hid behind it, could hear some scuffling, but couldn't make out what was going on. There was another shot, then silence.

I couldn't stand the wait; I crawled to the edge of the island and very slowly peeked around the corner.

McElone had Lenore pinned back. She was holding Vinnie's gun, and she was the very picture of serious attention. "Hands behind your head! Now!"

"No! You can't get my son killed!" Lenore was crying. But she wasn't moving.

"Nobody's going to do that if you cooperate. Now."

McElone didn't have handcuffs or zip strips, but we had the cord with which she'd been tied. McElone held the gun—thank goodness—and instructed me to tie Lenore. So I got behind her and reached for her wrist. That's when I saw the razor blade concealed in her right hand, but not soon enough.

Before she could move, though, my father flew through the dining room wall wearing a long hooded robe I'd only seen him in once before. It went all the way to his feet and was shrugged off before he was in the room a second, and it turned out he'd been concealing inside—

A shovel! Which hit Lenore in the back of the head, hard. She looked unbelievably stunned, then dropped to the floor.

McElone gaped at the sight and turned to me. "Was that . . . ?"

I nodded. "My father."

Dad floated over. "Sorry it took me so long," he said to me. "I chased that kid for five blocks before I realized he was just trying out some new binoculars."

"How long do you think she'll stay out?" I asked the lieutenant.

"I can't say. I've never seen a woman hit with a shovel by a ghost before." McElone started looking around the room.

She was checking the ceiling, but Dad said, "Let me," and began wrapping the cord around Lenore's hands. That caught her eye.

The lieutenant shook her head in disbelief. "Maybe I'm still in the locker and I'm hallucinating," she said.

"I was trying to make it look like I didn't care about you at all," Lieutenant McElone said.

"It worked," I told her. "I was totally convinced."

McElone looked impatient. "I was trying to save your life. No need to thank me."

"I got you out of a locker. Don't fall all over yourself paying me back. By the way, you dropped your handcuffs in the toilet?"

McElone grimaced, probably trying to figure who'd ratted her out, and remained silent.

We were in my car heading toward Martin Ferry's apartment building. I had plugged my cell phone into the car outlet, so McElone had been able to let Thomas know she was all right ("mostly," she added for me when the call was completed) and I had called Melissa, who informed me that Jeannie and Tony had taken Oliver home after he'd walked three more times, and that she was currently out back-to-school shopping with her grandmother. Eleven-year-old girls don't like to think about summer vacation ending, but shopping for clothes softens the blow a bit.

Before this, McElone had also called the police department in Harbor Haven, and Lenore Mancini, nursing a massive headache, was carted off for arrest, but not before the lieutenant had a word with her alone, and Lenore made a phone call.

McElone said we had to get to Ferry's place right away because she'd had Lenore tell Buster's "receptionist" (whom I was guessing was Vinnie) that the data everyone was looking for had been in Ferry's apartment the whole time.

"Who's after this data? What the heck is on that thumb drive?" I asked her.

"Actually, there's not much of anything," McElone answered. "Martin had some files about Buster, Harry 'the Fish' Monroe and Lay-Z, but nothing everybody didn't already know. It's mostly just redundancies."

"Then how come everybody's all hot and bothered about finding it?"

"Because they don't know that."

"But wait a second. Buster knew where you were, but Vinnie didn't. Vinnie was running around trying to find out so he could tell Buster, who already knew. What am I missing?"

McElone just shook her head slightly. "Buster being Buster. Selective information for selective people. That's why it was driving him so nuts to find out what was on the thumb drive."

"And you were willing to stay in a locker and endanger my life to protect not much of anything?" I made an effort to keep my eyes on the road.

"What's your question?"

I drove in silence for a while (I was going in case we needed to talk to Ferry), pondering the concept that I'd been protecting something relatively unimportant with my life simply because some fairly stupid bad guys had thought there was some value to it. "You could have called me back," I said to McElone.

"Yeah. I'm sorry about that. I probably should have. But I didn't know Vinnie was in touch with you."

"You would have known if you'd called me back. You have to trust me a little bit more."

"I trust you. I just don't have any confidence in you as a detective."

That wasn't much better. "I found you, didn't I?"

She nodded. "You make a good point."

"Did Lenore kill Detective Ferry, too?" I asked.

I couldn't look because I was driving, but Dad, from the backseat, said, "She's shaking her head. And stop being so sensitive. She's being a good cop."

"We don't know Lenore killed anybody," McElone said. "She took me hostage because she didn't want her son to do it. That was days after the two murders. And I'm not convinced Harry the Fish's wife didn't put out the hit on him."

"I take it Harry was getting around."

"And around and around, if you believe the gossip," she answered. "So his wife decided to forgo divorce and take the quick way?"

"That is what Vinnie told me, but I just assumed he was lying."

"A decent assumption, when it comes to Vinnie."

"Who else had access to the detective's apartment and his desk?" I asked.

"We'll find out."

It wasn't a terribly long drive to Ferry's apartment, but with the "air conditioner" in the Volvo at full blast, we were relieved to pull up. Ferry was not on his front stoop, but it didn't matter. McElone, not expecting to see him, bounded up the stairs and into the building.

We felt for the key behind the molding at the apartment door, but before McElone could insert it into the keyhole or Dad could slip through it, the door swung open and a young woman, looking very startled, stood in the doorway, dressed for the beach. Like in the south of France. Her whole bathing suit would cover my left instep. "Can I help you?" she asked.

"I'm sorry," McElone said. She reached into a pocket where her badge had no doubt been, but Lenore had taken all her possessions when she locked the lieutenant up, and McElone hadn't taken the time to go back to her station. "I'm Lieutenant Anita McElone of the Harbor Haven Police Department, and this is—" She turned and looked at me. "May we come in for a moment?"

Ferry came down through the ceiling and looked at us. "Anita!" he shouted. "You're okay!" He smiled broadly.

"What's this about?" the young woman asked McElone. She sounded nervous.

"It's not about you at all," the lieutenant answered. "But we think there might be something the previous tenant left in the apartment that could be evidence in a criminal case. Is this your apartment?"

The girl, who didn't present as a Phi Beta Kappa member, stood and stared at McElone for a moment. The lieutenant, who was accustomed to people treating her like a police officer, held up a hand. "You're not in any trouble," she said. "We just want to come in and look."

Her comment had given the young woman time to think. "It's not really my apartment. I'm a . . . friend of the landlord," she said. "He lets me use empty apartments when I'm going to the beach, you know?"

"Oh, I know," Ferry said, a leer in his voice. "She changes clothes in my old bedroom." I shot him a look, and he appeared defensive, holding up his hands.

"It's fine," McElone reiterated to the girl.

"If you're sure," the girl said. She stepped aside, which gave Ferry a better look at her profile. I glared at what the others thought was a blank wall as McElone and I walked in, and Dad floated behind us.

"We don't want to hold you up if you're going to the beach," McElone told her. We really weren't looking for anything in the apartment, and having no one there would make it easier for me to talk to the dead detective.

"I don't know if Larry would want someone in here without me watching," she answered.

"Larry?"

"The landlord." Right. Her "friend."

"Don't worry," the lieutenant told her yet again. "Nobody's getting into any trouble here."

The woman thought. It was an effort for her, as she clearly hadn't stayed in practice. "I do want to get out there before I lose the sun." It was going to be ninety-seven degrees today, and she was worried that she might not tan.

"Absolutely," McElone told her. "Go ahead, Miss . . . ?"

"Fiona."

Fiona flounced at the door with a beach bag hung over her shoulder. Ferry watched her from behind and, in a triumph of restraint, made no comment. I waited until the door was closed behind her and her footsteps faded on the stairs.

"She's maybe two years older than your daughter," I said to him. McElone stared at me for a moment, then saw where I was looking.

"Is Marty here?" she asked.

Ferry pulled a handkerchief out of his pocket and waved it at her. "I'm right here, Anita," he said.

She stared at it for a moment, then waved her hand. "Get that thing out of my face, Marty. I don't have time to be freaked out right now."

Ferry, chastened about the handkerchief if not the leering, put the cloth away. "Sorry," he mumbled. I did not pass it along, deciding he was apologizing to all women everywhere.

McElone scanned the large—now, since it was empty—living room. "We can set up in here," she said. "Anyone coming in will come through that door; it's the only entrance. And hopefully we'll have surprise working for us."

"What are we waiting for?" Ferry asked.

"We've let it be known that there are some very sensitive computer files hidden in this apartment," I informed him. "Whoever comes looking for them is a decent candidate for who shot you."

"That's not a whole lot to go on," Ferry said, slipping into thoughtful detective in a flash. This was business. "How are you going to make it stick?"

I passed the question on to McElone, the professional, who answered, "We're hoping for a confession."

Ferry snorted. "Like that ever happens." Assume I only echoed useful comments back to the lieutenant.

McElone had held on to the gun I'd gotten off Buster, and she took it out of her pocket to check it. "Only three bullets," she said. "I should have stopped back at the station house."

"There used to be a gun in the desk," Ferry reminded me. "But the desk is gone now anyway."

"What's left?" I asked him.

"Not much. What Natasha didn't take, the landlord carted away. I didn't know then he was going to use the place to hide his little pal away from his wife."

"Larry is married?" I said.

"Grow up," Ferry answered.

"Quiet," McElone hissed. "I hear something."

The ghost and I fell dead silent—one of us more so than the other—and we listened. Sure enough, there were steps on the stairway outside the apartment, getting louder. None of us said a word. I figured the footsteps would either turn at the landing and walk in the other direction or keep going up the stairs to the next floor.

They did neither.

Instead, the steps came as close as they could come, and I heard some fumbling around the door. McElone felt for

the key she'd taken from the notch behind the molding outside and found it in her pocket. She put it down on the
windowsill next to her and removed the gun from her
shoulder holster. She checked it again, to be safe.

The fumbling around the door stopped. Ferry's eyes
narrowed, anticipating the sight of the person who had
shot him.

"We can't catch them if they can't get in," he noted.
What the hell; the killer couldn't hear *him*.

After a moment, there was the sound of metal scratching metal, very faintly, from the direction of the door. It
didn't last long. Something clicked inside the lock, and the
doorknob turned.

McElone motioned me behind her, and I was all too
happy to comply. She stood in an anchored position, legs
apart but not spread, the gun in her hand pointed in the
direction of the door, which was swinging open toward us,
shielding us from view.

"Dammit," Ferry said.

Lay-Z, dressed in a loose basketball shirt with the number 65 printed on it and a pair of shorts that almost reached
his skinny ankles, walked straight into Ferry's former
apartment as if he owned the place. By the time he recognized there were people in the room (although two more
than he might have been able to see), it was too late.

"Freeze," McElone said in a normal conversational
tone, as if she were thanking him for bringing the pizza
and asking if they'd remembered the extra pepperoni. "Just
stand still and you'll be okay."

But Lay-Z just looked surprised. Unfortunately, he wasn't
nearly as surprised as we were when Vinnie 'the Goldfish'
Monroe appeared behind him in a sharp suit. Behind him was
a tall, slender man with a shaved head and a goatee dyed blond.

"Buster," McElone said.

The problem was Buster Hockney was holding a gun,
which he pointed directly at Lay-Z's head.

"Hey!" the kid protested. It was the most intelligent thing I'd ever heard him say.

"Thanks for getting the door open, Lamont," Buster told the skinny kid. "Now just stand there and be a nice human shield."

"Gun!" my father shouted. I don't think he believed we hadn't seen it. It just surprised him.

The sweat that popped up on Lay-Z's face wasn't entirely due to the ovenlike conditions in the apartment. Did Larry have to turn off Ferry's air-conditioning, too?

"I expected you, Buster," McElone said in a conversational, almost friendly, tone. "But I am disappointed in you, Vinnie."

But Vinnie was staring at me, no doubt remembering our previous encounter. "You can do what you want with those," he told Buster, gesturing toward Lay-Z and McElone. Then he pointed at me. "But that one's mine."

"Stop pretending you're in a Tarantino movie," Buster told him. He kept his gaze on McElone. "Now I'll ask, and then I'll shoot: Where is the flash drive?"

"I could grab him, but not before he could fire," Ferry said. He was moving around like he had drunk too much coffee, trying to figure out what to do. Dad, by contrast, was stock-still, just a different reaction to the same stimulus.

"There is no flash drive," McElone said. "We put that out so you'd come here and get caught. Nice work, Buster."

Buster's eyes took on a steely look. The more intelligent of the two, he believed the lieutenant.

But Vinnie had no such insight. "You're lying."

"She's not," I said. "There's no flash drive here."

Buster jerked the semiautomatic pistol up to Lay-Z's temple. "Well, that's a problem for our friend Lamont," he said.

McElone had not lowered her weapon, so the standoff continued. "That would be stupid, Buster. All I've got you for now is your drug business. You shoot the kid in front of me, and I can put you away for homicide."

Buster's voice was quiet and controlled. "You'd have to be alive to put me away."

"You fire at the kid, and I fire at you," McElone told him.

Martin Ferry circled around (and, to be honest, through) Buster, looking for a way to get his hand away from Lay-Z's head. The kid, for his part, whined, "Come on, Buster, I didn't do nothin'."

"You're right," Buster said, and, amazing everyone, released the kid, who fell to his knees and just stayed there. Buster trained his gun on McElone.

The situation was not looking better, and our reaction to Buster's move meant Vinnie had time to grab me by the arm, swing me around and put his gun to my head.

"Hey!" I shouted. Well, it had worked for Lay-Z.

"Baby girl," Dad said quietly.

McElone gritted her teeth. "Don't be stupid," she told Vinnie. "You killed your own grandfather. You and a couple of your guys, maybe even Lamont here, found him at my bungalow. You thought he was my CI, but you were wrong. I'd never met the man before. So you drowned him because he hated the water, then you drowned him again, and you stuck him in his car—why? Because you thought it was funny?"

"Come on," Vinnie said. "You have to admit that was funny. A drowned guy in a car?"

Buster turned, still keeping the pistol pointed at McElone. They weren't circling around each other but keeping very still, and yet Buster could turn his head just enough to sneer at Vinnie and say, "Will you shut up? They don't know anything."

I was still feeling the barrel of Vinnie's gun against my temple and watching the two ghosts in the room try to figure out how to act without getting someone they liked shot.

McElone knew I had my voice recorder in my pocket.

We'd already gotten Vinnie to confess to the murder of
Harry the Fish; why not go for broke? "Yeah, Vinnie. You
already said you drowned your grandfather. Don't add that
you killed Martin Ferry. Don't make it worse."

"He killed me?" Ferry said, mostly to himself. "I
remember Lay-Z coming in, but then it gets hazy."

"I didn't kill the cop," Vinnie said, and Buster looked
annoyed.

"Why'd you kill Harry?" McElone demanded of Vinnie. "He was cutting you in."

"Peanuts," spat Vinnie. "Two percent. Nothing. But I did it
because my 'grandmother' paid me sixty grand. She'd had
enough."

"But you didn't kill Martin, huh?" McElone tried to
circle around to get a clear shot. I was getting tired of having Vinnie's arm around my shoulders and thought I might
be able to squirm out just from the sweat. I pictured myself
doing that but couldn't raise the nerve. Do it wrong, and it
would be my last mistake. Melissa would never forgive me.

"How about you, Lamont?" McElone said. "Your
mother tried to cover for you, and now she's going to jail.
Are you going to let Buster say you killed Detective Ferry?
Spend the rest of your life behind bars?"

"I just picked the lock for him," the skinny kid said
from the floor. "I didn't kill nobody! Marty was in his bedroom, so I picked his lock and then opened his desk drawer.
Buster wanted his gun so it would look like suicide. I
swear, that's all I did!"

"Will you shut up!" Buster hollered. He stared at
McElone.

By now, I was hot, I was terrified and more than anything, I was spitting mad. If Vinnie killed me, The Swine
would get custody of my daughter. That was not accept-
able. I looked up at my father. "Get him," I said.

"I'm not playing that game again," Vinnie said.

"It's no game." I decided Ferry was the better bet. "Detective, I need your help."

Lay-Z looked up. "What detective?"

McElone looked at me like I was in need of mood-altering drugs, then glanced in the direction I was looking.

At Ferry.

"Okay," she told Buster. "You win. I can't give you a drive that doesn't exist, but I'm putting my weapon down." And she lowered her gun and let it fall to the carpeted floor. Vinnie was so busy looking at that he didn't notice her put her hand on her belt.

"That's my daughter," Dad told Ferry. "I don't have time for you to be stunned."

Ferry swooped down in a nanosecond and took the gun from the floor. McElone smiled just a bit as the gun raised itself (in her view and that of the three living men in the room) and leveled itself directly at Buster's eyes.

"What the hell!" Lay-Z yelled.

Vinnie said something a lot stronger. Then he added, "Not again." I heard something click next to my ear.

"That's it," my father said.

I couldn't see what he did, but I felt him move to my right and suddenly the barrel of the gun was gone from my temple. Vinnie's arm loosened its grip, and I dropped to the floor, remembering that that move had saved me in the pizzeria.

"This trick is getting real old," Vinnie said.

What I saw was Dad holding Vinnie's arms behind him, and Martin Ferry holding the gun on Buster. Ferry had a very serious expression on his face.

"Marty," McElone said.

"Tell him to let you go or I'll blow his brains out," Ferry told me.

McElone was already grabbing her belt and advancing on Buster, who had not dropped his gun.

"Detective Ferry is very mad at you for killing him," I said. "He says you'd better let me go or he might return the favor."

"I might anyway," Ferry threw in. I saw no reason to pass that bon mot along.

"Don't do it, Martin," Dad said. Dad becomes friends with everybody he meets; he hasn't lost that salesman's talent even after dying.

"Why not?" the detective asked. "What are they going to do, execute me?"

McElone was already grabbing Buster's arm and twisting it behind his back. There was some talk of remaining silent and what could be used in a court of law. But Ferry didn't move the gun from Buster's face.

Lay-Z, true to his name, sat on the floor looking dazed. It's possible he'd been sampling some of his product before Buster and Vinnie had brought him here.

"Marty, put the gun down." McElone was looking up, toward where Ferry's gun was giving him away. "We have him."

"His lawyer will get him off," Ferry said, shaking his head. His finger was looking awfully itchy.

I looked up at him. "If you do that, they'll think the lieutenant shot him with the gun I gave her," I told Ferry. "We'll probably both end up doing time. Because our alibi will be a ghost."

"Get him to confess," Ferry said. "Get him to confess and maybe I won't kill him."

I got the voice recorder out of my bag. "He says you have to confess," I told Buster.

But Buster was a tough nut to crack. Already tied up, staring at two guns in his face, he said only, "I want to see my lawyer."

Martin Ferry pulled back the hammer on the gun he was holding. "Stand aside, Anita," he said.

I told McElone what he'd said. She didn't hesitate at all. She stood directly in front of Buster Hockney and stared, for once, directly at the spot where Martin Ferry was floating.

"No," she said.

Buster grinned. For a second. Until the gun swung around McElone and lined itself up with the back of his head.

In shock, Buster blurted out a confession. And Martin Ferry, looking at his ex-partner, took the gun down and handed it to me.

I gave it to McElone. She's the cop.

She immediately called for backup and started to lead Buster and Vinnie out of the apartment. Lay-Z was fine but passed out on the floor. We figured the cops could handle him when they got there. I followed the lieutenant, carrying the voice recorder that held the evidence against Martin Ferry's killer and the murderer of Harry 'the Fish' Monroe. Behind me, Dad and Martin Ferry floated down from their respective perches and beat us outside, having the advantage of being able to pass through the walls and fly.

The police cruisers were already at the curb when we got downstairs; apparently McElone's reputation commanded respect in Seaside Heights, too. Vinnie and Buster were in patrol cars being taken in for booking before we could think about it, which was fine with me. I'd had enough weapons pointed at me for one day and just wanted to go home and hug my daughter for a couple of weeks.

It was, then, something of a surprise to see McElone allowing a tear to drop from her eye as the cruiser drove away. I didn't ask, but I assumed she was thinking about her children like I had been about Melissa.

She didn't look at me but stared straight ahead. "Thanks for coming to get me," she said.

I didn't know exactly how to respond. "You'd have done it for me."

"It's my job." McElone never did anything the easy way with me.

"It's what a friend does," I said.

Behind me, I heard Martin Ferry. "Awwwww . . ." he drawled sarcastically. "I might cry."

"Don't stomp on the moment," I warned him.

McElone looked down at me; the woman is tall and imposing. "I can't hear him, but I'm willing to bet Martin said something rude," she said.

"You're getting the hang of it," I told her.

"Swell." McElone shook off the emotion she'd exhibited and looked at me. "Can you drive me to the Seaside Heights department?" she asked. "I imagine they'll have a few questions for us."

"I just want to go home," I said, trying unsuccessfully not to sound whiny.

"Nothing I can do about that," she answered. "But if there's anything else I can do . . ."

"As a matter of fact, I have something in mind," I told her.

McElone's eyes narrowed. "Is this a ghosty thing?" she asked as we got into the convection oven I called a Volvo.

"You bet it is," I said.

Thirty-one

"This is gonna blow your mind." Maxie was smiling so broadly that I was afraid her lips would meet at the back of her head. Which in Maxie's case would only be the third weirdest thing to happen that Monday morning. "You'll just be completely amazed."

I didn't think I'd be surprised at all, but I was letting Maxie have her moment. This was the last spook show the guests would see before the Senior Plus van came to pick them up and take them home, and I wanted the ghosts to be loose and happy to participate.

Melissa looked up and smiled knowingly. She and I had exchanged folded pieces of paper on which we'd written what we thought Maxie's surprise might be. We'd vowed to open them once it was revealed.

Kitty Malone, finally cleared by her daughter to visit again, was standing by the entrance to the room, looking a little baffled. I'd asked, but Maxie hadn't told her mother the big secret she was about to reveal. I hoped Kitty would be pleased.

The movie room wasn't entirely ready yet, but it was functional enough. I needed to stain the paneling and cover the floor, but the giant flat screen was up, even if not running at the moment. The room-darkening drapes I'd gotten for the windows were open, so sunlight was streaming through, no doubt causing my air-conditioning bill to skyrocket.

Joe and Bonnie, arms wrapped around each other's waists, watched the hanging light fixture turn itself on and off. Paul, enjoying his new role as animated battery, was pointing a finger and powering various devices. It was, frankly, more interesting if you could see Paul. Otherwise, it was just lights going on and off.

Don and Tammy didn't seem as fascinated in the show. They were staring into each other's eyes with oddly sad expressions on their faces. I've seen it when people have especially enjoyed a vacation and are sorry to see it end. Don put his hand on Tammy's, and I thought she might actually start to cry, but she held it together.

Maxie, still with the cat-v.-canary smirk, descended from the ceiling wearing a khaki T-shirt reading "Army Strong." I nodded knowingly at Liss, who did the same back. "Here we go," she said.

Kitty perked up when Melissa told her what Maxie had said.

Rita and Stephanie had walked in, iced teas in hand, and took part in the audience-participation part of the show, when guests were encouraged to toss stress balls in the air, where a ghost would catch it and lightly toss it back. Rita, having lost her nervous scowl, especially delighted in this, throwing one ball behind her back and having Maxie fly it directly over her head and drop it.

"Are you ready?" Maxie shouted now.

Dad, hanging back at the entrance, rolled his eyes. "We're ready! We've been ready for half an hour!"

My mother, just to his left side (and two feet down from Dad), pursed her lips. "Stop, Jack," she said quietly. "Let the girl have her fun." Dad looked suitably admonished.

Even with Maxie's huge reveal happening, my mind was elsewhere. Josh had given me a hard time for getting myself into danger—twice—even if McElone had been there with me. He liked the investigative part of my work but wasn't crazy about me getting guns pointed at me. I resolved only to get involved in things like tax evasion from now on. He reminded me that tax evasion had been used to jail Al Capone. I don't always use the best examples.

Jeannie, sounding more relaxed than she had in over a year, had called to thank me again for watching Oliver while she and Tony were gone. And she mentioned something about she and Tony taking another trip in six months or so, but I did not take the bait just yet.

I'd also heard from Phyllis Coates, who was running a story about the murders. Lenore Mancini and her son were both likely to go to jail, she said, although not for as long as Buster Hockney, Vinnie Monroe and Harry's wife, Teresa, against whom evidence (including Lay-Z's testimony, which had been painstakingly obtained from him in under three minutes) was building.

Paul had been in touch with Martin Ferry a few times since the arrests. Ferry said he was able to get out of the apartment building before his place was permanently rented out, though he seemed restricted to Seaside Heights. He was now happily haunting his old station house, taking special pleasure in annoying those cops who hadn't cared for him when he was alive.

I'd gone out to see Harry the former Fish at the end of the pier, and he had not been pleased to hear his wife had hired his grandson to drown him, then drown him again, and then stick him in his car. All in all, he said, "a bullet to the head does the job, for cryin' out loud." It was difficult to argue. "That's why Vinnie was never going to get my territories. The kid has all the brains of an anvil."

Phyllis had been told to keep my name out of the story but had gotten enough from McElone and the police records that "I wouldn't havê had room for you anyway." It was, somehow, both comforting and insulting at the same time.

Maxie flew to one of the windows, looked out, smiled even wider (she could have been an ad for a ghost toothpaste) and then closed the drapes. That part of the room went dark.

"That's it?" Rita said. "That's the big surprise?" Rita was making up for lost time ghost-fearing-wise.

"No," Maxie responded, as if Rita could hear her. "There's *this*!"

She pulled the drapes apart again, and there, looking sheepish while trying to preserve some semblance of his dignity, was Everett Sandheim in his Army fatigues and a camouflage poncho, standing in an "at ease" position.

I held out my hand. Melissa low-fived me.

"So the drapes are open," Tammy said. She sounded a little baffled.

"It's my boyfriend, Everett!" Maxie shouted. She got a look from Paul, who seemed stunned, applause from Mom and Dad, who appeared to think that was what she was expecting, and folded arms from Melissa and me.

"I don't see anything," Stephanie called. "Did we miss something?"

Melissa was holding up my slip of paper, on which was written, "EVERETT." I unfolded hers, which bore the same message, and flashed it back at her. I gave Maxie a look that indicated we'd have to talk later.

Paul, however, was dumbfounded. "You . . . he . . . I just . . ." He smiled—he really does like Maxie and was happy for her—and shook his head.

"Everett," I said to the deceased soldier, "may we see some evidence of your presence, please?" I didn't know Everett that well, especially in his nonhomeless role, so I was treading lightly.

"Roger that," he said. From inside the poncho, which vanished, he produced a drill rifle. A couple of the guests gasped.

"Everett," I cautioned.

"There is no ammunition in the rifle," he said, and I passed that information on to the gathering. They seemed to relax.

Then Everett did a drill routine, twirling the gun expertly, holding it out and then pulling back in rhythm only Everett could hear, impressing everyone with his precision, particularly those who saw the rifle performing all by itself. There was a rousing round of applause when Everett finished with a flourish.

In true military fashion, he did not allow himself a smile until after the ovation had ended (not, again, that most of the audience could see anything but the rifle anyway) and Maxie yelled, "At ease!" Then Everett's shoulders softened, and he reached out a hand to Maxie, who took it.

"I guess that does it, guys," I told the guests. "The van will be here in about a half hour. I really do hope everyone enjoyed the stay. We loved having you."

They gave *me* a round of applause, and I felt my cheeks get warm. There are moments in this business that really do make it all worthwhile.

The guests went off to pack their things, with Tammy and Don especially lagging behind, never letting go of each other's hand. It was inspiring to see a couple so dedicated to each other.

"You guys are really something," I said as they ambled toward the stairway. Don turned to look at me.

"What do you mean?"

"I just love the way you hang on to each other," I said.

"Some couples, by the end of a vacation, would rather spend a week apart just for the change of pace."

Tammy laughed a little. "Oh, we're not that special," she said.

"You seem so sad to be leaving," Mom told her.

Don shrugged. "It's just that after this, I have to go back to my wife, and Tammy'll be with her husband." Tammy bit her lip; they held up their joined hands and walked to the stairway while we stared at them.

"Did he just . . . ?" Melissa asked.

"Later," I said.

Once the civilians were out of the room, the rest of us gathered around Maxie and Everett. "I started trying to teach him how to move around, remember?" Maxie said. Of course I remembered; it had been my idea. But never mind. "So we got to know each other and, well, here we are."

"Yes, we are," Everett told us. He looked over at Paul. "You should let Maxie show you how to escape," he offered. "She helped me."

Paul shrugged. "Sometimes it's not so bad to be in one place," he said. I smiled at him. Then he looked at Maxie. "Besides, she's tried. I think it's all about the pupil."

"Why didn't you tell me?" Melissa demanded of Maxie.

"I didn't want your mom to make fun of me," she answered, looking directly at me and adding, "You know how you are."

"How *I* am?" I was having a hard time believing this whole conversation.

Maxie turned to face Liss. "And *you* just can't keep a secret from her," she said, once again indicating that any negativity here would be seen as my fault. "I didn't want to say anything until I knew for sure Everett was interested. And I didn't know how to tell my mom, either," she continued, swooping over to Kitty and waving a scarf to indicate her position.

"A military man," Maxie's mother beamed.

"Roger that," Everett confirmed.

"I'd always hoped you'd find someone responsible," Kitty said.

This time it was Maxie who beamed.

"So I'm betting the cap Rita saw by the beach was Everett signaling you, Maxie?" I said.

Maxie very uncharacteristically looked away, but Everett said, "Yes, ma'am. I didn't think anyone saw me. I hope I didn't scare your guest."

I tilted my head. "Not too badly. Don't worry about it."

Before the adorableness became too much to handle, I had a text message buzz on my phone. I looked down.

McElone.

"I'm right outside your house. Have something for you."

Some things never change. I excused myself and walked out to the furnacelike heat of the porch, where McElone was standing with her husband, Thomas, by her side. She was holding a messenger bag in her hands, flat.

"I never got the chance to thank you," Thomas said before I could greet them. "You did an amazing thing, getting Anita back."

I'm not comfortable with praise. I avoided eye contact. "Anybody would have done it," I said.

"I doubt that, but even so, you *did*." Thomas reached over and gave me a hug. "Don't you want to say so, too, Anita?" he asked.

"Yes, I do." McElone looked like someone was suggesting she give up her front teeth, but she considered me straight in the eye. "I wasn't properly appreciative of what you did," she said. "You probably saved my life. I am beholden to you." And then *she* reached over and gave me a hug. Now I was *really* uncomfortable. Once we stood up straight again, I gestured toward the bag McElone was holding.

"Is that it?" I asked.

"Yep. It was still in the evidence room after all this time." McElone looked around me into the house. "Is she in there?"

I must have smirked just a little bit, but I tried to hide it. "Yeah, but you don't have to come in if you don't want to."

"Oh, I don't mind," she said. "But I haven't been invited."

Okay, so I was a bad hostess. I gestured them in and then led them to the movie room, where the mood changed noticeably when the crowd saw the lieutenant and her husband there.

"Fuzz," Maxie said.

"I know her," Everett told her. "She's a police officer, right?" Everett's memories of his homeless days are sketchy; he remembers his military years better.

"Yeah," Maxie answered. "And she doesn't like people like us."

"She doesn't like couples?" Everett seemed truly puzzled, but Maxie grinned at the word *couples*.

"Ghosts," Paul corrected him.

"I think you both know my mother and Melissa." But McElone was looking up into the air in the room, not toward any of the ghosts in particular, but she didn't know that.

"I have something for you," she said too loudly. "To say thank you for helping."

"Who's she talking to?" Dad asked.

McElone reached into the bag and pulled out the item she'd rescued from the Harbor Haven Police Department's evidence bin, probably long forgotten. But when it became visible, Maxie gasped audibly, which was impressive, given that she doesn't actually take in air.

"My laptop!" she squealed. Sure enough, the notebook computer McElone had confiscated from my first investigation—finding Paul and Maxie's killer—was in the lieutenant's hands. For a moment. Maxie swooped down and took it from her. McElone looked like someone had deliberately given her an electric shock. I looked over at Paul, but he wasn't even pointing a finger.

Thomas was also staring, but he seemed more amused than unnerved at the "flying" laptop.

"I did a little digging, and it was still there," McElone said to the laptop over her head. "I'm sorry it hasn't been returned for so long, but for a while it was evidence, and you were . . ."

"I know," Maxie said, even though McElone couldn't hear her. She showed the laptop to Everett, who seemed a little baffled at all the fuss but pleased Maxie was so thrilled. She showed it to Kitty, who also seemed confused as to its great significance.

"It's lovely, dear," she said.

Maxie rolled her eyes, but in a playful way. "Moms," she said.

I looked over at McElone. "You've made her very happy," I said. "She thanks you from the bottom of her heart."

"It's true," Maxie said, hugging the laptop to her. "Thank her. Over and over and over again. She's so *nice*!" Forget that this, too, had been my idea. A boyfriend and a recovered computer, yet do I get any credit? The world is a funny place.

McElone reached into the bag and also pulled out my own beaten, battered, ancient notebook computer and handed it to me. "We might need it for evidence against Vinnie, but I doubt it," she said. "Thank you for your help."

"Her help?" Maxie swooped back down, laptop in hand. "I did it all!" And then everyone who could hear her— including Maxie herself—laughed.

McElone looked up at the laptop, which to her eye was floating in midair and clicking on its keys by itself.

"I'm not ever going to get used to this," she said.

M2G0610